# Non-Return

Also by Dai Vaughan

Fiction
*The Cloud Chamber*
*Moritur*
*Totes Meer*
*Germs*

Non-fiction
*Portrait of an Invisible Man*
*For Documentary*
*'Odd Man Out'*

# Non-Return

## DAI VAUGHAN

seren

Seren is the book imprint of
Poetry Wales Press Ltd
Nolton Street, Bridgend, CF31 3AE, Wales
www.seren-books.com

ISBN 1-85411-391-7

A CIP record for this title is available from
the British Library.

This book is a work of fiction. Apart from
historical figures and events, the characters
and incidents portrayed are the work of the author's
imagination. Any other resemblance to actual persons,
living or dead, is entirely coincidental.

The publisher works with the financial assistance
of the Welsh Books Council.

Printed in Plantin by Bell & Bain, Glasgow

Cover photograph: Brian Gaylor FRPS, BA (Hons)

This book was written in fulfilment of a promise made to myself in 1956 – a promise which the passage of time has rendered meaningless.

tobacco ash, of damp plaster – a sort of gritty damp plaster
– and of sodden wool, with now and then a waft of menthol
from someone trying to leach chemical benefit from a
lozenge. *Horse? Go Suck a Zube.* A long, bony face. I try to
imagine these passengers in other contexts: corpulent men
lathering their hairy bellies; women with a pattern of red
indentations where they've removed their bras. It's funny
how you can visualise things you can't see and can't know. I
expect I'll see a woman without her bra one day. Most men
do, eventually. It's one of the rewards. God knows what the
others are. 'Hey, what you doin' standin' on top there! Get
me sacked, you will.' A faint wash of sunset reddens the
backs of the people in front of me, and I glance over my
shoulder at the ruddy smudge sliding across the rear window
where somewhere over Bayswater the clouds have briefly
parted. I wonder what Mum'll give us for supper tonight.
Halibut if I'm really lucky and she's decided to lash out. Or
even Wiener schnitzel. It's amazing what things you can get
to eat nowadays. I tried once to persuade Mum to try red
cabbage with it, which one of the chaps at work said he'd had
when he was stationed in Österreich, as it's spelt on those
stamps I used to collect; but she drew the line at that – said
Dad wouldn't put up with it. 'But he never complains – never
says anything in fact.' 'No, he simply wouldn't eat it, that's
all.' People's backs can be surprisingly eloquent. Of what?
Well, of docility mainly; but of a measure of resentment too.
Resentful docility. Or docile resentment. Those aren't quite
the same thing; but I can't put my finger on the difference. I
wonder if women let you touch their nipples. Oh come on
now, concentrate: 'The position in the jet where the area is a
minimum, the velocity a maximum and the stream-lines
parallel is known as the *vena contracta...*' No. It's no use.
Once you start feeling randy, everything seems to contribute
to it. *Vena contracta* – corrr! I'll just have to give up for the
present and enjoy the view – and the company. Wasn't there
a bit about a bus going up Fleet Street in that book by
Virginia Woolf I was reading during the summer break from

nightclass – part of my campaign to educate myself? Only in her day buses were open-topped; and sometimes you'd stop alongside one coming the other way, and you'd be almost face-to-face with someone you didn't know from Adam, and the etiquette was to pretend you couldn't see each other. Question: What would you call somebody if you didn't know them from Adam? Answer: Adam. The crush is thinning now as passengers begin to reach their destinations and the bus veers into broader, treeless streets towards the marshes where the air is noticeably fresher – or almost noticeably – except when we get near that cosmetics factory which out-pongs all pongs in its vicinity. Perfumes for export to the Middle East, so it's said: a brand called *Bint al Soudan*. I thought that must be a joke until I mentioned it one day to Bill Newcombe, who said it might not be. 'Bint', he said, isn't a dirty word, it's just the Arabic for 'girl' – 'though of course any word soldiers use turns into a dirty word in less time than it takes to skin a cat.' Right, now: what's the formula for frictionless, adiabatic, laminar, horizontal flow of a compressible fluid?

They're quite right, it doesn't look a bit like Stalin. If it weren't for the moustache you wouldn't know it was supposed to be. None of the foxiness. There is the hint of a squint; but then Picasso often has eyes looking in different directions, doesn't he. So this is being taken as proof that he's a fraud, can't actually draw, is having us all on; and I'm coming in for a good deal of flak on his account. Ironical, to say the least, when most of his stuff is beyond me too. But whenever the subject has come up, I've taken the view that you have to make the effort to understand; so I suppose they've got me marked down as a bit of a pompous twerp. Anyhow, I've been cast in the role of apologist for modern art, and I'm expected to be able to defend the corner they've put me in, or at least to show willing and try, and to take the ridicule if I don't succeed. All right, then: make the effort to understand. You could say everyone makes mistakes; but Picasso evidently didn't think it

9

was a mistake – after all, no-one forced him to release the drawing. He could have chucked it in the waste-paper basket. So what was he actually trying to do? Trying to work out what Uncle Joe must have looked like as a young man? Or trying at least to cleanse him of all the murk of his misdeeds, that fluffy flock that seems to have crept slowly over him, coating his face, if you look at any recent photographs of him taking the salute on Mayday? One thing I've only just noticed: the head isn't resting on shoulders but on a horizontal surface. It's meant to be a piece of sculpture, then – marble, probably. So it's sort of doubly distanced from us. And there's something else: all those rubbed-out lines where he's been changing the position of the cheek, the hair-line, the moustache. He could easily have rubbed those out properly, or even started again if he thought he'd got it so far wrong. But they're clearly visible, even on this snip of newsprint; which means that he wanted us to see his indecision, as if saying, 'Nobody knows what Stalin really looked like. All that was left by the time he died was the *idea* of Stalin.' I don't somehow think I'd get far trying to convince the blokes with an explanation like that. So what are we left with? Moon-faced Malenkov. Mechanical, melancholy Malenkov; lunar balloon. That's better.

There's the usual murmur of undemanding conversation as we work all bent over our boards, perched on our stools, occasionally pausing to wipe our pens on the cuffs of our white coats: marks which survive successive laundering to present a cuneiform palimpsest, fading and indecipherable. Now and then a quiet crescendo of chatter from the lady tracers on the floor below becomes audible, and less frequently the mosquito hum of the lift and the clang of its cage doors as a client arrives to visit the boss in his office which has the suggestion of a barrister's chambers or of a Harley Street consulting room – though that's only my imagination, because to be honest I've never set foot in either. With its north-east facing studio lights admitting the merest purr of traffic and the muted pandemonium of a near-by building site, this space confers on us an undeniable quality of tranquillity, of placidity even: a quality that impressed itself upon me almost the moment I entered as a fifteen-year-old straight out of school and proudly clutching my dad's old scale rules with their genuine ivory edges, pens with turned ebony handles, all folded neatly in a Selvyt. What struck me first, I remember, was the resemblance to a Roman galley: the two files of drawing boards either side of a central aisle. But the draughtsmen were facing alternately fore and aft, denying any crude unanimity of effort; and instead of the familiar Hollywood pace-keeper, muscular at his drum, there sat at the far end the Chief Draughtsman, Mr Brightwell, mild of disposition, ascetic in his concentration, his pipe maintaining such a fixed angle that it is rumoured – in whispers only, mind you – to be permanently fused to his dentures so that he must remove both together when he goes to bed. But for all that, he's no fire hazard. It's common knowledge that not a trace of dottle has ever dropped to singe one of his drawings. And he's so sure of his capabilities that he often works directly in ink without bothering with a pencil underlay. Indeed, he'll sometimes work straight onto linen so as not to have to take up the time of a tracer; and only occasionally do we hear the scratch of a razor blade erasing a wrong line to the accompaniment of murmured curses prompting a quip from somewhere, 'I've heard of scraping a living...' Recently, however, an unsuspected weakness was discovered in him when he turned up in a new suit and the blokes said, 'A bit loud, isn't it – those red lines?' and he said, 'What red lines?' I suppose he'd argue, though, that colour vision is inessential to him in his occupation; and, since his occupation is all that matters, evolution has unburdened him of that faculty. Mr Brightwell seldom takes part in the office chat, which has now turned to the mystery of soundproof wall tiles.

'Why do they have all those little holes in them? I mean, why does having holes in them help make them soundproof?'

'Well, that's where the sound goes, you see. It gets lost in the holes because they're so small.'

'That's right – they're so small it can't turn round to get out.'

'So what happens when the holes get full of sound?'

'Then you have to have them stripped out and replaced.'

'No, you don't. There are people you can get who come round with vacuum cleaners with very fine nozzles, and they suck all the sound out.'

'Yes. Then they have to take the vacuums and empty them somewhere quiet.'

Meanwhile Bob Bobson – real name Robert Robertson, of course – is intent as always on the design and construction of paper aeroplanes, an activity which seems to occupy him for most of the working day. Lazily gliding, they slide to a halt on someone else's board; by which time he's got his head down, all innocence.


'You oughtn't to be so hard on your old dad, you know. You really shouldn't. He's been a good father to you.'

'I don't want to be hard on him. It's not that. It's just that I'd like him to talk to me once in a while. Most people's dads talk to them, impart the wisdom and all that. I mean, all my childhood. He must have God knows what stashed away in his noddle.'

'You used to go down to help him on his allotment when you were small. You used to enjoy helping him.'

'Yes – well, pottering about. But even then he was pretty hard to get a word out of. The odd aperçu once in a while, fruit of long cogitation.'

'Don't be sarky about him. I won't have it. Here, hold this blanket level while I put it through the wringer.' Every sinew tautens, and she shuts her eyes tight with the effort. Beyond the rubber rollers the fabric falls in concertina folds, a map of a long journey, the wet side swelling like puffed-up cheeks as the water cascades into the tilting wooden tray then back into the tub.

'I saw in a magazine you can get machines now that don't

need wringers. The drums vibrate, or something, and hot air blows through them.' Water cascading. A gorge somewhere. A holiday we once took. 'Do you see us being able to afford one?'

'We won't be wasting money on one of those so long as I'm fit and capable.'

Where can it have been? 'When I've got my qualifications, and I'm making my fortune...'

'Yes.' She takes a breather, leaning on the sink and brushing the neatly cropped hair out of her eyes with the back of her hand. 'He's not negligible, your dad. Far from it. I don't know if I've ever told you: it was some time around 1934 – we weren't yet married – he was Second on a cargo ship bound for Montevideo, still studying for his Chief's ticket. They'd got half way across the Atlantic, ten days out; and he was on the midnight watch; and in the early hours he noticed something, something to do with the sound of the engines, that wasn't right. So after a bit of hesitation he woke the Chief, and it turned out there was some sort of a fracture in the bearings. The Chief ordered the engines to be shut down there and then, and before long the skipper was up wanting to know what the hell was going on, why the engines were dead. Anyhow, the upshot was it took them a day or two to fix the fault; but if your dad hadn't sounded the alarm the shaft would have seized up and the whole thing would have ripped apart and there'd have been no end of damage, and they'd have had to be towed back to Liverpool for a re-fit and all the cargo transferred to another ship and it would have cost the company a fortune. Your dad got a letter of commendation from the head office of the shipping line. I think he's still got it somewhere – probably keeps it in that shed of his.'

'Did he get any financial recognition?'

'What, a reward you mean? No; I suppose they took the view he'd been doing what he was paid to do. That was why he was there. Here, there's one more blanket. Grab hold of that end.'

'I suppose it's understandable him not telling me about

that. He did once talk to me about when he was torpedoed – well, "talk to me", that's putting it a bit strongly, but he did tell me how so many of his mates who were clinging to scraps of wreckage just gave up after a while and let themselves sink into the sea. He still seemed to be trying to puzzle that out, even as he was describing it.'

'I know. I know.'

'How long was it they were in the water?'

'Five days, I think. Frozen stiff. They'd somehow got separated from the convoy; but a plane spotted them and radioed back, and a destroyer came to look and see if there were any survivors.'

'And he left the sea after that?'

'Not straight away. You were expected to be able to take that sort of thing in your stride in those days. So he signed on for one more voyage. But something had happened to him. He didn't actually get dismissed, but I think it was strongly recommended to him that it was time he looked for a shore job. That's when he got taken on by Comyn Ching as stores supervisor, and he held that down for a year or two, till people started crowding back from the forces... Just help me hang this lot out, then I'd better let you get on with your homework.'

Parents. Mothers and fathers. Marriage. That's how the mechanism functions, it seems: one coming up when the other goes down: Dad sinking into silence; Mum, who'd never been out to work in her life, getting a job as sales assistant at Peter Jones to help keep the family in shoe-leather, then promoted to deputy buyer when John Lewis's was rebuilt after the bombing. You'd hardly think it to look at her. As for Dad, what does he do all day? He could run a comfortable little smallholding with the time he devotes to that allotment. Chickens. A bit of an orchard. Pigs. 'Five Things Pigs Will Eat.' Nobody keeps pigs any more, do they?

It's like being a child again, sitting at these desks in rows, bruising your knees. They're meant for adolescents. This is a secondary school in the daytime: bulbous cast iron radiators painted brown; lights suspended from the roof beams with big green enamel shades each held by three dust-clogged chains; blackboards which howl painfully as they're raised and lowered; high arched windows uncurtained and giving out upon nothing but the deeper blackness of winter. A church of learning: penitential and utilitarian. I'm reminded suddenly of the first time I encountered logarithms, and was horrified because I assumed we'd have to learn the books of log tables by heart just as we'd had to learn our multiplication tables in primary school. The maths instructor is introducing this evening's subject, Solids of Revolution; and Graham, seated alongside me, gives me a covert clenched-fist salute. The instructor is monotonous in his delivery, verging on the inarticulate. Quite a few of them are, in fact; and Graham and I often share a surreptitious laugh at their expense. It helps keep out the cold. But at the same time we're both a little bashful about it. As he once said to me, 'I've really a good deal of respect for them. They're not trained teachers, they're ordinary people – motor mechanics, hospital maintenance engineers, overseers from Ove Arup – trying to make a bit on the side for a few luxuries. Yet they mostly seem to put more effort into the job than the pay probably warrants.'

Walking homeward, the spokes of our bicycles strobing through the fog in the violet light of the mercury vapour street lamps, we take the short cut through the graveyard where the tower, stocky and patched with cement, is all that's left of what was presumably the village church when this was a village. No moping owl, though. I try to imagine what the surrounding area must have been like: market gardens, perhaps: tilth and sobriety: the people semi-prosperous, very devout. But I'm only guessing. We turn to talking about hyperbolic functions, the odd way in which they parallel trigonometrical functions, yet you can make sense of trigonometrical functions by simple reference to triangles, whereas hyperbolic functions seem to refer to nothing you can visualise as an actual object in the world; and I begin to play with the idea that maybe it's the mathematics that is the ultimate reality, the real world only a shaky and imprecise expression of it. But that's too much for Graham:

'I can't go along with that. It savours of the worst sort of idealism.' At this moment we're passing an elegantly carved eighteenth-century tombstone. Above the text is an image of two skulls flanking an hourglass, and the hourglass has wings. The hourglass with wings is somehow straining towards an idea – the transitory – which it can't emotionally express; and that seems somehow to relate to my thought about mathematics; but I can't make the connection. 'So far as I'm concerned, the material is reality; it's what we've got; and mathematics is one language among others, though an extremely effective one, with which we try to describe that reality to ourselves in order to manipulate it. And that's what being human is about.'

'Yes, I can look at it that way too – in fact I usually do. But I'm troubled by what happens when the language starts developing by its own logic beyond anything that can be checked against common experience.'

Ivy drips leaf to leaf. *Sacred to the Memory of...* someone forgotten.

As we re-join the streets – these smut-choked thorough-fares wide as healthy lungs – a man in a long monkish overcoat steps from a shop doorway and peels a couple of leaflets from a sheaf in his hand. We each accept one, reluctantly impressed by the commitment of somebody prepared to give his evening to leafletting on such an unfrequented corner. The thought arrests me that one day such a swathed figure may turn out, in a swerve of passing headlights, to be ourselves; and, as if spooked by the same prospect, Graham winds his scarf more snugly around his neck. The leaflet is announcing a demonstration organised by the Communist Party for this coming weekend, and opens with the rousing call: SHOW WHERE YOU STAND BY MARCHING.

'Show where you stand by marching? How can you take a party seriously when they come up with a slogan like that?'

Graham laughs briefly, then adopts a severe expression. I

think he considers me woefully flippant in certain areas. 'If only that were the worst that could be said of the CP!'

'Why? I thought you were all for it – revolution, I mean.'

'In principle I am. But the cause has been put back by decades. Marx made it perfectly clear that the transition to socialism couldn't occur until a certain level of industrial production had been achieved under capitalism.' The gauzy roadside lights describe a sensuous curve as they rise to the brow of the hill then veer away into their own halation: a twin variable graph – would that be right? 'What the Bolsheviks did was to try and leapfrog straight to socialism from what was still substantially a feudal system. So what have they ended up with?' And beneath this tarmac, mere inches deep but acres broad, there is still soil, fertile soil: an alternative life; an alternative economy. 'It's obvious, isn't it: state capitalism: a system where a central bureaucracy creams off all the surplus wealth. It was a ridiculous enterprise from the start.'

Yet my surroundings breathe comfort. There seems to be something inherently consolatory, almost nostalgic, about the smell of coal – of coal-smoke trapped under fog – childhood, a fire in the grate in your bedroom when you're out of sorts. 'So how would the real thing differ – real communism?'

'Difficult to say. Since it's never happened, we've no way of knowing precisely what form it'll take. You can't draw up a blueprint for the outcome of a historical process. But my own guess is that money will have to be abolished.'

Chemistry of Combustion: molecules re-distributed and re-combined. As these evenings, so similar, superimpose themselves one upon another, I feel the acid of time beginning to bite, to etch the plates of our future memories. 'But money isn't wealth. You were telling me that only last week. It's only a convenience, a token which is easier to manage and distribute than herds of cattle or bushels of corn...'

'True enough. But it's hard to imagine a money economy without capitalism springing up from it – of its own accord, almost. There seems to be something about capital which dictates its own logic: an irresistible propensity to accumulate.'

This begins to sound oddly similar to the thoughts I was struggling with a few moments ago about the independent life of mathematics. But I'll keep quiet about that for now, as we've reached the corner where our paths diverge and I'm too tired to want to launch into a whole new level of debate at this time of night. Graham never gets tired of intellectualising. 'Well,' I say, 'I'll have to content myself with voting Labour when the election comes along.'

'Why, what's the point? With all the good will in the world – and that's assuming they've got all the good will in the world – there's nothing much they can hope to do without dismantling the system in its entirety; and they've certainly no intention of doing that.'

'But surely a government can make improvements to our day-to-day lives?'

'Marginal ones, I dare say. But you'd probably stand a better chance having a flutter on the bow-wows.'

Graham pedals off to the north, man in proficient control of machine as if his accomplishment were itself a parable on historical inevitability; and I, less experienced a rider, step out into the road to mount my bicycle from the right hand side. I can only do it from this side, and I know why. In my last year at school I used to stroll with a friend, a cyclist, down the asphalt path that led to the main road. He wheeled his bicycle between us with his right hand, as most people do; and often he'd let me take a turn steering it. Then I developed a habit of scooting it along with one foot on the pedal. One day I felt confident enough – confident of my balance – to risk swinging my left leg over and sitting on the saddle: and there I was, suddenly able to ride a bike. But I assume that for the rest of my life I shall always mount from the wrong side: historical inevitability of a less exalted order.

Frank Rillington, his name is. Yes, I'm no longer the baby of the firm. Frank, the new office dogsbody, with his velvet-trimmed powder blue jacket and his hair flopping over his forehead in the Tony Curtis fashion – 'Shirley bloody

Temple, more like,' Clegg mutters – is already demonstrating to the lads the latest way of walking, which involves thrusting your hands deep into your pockets and jerking your left shoulder forward in step with your right foot and your right shoulder forward in step with your left foot. Strictly speaking, the shoulders should be padded. It's termed the Tottenham flick. Very entertaining; but I can't spend all day listening to him. I turn my attention back to the specification I'm supposed to be checking, and out of the monotony of the prose a rhythm begins to assert itself:

The firebars to be cast hollow
From special heat-resisting iron
Chilled in the jaws where the cams operate
And along the heated zone.

'You writing poetry back there, or something?'
I must have been reading aloud. 'Well, it scans, doesn't it?'
'Oh for Christ's sake...'
I'm saved by Mr Brightwell calling me to the other end of the room. He's taking down one of the old-fashioned hanging files from the back wall: a wad of old blueprints heavy as an Axminster carpet and gripped together with a thick spring clip.

'There's a law...' He heaves the thing onto a plan chest and deftly unlocks it. 'There's a law against using these to trap rabbits.' He selects a faded old drawing of a multiple swivel bearing. 'Look, here's what I want you to do. This thing's been re-designed, but a good deal of it's the same. I've sketched out the new part, with all the dimensions. Just put some tracing paper over this and add in the new section to scale – make it clear how it fits in with the original – then you can get one of the girls to trace it, substituting your replacement bits. Only don't get one of the daft ones. That Alice Cave's got her wits about her. I'll tell her you'll be bringing it down some time tomorrow or the next day. OK?'

Back at my drawing board I discover the conversation has turned to limericks and clerihews:

'Here, he'll be able to help us. I heard him reciting poetry to himself a moment ago.'

'All right. We're trying to make up a verse about Gina Lollobrigida. What's a rhyme for Lollobrigida?'

'I suppose it would have to be "frigider", wouldn't it.' Nothing else comes to mind.

'Yes, well, we got that far by ourselves. How's about a verse, then?'

I'm on the point of backing off with as much grace as I can muster – something of a habit with me – when it pops into my head. 'Half a mo – try this:'

Rosanna Podesta
Will let no-one molest her
But they say Lollobrigida
Is frigider.'

The others laugh, and I realise my stock has risen. I don't necessarily have to feel intimidated by young Frank and his Tottenham flick. What's more, I'm going to have an excuse to talk to Alice Cave. She's a funny little thing, almost like a character out of Beatrix Potter – straight mousy hair, a perky nose – a hamster done in watercolour; yet I've always felt a distinct sense of personality about her, of individuality. No make-up for a start. It's beginning to weigh rather heavily upon me that I don't have a girl-friend to boast about in the office. I once remarked to Bill Newcombe that I didn't find girls very interesting to talk to, and he said to me, as if explaining an elementary fact of life, 'But you don't expect girls to supply you with intelligent conversation. You get that from your male friends. You turn to girls for the other thing – you know what I mean.' I knew what he meant; but it's not the sort of statement I want to be true. More fool me, I suppose.

I would be where the clams perpetrate
Their gristly and greasy sins
Not packed in olive oil in tins
Chilly and fallow and alone...

You could keep going like that for hours, couldn't you.

Gazing out at the backs of things: sooty galvanised cowling; paltry yards with washing hung out in zig-zags; upstairs windows half blocked by the scrubby backs of dressing table mirrors. I've got a compartment to myself – not many people travelling mid-morning – having been deputed to deliver some urgent bumf to Maxtead Milmans and now relaxing on the return to Waterloo, nothing for the moment demanded of me. It reminds me of something. I can't place what. A strong memory, but inaccessible. But if it's inaccessible, how can it be strong? Search me! I brought my copy of *The Years* to read on the train; but the view from the window does the same job, somehow. I can't make up my mind about Virginia Woolf. She's so swanky, sometimes I can't take it; yet I'm always drawn back. I saw somewhere she was supposed to be a socialist; then I read somewhere else a quotation from her to the effect that the worst thing about going down the air raid shelter – in the First World War, this was – was having to talk to the servants. Still, at least she had the gall to say it. Could be that anyone who looks hard enough at their own society winds up a socialist of sorts – though I can't see Graham buying that for a moment. 'Did she argue for a planned economy?' The view opens out onto a vista of allotments: a patchwork of oblongs, each with its own shed and its own indefinable character, which puts you in mind of the chessboard landscape in *Through the Looking Glass*. And suddenly I have a vision of Dad, multiplied, seated in the doorway of every one of those sheds, watching me with an identical expression of resignation and guilt, accusation and sorrow, as the train stammers and slams past.

I never cease to marvel at the slender, stone arches of Waterloo bridge – though of course I know it's an illusion, they're not really arches, the roadway is actually cantilevered out from either side of each of the piers to meet in the middle. As I set out across the Hungerford footbridge, trains alongside me rumbling towards Charing Cross, the white Portland stone begins to take on a tremulous intensity; and I realise that the sky is blackening, and all those women's coats which are fashionable this year, conical in cut and dyed in day-glo mulberry, lime or electric blue, are beginning to fluoresce wildly as if the world were an aquarium bathed in ultra-violet light. I crank up my stride in the hope of reaching shelter before the downpour comes. Once those coats have fallen out of favour, this particular visual experience, this particular component of all that adds up to 'London', will be lost.

I dodge into a shop doorway just in time. The rain is bouncing up like spears out of the pavement in that Greek story where the hero plants dragon's teeth; and suddenly – don't ask me why – I remember what it was that nearly came back to me in the train with that sense of being for a short while free of responsibilities, that thing that's always to a degree the magic of railway travel where no-one can tell you to change your destination and you can't be reached on the telephone. I must have been about ten or eleven, almost certainly travelling on my own by train for the first time in my life. I was on holiday at my grandparents', and Grandpa had seen me off on a journey – half an hour or so – to visit an aunt I'd rarely met who lived in an outlying village called Ryehill. It was five or six stops on a somnolent branch line, steam fraying past the window with its punched leather strap. She met me at the station: a wiry woman in a flowery apron, hair loose and touched with grey, striding down a sandy cart-track between fields of wind-combed cereal, presumably rye. But who was she? I seem able to account for all my aunts and great aunts and aunts by marriage on both sides of the family; and this woman is none of them.

I've finished the job for Mr Brightwell, and take it downstairs to the tracing room. Alice is putting the last touches to a complicated piece of work, and I notice she's one of the few people who still spurn the use of stencils for her legends and captions and has the confidence to rely on her own freehand lettering. It is firm and neat and legible. If it weren't, she'd soon have been instructed to abandon it. Indeed, the whole drawing has a crisp and individual quality.

'Is it dry?'

'Yes, it's OK.'

I unroll my composite. 'Mr Brightwell told you about this?'

'He said you'd have something for me. Didn't give me any details.'

As I start to spell it out, I notice Mrs Collingwood is gazing at me with an almost insolent smirk; and I realise there is nothing on her board, and she must be wondering why I didn't approach her first with the new job. She takes a deep drag on her cigarette and expels the smoke in our direction. 'Ahhh – the eternal substitute!'

Like a fool, not noticing till too late the suppressed giggles of the other girls, I say, 'Substitute for what?' And the giggles become less muffled as one or two of them give vent to choking coughs. Alice, keeping her eyes on the drawing, slightly flushed, is trying to ignore the situation; but she clearly knows that I can see she understands.

'Substitute for a lovely fat Havana cigar, dearie.' And with that, Mrs Collingwood slides off her stool, allowing it to pull her skirt up briefly and lewdly beyond her stocking tops, then waddles away towards the toilet. The merriment subsides; but I have to make a great effort of concentration to explain to Alice what is required. Luckily she seems to grasp it.

I return to my rightful place in the world.

'Here, Frank, you done them bleedin' whass'names yet?'

Frank turns slowly to face his tormentor: 'What you on about?'

'Them bleedin' whass'names – you done 'em?' There's nothing like normality to make you feel better. But it's difficult to get my mind back onto my work.

They gave me a silver rattle
They gave me a wooden gun
But time and tide disqualified
The hobby horse that won.

I've spent all afternoon with Graham in his living room – floral wallpaper stained with condensation, furniture surely inherited from grandparents or great-uncles – his wife tripping in and out in a wan floral frock coeval with the curtains – I'd never imagined Graham having a wife – to keep us supplied with tea and rock buns, evidently regarding our preoccupations as above her, or simply uninteresting, as we've struggled with the revision for our final exams, challenging each other on this and that point of detail, helping each other with things we thought we'd understood at the time and perhaps hadn't or perhaps had already forgotten under the weight of subsequent data, subsequent formulae, subsequent revelations of the nature of our sorry universe. Why do I say 'sorry'? I've no disrespect for science, certainly not for the truths that have been hewn out of the resistant rock of ignorance by one dogged experimenter after another. It's just the way it's all become a sort of square-bashing for the mind, all the excitement of discovery censored out of it. Graham suggests we jack it in and go for a drink. They'll just have opened. I'm not going to admit I've never been inside a pub before: so I brave the smell of stale fags and stale beer, assuming that, like most other things, one gets used to it. We sit down with our halves at a scuffed wooden table with cast iron legs. Graham begins to muse upon the wider value of what we are learning: how it primes the mind: how the revelation of how dimensions can be manipulated mathematically, quite aside from actual numerical values, makes it easier to grasp the concept of labour power as the fundamental unit of economics which enables economic theory to be re-built from scratch. I nod my agreement – I've had similar if less organised thoughts from time to time myself – but then I add that I'm beginning to think what I really want is to be a poet. Graham laughs, then cuts his laughter short and glances sidelong at me:

'The trouble is, being you, you probably mean it.'

'Probably, and at the same time probably not.'

'Well, I don't know anything about poetry; but my understanding is that you don't make much of a living at it.'

'No – I imagine it would have to be a sideline, at least to begin with.'

'There must be special magazines, I suppose, where you could send material.'

'I think they're called "little" – little magazines.'

'And publishers – specialist publishers?'

'Yes. Still, I'd have to write something first.'

'That would undoubtedly help.'

'What I've got in mind, though, is something that would be politically relevant: something founded on real people's experience.'

'Proletarian poetry. Poetry for the masses. They're rather keen on that in the Soviet Union. I wouldn't say, though, that the workers are all that keen on poetry – at least, not here they're not.'

'I'm not so sure… Well, hold on: poetry about working life and poetry *for the workers* aren't necessarily the same thing – and proletarian poetry may be something else entirely. But having said that, I'm still not so sure working people aren't keen on poetry. It may be true that they reject it…'

'You've lost me.'

'All right. Look. There are limericks, there are music hall ballads and advertising jingles, there are… I heard a song only the other day – the Mills Brothers – with the line, "Your disposition sours like a lemon on a tree." I mean, honestly! And you don't even have to go beyond the titles. Whispering grass…'

'Smoke gets in your eyes…'

'You'll look dapper from your napper to your feet…'

'That's not a title. But yes, I suppose the primitive appeal of rhyme has always been recognised. There was a poster during the war:

The sight of thick potato peelings

Deeply hurts Lord Woolton's feelings…'

'Exactly. And then there are all those off-colour epics like *Eskimo Nell…*'

'You surely wouldn't categorise that as poetry, would you?' For someone who claims no interest in literature, indeed tends to treat it as irredeemably bourgeois, Graham is remarkably quick to defend its honour. But it seems to me you've no choice but to start from what you've got:

'That's not necessarily relevant – only a question of nomenclature. The point at issue is that all these things use the same techniques, draw upon the same resources, as what we call poetry. And it's only when we *call* it poetry that people turn their backs on it. Wouldn't you agree?'

Graham is looking thoughtful. 'I'm trying to remember whether Marx had anything to say on the subject. Of course, there's a theory among some socialists that the arts will cease to be necessary after the revolution – the point being that the impulse to artistic expression is a product of the frustrations of life under an oppressive system in which we're alienated from any expression of our true nature.'

A roughly dressed, middle aged man who's been chatting quietly with a couple of others at a near-by table gets up and walks across to the battered upright piano close to where we're sitting. He opens the lid gently and performs one or two excruciating runs up and down the keyboard, filling the hitherto quiet room with a tumult of dissonance. Then he shakes his head, closes the lid, turns to us with an injured look and says, 'It's out of tune.' He returns unsteadily to resume his seat with his friends.

Alice is on her own in the tracing area when I go to collect Mr Brightwell's drawing. I've timed it just right. The others have already left for lunch. I compliment Alice on her work and succeed in engaging her in conversation as she deftly stretches a new length of linen onto her board, the chill blue light reflecting up onto her face, then sprinkles it with French chalk from one of those red rubber gadgets barbers use to puff talcum onto your razored neck, and rubs it across the surface with a soft cloth. It seems she's keen on cycling: a possible point of common interest if only I can put in some serious practice, though she goes on to tell me she has a group of girl-friends with whom she goes on weekend outings. Apparently she took up tracing because she was considered 'artistic' and her parents saw it as a way for her to reconcile her talents with the requirement to earn a living. I give her a quizzical look:

'A pretty far cry from the creative arts, eh?'

'Why do you say that? Have you ever been to the Science Museum? I used to spend hours there looking at those old machine drawings from the nineteenth century. They're pictures of something, aren't they? There's a wonderful longitudinal section of the Great Eastern: Brunel's ship, the Great Eastern. It's more than four feet long. I used to linger in front of it like a child in front of Selfridges' window at Christmastime. Isn't that art? It's exciting; and it's a way of representing things visually: so – ?'

'But it's a standardised way – impersonal.'

'Is it? Wouldn't you say you could tell the difference between one of my tracings and somebody else's?'

For all her soft voice and self-effacing manner, she's very firm in the expression of her views. It's a bit unexpected – even disconcerting. Eventually I find the opening I'm waiting for when she remarks that she likes music, goes to concerts. I happen to have noticed that the Proms are on, so I ask her if she'd like to come with me on Friday. I've never been to a Prom, and have no idea what they're playing on Friday; but she chooses not to call my bluff. So here I am, fixed up with my first date!

I take the drawing to the printers' round the corner and slap it down on the broad counter – broad enough to take an antiquarian-size sheet. The assistants are passing in and out between the doors at the back, shouting to each other about various orders. We've a theory that they lay bets with each other as to how long they can carry on like this without a customer being able to catch their eye. But for once I'm not bothered. The radio is playing a song:

*Answer me, O Lord above*

*Say what sin have I been guilty of...*

I've never heard it before. The tune is strangely compelling, the beat somehow tugging against the metre as if flying a kite in a stiff breeze:

*Tell me how I came to lose her love*

I've a feeling it'd be there without the music, too: there in the words on their own...

*Please answer me, I pray...*

The corners of the drawing boards at night-school are spongy from generations of pins, so that it's difficult to fix the tracing paper firmly. A dab of chewing gum might help; but then it would probably tear when I removed it. At least I've managed to grab myself a half-way decent T-square, having spent all year methodically assessing which were the least damaged. Everything counts. This is the drawing on which we're to be judged: an exploded isometric of a non-return valve. Some people get flustered, can't decide where to put the first line. Put it in the wrong place and the final drawing will be badly centred. Of course, if a thing's going to be traced, a fault like that can be corrected. But there aren't going to be any second chances this time. Anyhow, whether by skill or by luck, I seem to have cleared that hurdle. It's going well so far. Glancing around, I see nineteen other men, arrayed at boards equidistant from one another in the gentle light of an early summer evening, all engaged upon drawing the identical thing. There's something mildly unsettling about it. Yet I can't deny I'll miss nightschool: the camaraderie of a shared effort, of shared specialist learning. Question: Why did God give us left hands as well as right hands? Answer: Because he wasn't sure whether the drawings were done to first or third angle projection.

Help me, left hand, help me
In my hour of need
Right hand doth forsake me
I am thine indeed...

I may, assuming I pass, decide to move on to a higher level. I think you can even do a degree part-time these days – though that must be a real sweat. I'm not sure what use a higher qualification would be. It's not required in my present job. But then circumstances change. The other thing I'm not sure about is whether they'd defer my National Service for another three years, or beyond the completion of my apprenticeship. Still, the problem for the moment is to get this drawing completed within another hour and a quarter. Should be OK. Looking good so far. If I do pass, I'll have a print made of it and frame it: All My Own Work, as the screevers like to insist. Nice word, 'screever'.

It's Friday. Today I shall spend my first ever evening with a woman. The thought tantalises me, seeming always to slip just inches out of my grasp. Going to work on the bus, seated next to a hefty workman with a bag of tools at his feet, I visualise Alice and her pert movements. I think of her weekend cycling, her liking for music, her pride in her draughtsmanship, her solitary visits to the Science Museum, and I foresee myself as – what? – not as possessor of these things, but somehow as being allowed privileged access to them, as being able to explore through them, and through her, an enlarged and enriched version of my own life. I'm not particularly expecting her to be here already as I pass through the tracing area on my way up to the top floor; but in fact she's over at the other side putting on her white coat; and, as she turns in my direction, I see that her hair is coiled in strange little shells all over her head. She's had it permed. I return her smile, and hope she didn't catch my immediate reaction which I'm sure must have been visibly one of shock. She's not the same person – rationalise it how I may – whom I've been looking forward to taking out this evening. And then the awful truth strikes home: that's why she's done it: she's done it for me.

Word has got about. It was bound to. And half way through the morning Frank Rillington sidles up to me with a morsel of confidential advice: 'One thing to remember: when you sit down beside a bird, make sure you're sitting on her left hand side.' Why's that? 'Well, a bird's clothes button over to the left, see. Means it's easier to slip your hand in and feel her tits.' I think he's genuinely got my interests at heart; he's not trying to embarrass me. But the fact is – and in my anxious state I find myself registering this as a problem – I always feel more comfortable, in my fantasies, to the right of a woman. Rather like a bicycle.

I've found out what they're playing tonight: Dvořák, Mozart and Tchaikovsky. That sounds safe enough. I'm sure I've heard things by Mozart and Tchaikovsky, though I'm not quite sure who Dvořák is – or was. We've agreed to leave on the dot, so there'll be time for a bite to eat before the concert; and, when I go to pick her up from downstairs, I receive another blow. She's put on face powder and lipstick. Why, for heaven's sake? I obviously can't tell her, without offending her, that the person with whom I wanted to spend the evening was someone who didn't doll herself up like this – that that was precisely what I found attractive about her, or part of it anyway. I can't tell her how hurt I feel that she should have thought this necessary. Again I ask myself why; and the only answer I can come up with is that this is what you do. If you're going out with a boy, you do yourself up for it. And there's nothing special about me – nothing in the way we've talked to each other – that might make any difference. I get the same treatment as anyone else. In fact I'm being self-centred in thinking I enter into the equation at all. It's what you do, and that's all there is to it.

As Alice tells me we'll have to queue, and ought to get there early, we settle for a skimped meal. 'Some other time,' I say, trying to appear positive. There was one of those news items the other day about someone being arrested for climbing the Albert Memorial. As we skirt around it, cutting across Hyde Park on foot, we pass a young couple and overhear the woman saying to the man, 'OK, you go up those steps. Then what?' – and we glance at each other and laugh. It's the first suggestion of a relaxation of the unease between us, an unease for which I blame myself entirely but which I've seemed powerless to do anything about. The queue for the gallery already seems long when we arrive; but Alice says there are several staircases and she knows which one to head for to ensure the best position. Behind the Albert Hall, strangely, is another and smaller Albert Memorial. It's the sort of thing you'd encounter in a dream, then wake up wondering whether such a thing really existed before coming fully to consciousness and realising that no – don't be silly! – of course it didn't. Equally dream-like, in another way, is a square chimney – must be all of a hundred feet high – which rises straight from the pavement as if gnomes or Morlocks had set up industry right under our feet. We join the queue and wait alongside the buff wall which looks from a distance like glazed ceramic tile but is in fact coarse-fired brick cast in relief with scutcheons and trophies, newts and swallows. 'Typical of the Victorians,' I say. 'No sense of what's an appropriate use for a material.' But Alice bridles: 'I don't think we should be so superior about the Victorians. We may find them fusty, but they didn't feel fusty. They saw themselves as exploring all sorts of possibilities, trying everything.' As the doors open, and the queue jogs forward like the start of a marathon, I notice that one of the shields on the wall bears the device of an hourglass with wings. Up and around and up and around, an invasion force of us clatters up the stone staircase until finally emerging high under the roof on a continuous walkway where there are no seats, but Alice steers me quickly to a point where we can lean on the rail and the enormity of empty space engulfs us. 'But it looks so much bigger than it did from the outside!' 'Yes,' Alice says, 'I've often puzzled over that. I think it's to do with the effect of perspective on a curved building. Your eye doesn't take it into account the way it would with a square one. It makes the outside look a lot smaller than it really is.' The conductor – Malcolm Sargent – steps up onto the podium and raises his curiously overgrown hands; and the sudden hush seems in its own way to deform space: to bring us measurably closer to the orchestra.

It's supposed to be something about a water goblin. We didn't get around to reading the programme notes before it started; but the surge and eddy of a river is obvious from the beginning; and then, before very long, I find myself carried away by a most beautiful tune, at once a majestic, irresistible current and an intoxicating shimmer which makes me think of water rippling past the piers of a bridge and catching the sunlight. The mood of the river keeps changing, though, and eventually it develops into something quite threatening which I suppose is the goblin; and then it gets sort of hollow, as if we were being pulled under and possibly even drowned; and I'm waiting for the beautiful tune to come back, but when it does it's ghostly and hesitant; and then the music dies down to what's obviously a tragic end. The Mozart piano concerto feels a bit lightweight after that; and I'm thinking that people who understand music would probably consider me very vulgar for being sorry that Dvořák's opening tune didn't come back in triumph as I was assuming it would. When the interval comes, I buy us each an ice cream from the little kiosk at the extremity of the gallery and we get our heads together to read about the Water Goblin. It turns out that he married a young girl and they had a baby; but then she got bored and went back to her mother, and the goblin was so furious that he banged the baby against the mother's cottage door and killed it. Alice, to my surprise, has some sympathy with the goblin: 'After all, it was his baby too. He must have been desperate with sorrow. I think the music's trying to express his feelings as well as the girl's.' Possibly. Then she voices my own thoughts: 'Strange, wasn't it, how the big tune never came back...'

We spend the interval discussing the upside-down mushrooms that hang from the ceiling, which I remember reading somewhere were rigged up by the same chap as designed the acoustics for the Festival Hall in an attempt to reduce the notorious echo. Alice surprises me again by saying she wants to become an engineer, and is thinking of taking a course to get some qualifications. I tell her she'll need her Ordinary National for starters. She nods; but I get the feeling she's worked it all out for herself. The second half is devoted to Tchaikovsky's fifth symphony; and by now I'm beginning to realise that my evening with Alice is drawing towards its close and I've so far found no opportunity for any sort of an advance. Worrying over this, I make a fool of myself by beginning to clap before the symphony is quite over, and attract a few snooty looks from the people around me. When it is over, and we reach the bottom of the staircase, which seems far longer than it did when we came up it, we find the weather has broken. We shelter under the canopy from the torrential rain as people slam their car doors and turn on their headlights to depart, twinkling, in an aura of squalid comfort. I'm about to put my arm around Alice's shoulders in a gesture which I hope can be construed as companion-able if she prefers not to construe it as amorous; but at this very moment she begins to unfurl her umbrella and says, 'It isn't going to ease up. I think we'd better head for the bus stop.' She tries to share the umbrella with me, but our heights are too different, and I'm not sure whether it would be proper for me to take it from her and hold it over both of us. As we cross the road, she says, 'Here's my bus coming. You don't mind, do you? They're pretty infrequent...' and with all the courage in the world I'd have no chance to attempt a good-night kiss as she adds, 'See you tomorrow,' waves, and boards her bus for home. I while away my own journey trying to recall the 'big tune' from *The Water Goblin*; but all I can remember is Tchaikovsky's bombastic march.

'Get your hand up her skirt, then, did you?' There's nothing confidential about Frank Rillington's manner this morning. I'm in the spotlight now; and he means to set the wires vibrating – the invisible wires of mutuality, of respect and disrespect, ridicule, admiration, resentment and envy, which criss-cross any closed community in a complex web. I know the wise tactic would be to say, 'None of your business, old boy,' in such a tone as to imply that there were plenty of juicy details I could impart if I wished, but that I'd every intention of keeping them to myself. I can't be bothered. I say a flat 'No,' and suffer a day of banter with unfeigned indifference:

'You haven't understood the rules of engagement, mate.'

'Consider ye the beasties of the fields.'

'Lilies.'

'Eh?'

'Lilies. It's lilies – isn't it?'

What is the formula for love, I wonder. Is there one? Must be. There's a correct formula for everything. It wouldn't exist if there weren't.

I'm carrying on into the evening, because there's a drawing I need to get finished by tomorrow. Mr Brightwell, at the far end, is the only other one of us still at work, only the occasional click of his set-square keeping me aware of his presence. The lights over most of the boards have been switched off – the alternation of pink-white and blue-white fluorescent tubes supposedly approximating to natural daylight. The one to my right, about to give out, has developed at one end a perceptible violet flicker and the intermittent buzz of a fly trapped between window panes. I'm working directly onto linen. There's something in the tactile quality of pen on linen that I always find calming. My pen is adjusted to a very fine line as I trace the architect's drawing of a space in which one of the client's units will be mounted. Through the windows where no lights are reflected, a star is visible. The architect obviously tired of drawing the wall tiles. First the verticals peter out, then the horizontals, leaving only a blank space. And I find myself gazing at this blank space which signifies a wall in a building I have never seen, a building indeed which does not yet exist, yet which is nevertheless in some sense represented by this absence, this emptiness. The pink and blue tubes sometimes make me think of lupins. I remember an occasion when I saw a cat, its fore-paws buried in a clump of lupins, its eyes reflecting the headlights of the passing traffic with the green of toxic pools. I remember the white tiled wall of a place where, late one night, I sat alone on a high stool eating fish and chips with salt and vinegar. I remember the night-blue face of a clock with stainless steel casing which ticked away the seconds on a deserted station platform. I remember how the driver of a late bus waved a greeting to a colleague who was leaving the depot at the end of his shift. Could I make sense of all this by writing poetry? Graham believes that nothing is seriously worth doing until after the revolution – not even, if I understand him correctly, preparing for the revolution. But meanwhile, we have to spend our time somehow, don't we?

Bouncing a ball against a wall at twilight.

The smell of warm asphalt.

Laughter.

# THE PIANIST

He was not blind, the pianist, though he somehow behaved as if he was, gazing into the fretwork front of the old plonky-tonk with its two stiff keys and its dubious tuning and its one remaining pivoted iron candle-holder, with specks of the original gilt, swinging about like a useless appendage evolution has left behind. And he'd sit there all evening with his back to the racket of the crammed bar – my dad remembers when it still had sawdust on the floor to soak up the spew and the spittle – and the customers would make sure that he never had less than a pint and a half at the ready on top of the lid, and he'd never say a word beyond 'Thanks, George,' or 'How's the missus?' His name was Charlie, and he was getting on a bit. He smelt of fish glue.

So I'd often wondered about Charlie, about what made him tick, being so much a part of the community yet so much apart from it.

One day – the day of the general election, it was – I found myself sitting alongside the piano as I waited for my mates, who had taken a detour via the polling station. It was still quite early, and the pub was far from full. Charlie had just played *Answer Me,* and was taking a long draught of bitter to work up steam for his next number, when I said to him, uninvited, 'Have you voted yet, then?'

Though I didn't realise it till later, no other opening would have achieved the same results. In a breath between gulps, Charlie muttered, 'I don't vote;' and then, after looking at me over the rim of his glass as if checking my credentials for something or another: 'I'm an anarchist.'

'Oh?' was all I could say.

'Well, at any rate, that's what they told me I was. One of us, they said. May have been pulling my leg, of course; but I decided to believe them any-old-how.'

He was already rippling out arpeggios in the left hand, and was clearly about to launch into some favourite of his younger years, entitled... But the opportunity was too good to let slide.

'Come on, Charlie, you can't just leave it at that.'

The arpeggios hesitated. 'My glass seems to be getting empty.'

'Done!'

I brought him a full pint, just for good measure, and to make sure he didn't dry up too soon. He gripped it in his stumpy little hands like a squirrel gripping an over-large nut.

'I suppose it goes back quite a long time,' he said. 'I was bashing this piano here while you was still in nappies. No training, of course – just found out I had a talent for it – natural sense of rhythm, you sing it and I'll follow you, that sort of thing. Got better as I went on. Well, you'd expect that. Anyway, it gave me something to look forward to of an evening. Wasn't getting much out of my job – I mean, not just the money...'

'What is your job, anyway?' I'd never stopped to ask myself what he might do for a living. I'd always just thought of him as the pianist.

'Was on the docks till my lumbago took bad. Now I stir the glue in a furniture place down Hoxton way.'

'Spirit of craftsmanship, eh?'

'Craftsmanship my arse! The wood's so lousy it splits when it gets within sight of a cutting edge.'

'Never mind, you were telling me about the piano.' I didn't want him to get side-tracked onto things not being what they had been in his day. Old men are like that, give them half a chance.

'Yes, well, I was telling you. One day – and I'd been coming here for ages, mind – I thought of looking inside the piano. And right down the bottom, in the front, there was some dirty old sheets of music – *Alexander's Ragtime Band*, selections from *Chu Chin Chow* and *The Gondoliers* – stuff I still used to play in them days. Must have dropped in before my time when someone folded the music rack back into the lid, too far gone to notice. Anyway, I dusted these things down, and I started – just for amusement's sake – trying to fit all these blackheads and whiteheads on the page to the way I'd always played 'em. But it soon got too difficult, 'cos I didn't understand all the sharps and the flats. So I got on to this old oppo of mine who'd done the violin a bit when he was a kid – never got very far, but he remembered enough to clue me up on key signatures and what have you. You still with me?'

I nodded. My dad once tried to learn the trumpet, but the Sally Ann wouldn't take him on.

'Right, then. So far so good. I got to learn to read music that way, up to a point. But then I got dissatisfied – couldn't see my way clear to making any more progress. So I reckoned I'd just have to take proper lessons. Went to an old dear up Whitechapel High Street, Mrs Goldberg – *Madame* Goldberg, begging her pardon – like the variations.'

She sounded the sort who'd put pennies on the back of your hands and rap your knuckles with a ruler if they fell off. But I didn't interrupt to ask.

'So three half hours a week lessons, and practice, practice, practice.' He underlined his point with a run up the keys. 'Really got stuck into it, I did.'

'You got your own piano, then?'

Charlie laughed. 'You ain't seen our buildings, have you? I'm on the top floor, for a kick-off. And the roof leaks.'

'You could always put a waterproof sheet over it.'

'It's not that so much, it's the floorboards. Rotted away, they are – wouldn't take the weight. Anyhow, what do I need a piano for? I got one here.'

'Not exactly your concert pitch, though, is it?'

Charlie shrugged. 'Fred did have it tuned for me once. But the bloke said it wouldn't last – wooden frame, you see, all warped. It had gone again by the next day. Still, the thing is, it's here. And I've got used to it. Five hours' practice a night I can get on this – better than some professionals. That's how I started to look at it. Five hours of solid practice. After all, the customers here don't know any different – so long as you play what they want when they ask for it. I've often as not spent ten-thirty till eleven just rehearsing scales, and they've been none the wiser. So then I started reading books on it. Theory.' Charlie took a long, reflective swig at his bitter. 'I was the oldest one in the hall when I sat my first exams.'

'Exams?'

'Why not? Standard grades, they have. Starts out easy enough, but then it gets more difficult. Written work as well, not just playing: identify this chord, compose a canon on *Mother Kelly's Doorstep*. Have to make up tunes, too – and you're not allowed to whistle them or hum them, just do it in your head.'

Charlie's bitter was running dangerously low, but I could tell that if I went to fetch him another he'd start up on the joanna while I was gone, and that would be that.

'So what's this got to do with you being an anarchist?' I asked.

'That's what I'm telling you, isn't it. These three coves come here one night, and I didn't pay much attention at first, but I realised after a while they was taking a proper interest in me – you know, listening, like. So I started getting a bit more flash with the twiddly bits, and then I threw in a bit of Liszt just for their benefit. After a while they came over and said a few nice things to me – compliments – and they asked me did I think I was good enough to play on a platform. So, cocky with it, I showed 'em my diploma what I used to carry around.'

'Your what?'

'My diploma. I used to carry the thing around with me like a lucky charm after I'd just got it – pleased as Punch. That impressed them, and they said they was organising some sort of a fund-raising do for this anarchist group, and they was looking for genuine local talent. So I did it.'

'Just like that?'

'Just like that. A hall on an estate near Clapton pond. They only had three acts – some hairy fellows singing with their hands cupped round their ears, a street theatre bunch with big puppets, and me. I played *Liebestraum* and *The*

*Dream of Olwen* and my own medley of Spanish republican songs, which they'd asked for specially. Encored three times, that was. Shagged out by the time I'd finished.'

'And that's what made you an anarchist – getting shagged out playing to 'em?'

'They actually sat and listened. Just imagine that! Then after it was all over, they took me for a drink and they started asking me about myself. So I told them, just like I told you. And one of 'em says, "Well, I reckon that makes you one of us, really." That was it. I mean, was I going to tell 'em to get stuffed? I thought to myself, if this is my reward for years of trying hard, who am I to look it in the mouth, or count its teeth, or kick it in the teeth, whatever the phrase is?'

'How long ago did all this happen?'

'Two months it'd be now.'

I let out a low incredulous whistle.

'Oh yes. I only passed my finals last year. Fifth time lucky. Well, I had a lot of bad habits to get rid of, see, what with teaching myself for so long.'

'I wasn't suggesting you owed anybody an apology,' I assured him.

Already someone had deposited a fresh half on the piano top, and people were beginning to latch on to what was missing, and to call out things like 'Give us a tune then, Charlie!' and 'What you rabbiting on about over there?' Now somebody shouted, 'How's about something to celebrate tomorrow's landslide for the labouring masses?' Charlie winked at me. 'Wait for it,' he muttered.

Like the first crack of thunder after a day of muggy weather, he pealed out the opening chords of a Chopin Polonaise. The crowd fell silent, as if we were all at once chilled and stirred by some intimation from outside our lives. The silence didn't last. Conversation picked up again. But for Charlie it was a victory. And at the end, he received the first round of applause the pub had ever thought to give him.

# TWO

Taking a short cut through Mayfair to Piccadilly, I'm crossing the road when I notice a cluster of people gathered on the corner at a respectful distance from a posh-looking hotel. You can't quite pin a label on these people. They're scarcely the sort you'd expect to find waiting for a glimpse of Cab Calloway or Diana Dors. More casual, somehow, more random: teachers, trade unionists, errand boys, pensioners. I ask one of them what it's all in aid of, and he says, 'B and K – they're expected to come out soon.' And even as he's saying it, a shiny, buxom Rolls Royce slides up to stop outside the main entrance. So I decide to hang around for a little; and in so doing, I realise, I too partake of the indeterminate standing of this assembly, and am even a trifle puzzled by my own motives. But still, it's not often you get the chance to observe world leaders at such close quarters, the men whose decisions affect our lives, even if they are ultimately, as the saying has it, only the agents of dialectical necessity. Here they come. The flunkey, having held the glass doors open for them, glides forward with no fluster of haste to open the door of the car. Bulganin and Krushchev, unsure whether they ought to wave to us – K allows us a sheepish, wolfish smile, while B maintains soldierly eyes-front – perhaps because they're unsure of our attitude or perhaps because our numbers are so small as almost to constitute an insult in their terms, take their two or three steps across our gritty London pavement. They are utterly without charisma in their identical grey trilbies and their grey mackintoshes unbuttoned to reveal identical blueish suits which remind me of something. That's it: demob suits. They look as if they're wearing demob suits.

My head is the crucible for an experiment.
Alien fires float their sulphurous flames
Around its inner crust.

41

'I was a major by the end of the war. And I'll tell you one thing. In May 1945 my orders were to remain in readiness for a continued advance to the east. I've often wondered whether that order was ever formally rescinded.' He's a taciturn bloke, Stallworthy; but, if you pay attention, you get info from him that you never got from the nine o'clock news.

The character of the company seems to have altered in subtle ways since we moved. It may be because so many of us are now congregated in this big back room with its central lantern light: eleven drawing boards, with Mr Brightwell off in a sort of side-chapel with a high, narrow window. Or it may be the different distribution of personalities. Or again, it could have a lot to do with the new recruits: Ron Cottle, for instance, who has already de-throned Frank Rillington as resident cheeky chappie. It's odd how he does it, actually: manages to be both foul-mouthed and self-important without ever quite giving anyone cause to reprimand him. Still, he's never once been unpleasant to me – though I might seem on the face of it to offer him a natural target. Never unpleasant when we're chatting in private, that is. The theatre, the arena of the office, is a different matter, where everyone's fair game and where we forge and temper our ambitions. Here's where he thrives, and where he soon revealed Rillington as a mere rustic. The other odd thing, though, is how he combines the tearaway image with a certain military rectitude. He evidently landed himself a cushy number in a drawing office during his National Service; yet he also claims the exalted rank of Chief Petty Officer in the RNVR. Stallworthy, having perhaps unwittingly silenced our debate about the Red Menace, pauses to light up a cigarette; and Cottle, never one to resist an opportunity, says, 'They kill you, those things do;' to which Stallworthy replies, 'D'you think anyone would bother smoking them if they didn't know that?'

Some things remain unchanged. The Phonotas girl still visits fortnightly in her matt chocolate and margarine uniform to wipe inside each of the mouthpieces with a tissue smelling faintly of disinfectant. We could do this ourselves. It's the ritual that matters. Taking a completed drawing to the tracing department, which now comprises several small offices on the first floor, I pass Bob Bobson, who has been leaning on Bill Newcombe's board for the past half hour. It turns out he is regaling him with an account of his wine-making adventures: 'I succeeded once in concocting a vintage – a small one, but still – out of old Christmas pudding water. Well, when you think about it, it's got all the necessary ingredients. Decidedly delicious, it was.' Betty Hammond is the next tracer free. She was always very friendly with Alice Cave, so I take the opportunity to ask if she's heard any news of her.

'Yes, I saw her a couple of weeks ago. She's studying full time now – you knew that, though. You didn't? Oh yes. She's decided to go for her Mech.E. It's not going to be easy for her. She's the only woman in the class, and I get the feeling the fellows are giving her a pretty rough ride. You know how it is. They're either chatting her up or jeering at her – some-times both: I mean, the same boy, as it were. They don't seem to know how to handle it. Still, I think our Alice will see it through. She's got what it takes. Says she wants to work on aero engines. Or is it ships?'

No doubt she has plans to re-design the Great Eastern. No, come on, that's mean. Something in Betty's tone has left me feeling she was being critical of me; but I've no real reason to think so – just my own bad conscience. Yet why? Betty reckons Alice knows her own mind; but if that's so, why did she... Oh, what the hell! The saying, 'She's got what it takes to take what you've got' is jogging irrelevantly through my head as I return to the big office where Bobson is still talking to Newcombe, who is clearly anxious to get on with his work while trying not to seem uncivil. Cottle is in the throes of an anecdote about his National Service, when he was instructed to paint a notice of some sort:

'High-ups don't know the difference between a draughts-man and a sign writer. But it's not in your interests to try and enlighten them. So I get the thing laid out all neat and symmetrical, best of my ability, like, and at that moment he comes in and stands over me and he says, "Are you by any chance aware that you've spelt the CO's name incorrectly?" Fuck me, he's right! So: "I'm very sorry sir. I'm extremely grateful to you for pointing it out to me in time, sir. I'll see to correcting it straight away, sir." And then, like an idiot, I get carried away and add: "After all, sir, they say only God can make things perfect." And as soon as I've said it, I'm thinking, Bloody hell, what d'you want to say that for? It's the glasshouse for you this time, Cottle! But he simply smiles and says, "I don't think God would object too strongly if you were to get the CO's name right, do you?"'

We all laugh. It's a good story. But it's left a residue, something I can't quite get a hold on, like a name on the tip of your tongue. And, as in such cases, it's not until I've stopped fretting about it that the thing comes and taps me on the shoulder from behind. I'm a child of about ten. I'm sitting sipping tea in a room furnished with exotic fabrics and statuettes. Hanging in front of the door, presumably to keep the warmth in, is a length of fabric made from stitched squares and triangles: indigo, maroon, a dark citric yellow. I notice that there is an error, an asymmetry, in the design; and, with a child's want of tact, I point this out. At once I regret having said it, thinking I may have behaved rudely. But the woman with whom I am taking tea, who is plump and gentle and resembles a benign headmistress but who in fact has spent most of her life as a missionary somewhere in southern India, tells me it is deliberate: 'They believe that only God can make things perfect, and it is therefore presumptuous for human beings to try.' The woman who is saying this to me is a distant aunt. And in a flash the truth dawns on me that this is the aunt whom I went to visit all those years ago in Ryehill. So where did I get the other image, that image that's been haunting me since I don't know when: the image of a windblown woman in a flowered apron, lean as a whippet and tough as a herring-gutter, approaching down a sloping path? This can only have been the image I held in my mind when, having not seen my real aunt since I was four years old, I set out on my first solo train-journey to meet her. For some reason or other, that vision, that woman striding along the rutted track between the cornfields, lodged in my mind and was never totally erased by the subsequent reality. I have been gazing into space for minutes on end, juggling these two truths: because truths they both are, in their different ways. I have got something back: something from my past: something never realised, but existing nonetheless as a potentiality, as something striven towards. Would that be right? I want to lay claim to this aunt, even though she did not come down that path to meet me. It is not my fault that you didn't. Nor yours. I wanted you to. I shall call you Cassandra, because you were evidently the bearer of some truth the gods did not want me to hear and therefore suppressed by deleting you. Cassandra. Cassie for short, because 'Sandra' is too suggestive of soft curls and tenderness.

Across the sky
Chimney pots brood like charred paper
Ideas crumble
Others tumble to sleep

'Carrots'll be ready for lifting soon.'

I glance at their feathery heads and nod wisely. For all the time I used to spend here as a kiddie, I never picked up on the arcana of it all. I suppose it was that the idea of the soil never took on the necessary emotional or symbolic significance. My engagement with horticulture never passed beyond the childhood stage of growing mustard and cress on a piece of damp flannelette as a contribution to the war effort. But I realise now that there's something about this allotment of Dad's which I've always been more or less aware of, but I've never tried to put into words. To say it's tidy wouldn't be enough. Lots of them are tidy. It's more to do with a sense of spacing, of distance, of the relations between objects. Look at those bean poles – hazel at a guess. They're none of them quite straight, and no two are of exactly the same diameter; yet you'd be prepared to swear the gaps between them were identical. Then let your eye travel from the rainwater butt – an oil drum painted dark blue – to the lidded wooden tub which has the soot bag suspended inside it, centre of its known universe, and to the compost heap which is far from being a heap but is shuttered on all four sides with corrugated iron held in place by lengths of gas piping hammered into the ground at regular intervals; and then, on the other side of the shed, the potato clamp perfectly formed as an old-style beehive, a moated beehive, with its little tuft of straws at the top for ventilation. 'Ship-shape' is the phrase that comes to mind, though I have to say there's also a hint of the alchemical about all these structures with their several and distinct purposes. The paths between the beds are paved, in herringbone pattern, with bricks which he collected, one by one or two by two, over many months, from bombsites, always careful to find unbroken ones. Grass is allowed to grow in the cracks, to hold the bricks in place and perhaps to make them look as if they've been there for centuries; but it's kept very short, and there are no weeds. Does Dad, I wonder, ever think about the houses, the destroyed houses, which these brick pathways commemorate? Houses, after all, carry as much emotional freight as the soil – at least, for most of us. And suddenly I notice a visual echo between the herringbone pattern of the bricks and the alternating growth of the leaves of the leeks, which Dad is at present earthing up between their lengths of planking 'in order to blanche the stems,' he tells me. The echo is surely not intentional; yet it somehow typifies what is special about this plot.

He straightens up and flexes his back; and at once, as it seems, his eyes take on that blankness, that look of indiffer-ence with which he gazes at anything that is not his produce or his implements. The world has long ceased to engage him.

'I suppose you think I was a bit neglectful of your mother – always here with my vegetables.'

He's obviously noticed – well, yes, obviously – that I've

been making a point of coming out to spend time with him here since Mum died. Is it that I'm trying to repair something, to patch something up? If so, what? Am I trying somehow to make amends for having left him to his own devices since those childhood days when I'd pester him every weekend to bring me here with him? Or is it more simply that I feel duty-bound to try and fill at least a little of the gap Mum's absence must have left in his spirit? Yet again, is it in some measure an attempt to compensate for her absence in my own life, to reaffirm family bonds? What's never crossed my mind, in all this, is that Dad might have his own ideas and uncertainties about my motives: that he may even suspect some sort of a veiled rebuke.

'It was difficult. There was no hostility, you understand. We still cared for each other just as much; but it was difficult, because we saw things different ways. You do understand, don't you?'

'She had her own concerns, I'd imagine – yes – once she was out at work, leading her own life. Was that it? Bound to happen, really, at least to an extent.'

'More so than in most cases, what with the meetings and that. A lot of meetings. She took it very seriously, the social side of it.'

'The partnership aspect, you mean – all the employees being partners?'

'Yes. The 13 points – or 21 points, was it? I don't remember. All those back numbers of the weekly *Gazette* we had to turf out when she'd passed away. Great bundles of them. But no, it was all very important to her. Not that I didn't agree with it in any way; but of course I wasn't part of it. Couldn't be. She even dragged in the architecture. You know, Peter Jones, one of the first progressive buildings in London.'

'Curtain walling.'

'That's it. Saw that as the future – the future for us all. That's what I'm talking about.' Graham, I realise, would have called it paternalism. Possibly so. But what harm did it do anyone? If it gave Mum some meaning for her life. After all, she wasn't going to live to see the revolution. Who's to say any of us are? Mum: a face I took for granted concealing a person the two of us perhaps scarcely knew. Or is that merely a platitude, equally true and untrue of everybody? Dad cuts across my thoughts:

'There's something you could do if you want to be helpful – little job you could do for me.'

He beckons me into the shed, with its smell of dryness. On the bench are several shallow, slatted apple boxes full of plump onions, each with its leaves bent over like a chicken with its neck broken. Dad ties a knot at the bottom of a length of twine that's hanging from a roof strut, then shows me how to loop the leaves of an onion around and under so that it hangs by its own weight against the knot. 'You can go on adding them, and they'll fall into a sort of spiral, each snuggling between the two below – see?' It looks easy, except that sometimes the leaves are so brittle that they break off where they've been kinked before I can get the onion safely into place. Flakes of dried skin fall away like the paper of a book in the farthest recesses of the basement of a second-hand bookshop. I haven't been at it very long before I become aware that the spiral I'm making is already looking knobbly and uneven. If Dad were doing it, he'd have graded the sizes – intuitively, without even having to think about it – and the result would look as neat as a Turk's head knot on the prow-post of a barge. Another of life's small defeats. Thinking of which, I realise Dad's explanation, his apparent opening up, has really not got me very far. I know the sense of estrangement – for want of a better word – between Dad and Mum began before Mum went out to work; in fact it was largely why she did go: that and the economic pressures when he became unemployed. It all goes back to the sinking of his ship. But how to broach the subject?

'I was thinking, Dad, about when you were torpedoed. I was only a kid when you told me. Did you say you were the only survivor – left clinging to a spar?'

'A spar? "Two Years Before the Mast" sort of thing?' He

chuckles. 'It wasn't a sailing ship. But we did still have wooden bulkheads. Just as well... No, I wasn't the only survivor. There was one of the greasers – a Chinaman. And that's not counting the ones who got away on one of the rafts – hardly had time to cut it loose – a dozen or more on a raft meant for eight, but they managed to stay afloat, I found out later. I'd been with a bunch of us trying to lower a boat, trying to clear the falls, 'cos we were listing heavily after the first torpedo – well, there wasn't a second one, there didn't need to be – the cargo shifted, and that was it. I was thrown over the side, and I started to swim away as fast as I could, 'cos she was sinking like a stone, and I did feel the drag as she went down, but I was just far enough away not to get sucked under. It was a close thing – very close. So then everyone was left flailing and floundering, swimming towards whatever we could see – nearly daybreak it was by this time – and I found this wooden panel with a baton which I managed to get a grip on. So here I am. Thank God we weren't carrying aviation fuel, that's all.'

'But I seem to remember you telling me something about how the others all gave up – I mean, didn't seem to want to hang on to life.'

'Maybe. Certainly they were going under one by one. Didn't have a good enough hold, I suppose. The Chinaman had found a bale of something – I don't know what – with rope around it, which helped; but it looked as if the water must be soaking into it, 'cos I could see him a way off, and the thing seeming to get lower and lower in the water. My fingers felt as if they were locked in place on that baton; but as soon as I began to doze off, my grasp slackened and I woke up to find myself sliding down. That was the worst thing, having to keep awake all the time. Ended up in a sort of hallucinatory state. Exhaustion of every cell and fibre. Failure of every chemical process. It felt like a bloomin' miracle when the Cat came out of the clouds.'

'A cat?'

'A Catalina. It tried to come down, made a couple of

attempts, but the sea was heaving too heavy; so then it dropped something, probably food and water with a float, but they were afraid of scoring a direct hit on me, so it fell about 20 yards away. I couldn't control the panel I was on, not to any sense, and I was too frozen to risk swimming off for the thing, afraid I'd never make it back. All I could do was wait. I could be pretty well certain they'd have reported my position, so it would only be a matter of time. But that was when I learned something I didn't know. You'd think it would be easier to wait when you knew help was on the way, wouldn't you? But it wasn't. It was torture. Previously I'd felt I could have held on in that dulled condition for ever, alive or dead; now I was all the time slipping and slithering, cursing, losing my grip, counting the seconds – and it was the best part of a day – before the destroyer finally showed up. It taught me something. That's why I could never quite have your mother's belief in politics.'

Funny, I never really thought of Mum's interest in the Partnership as 'politics'; but I suppose it was. The fact that she chose to keep all those Gazettes: fulfilling the management's commitment, year upon year, to share all information with the workforce: one step, to be sure, towards a different way of doing things. For a moment it seems as if Dad may be about to develop his thoughts further. But all he says is, 'That's what you wanted to know, isn't it?' He gazes around the allotments, then adds:

'This'll do me. Like the world, when you think about it. I chat to the people on the adjoining plots; I nod in passing to those on the next plots on. After that – well, they're not really any concern of mine. All you need in life is enough to eat and a modicum of shelter. I've got that here. And that'll do me. You understand, don't you?'

I assure him I do; but when I scan my surroundings, the mediaeval strips of land with their isolated huts and the odd head bobbing up and down absorbed in their cultivation, what I see reminds me more of a vista of survivors at the mercy of the waters.

I spit into the waters
Waste sentences
Fixing with sulky eyes
Dead eminences.

There's something I noticed a year or two ago that's preying on my mind. In a graveyard, it was, carved on a tombstone: an hourglass with wings. Well, it's simple enough: Time flies. But the thing is, you see, it just doesn't work for me. Yes, I get the message all right; but it doesn't carry any emotional force – the force of recognition, I suppose you'd have to call it. The question is, though, did it have that force for our ancestors? Is it that we see things differently now – bring a different mind to bear on them? Now then, here's something that may be the same question or may not, or may be a similar one – or, again, may not. I wrote a poem the other day consisting of only two words: 'Extant. Extinct.' How about that? I can't answer for anyone else, but for me that does have emotional force. It's to do with the fact that the words are so similar to look at – five letters the same, after all, in a six and a seven letter word, which surely has to stand for something – yet mean virtually the reverse. So again, you've got two elements, in this case the look and the meaning, which are set in apposition to each other. So why does one work and the other not; and would it have been the other way round in, say, the eighteenth century? Is this an example of the contrast between what they call the Classical and Romantic sensibilities? That's the sort of thing they'd tell you about in a university, isn't it? So does that mean I ought to try and get into university? How's that done – and what do you do for money? I worry more and more about all this. And you, Cassandra – what would be your slant on things?

'There's a chap at work called Bill Newcombe – easy-going, not always trying to score points – who's the only one I've ever mentioned my poetic efforts to, and I made some remark the other day about not being sure whether I oughtn't to take some sort of a course, and he said, "Well, there must be some sort of expertise involved. I mean, you wouldn't expect someone to be able to design a triple expansion engine who hadn't got their letters, would you?"'

'And what did you say?'

'I said, "I shall require notice of that question." It's a phrase people have started using recently – a sort of catch phrase. So he laughed. And that was that.'

You glance indulgently at me as you lift the dough, slam it down on the board, turn ends to middle and thrust your knuckles into it until it squeaks.

'Sounds like a mouse,' I say.

And you say, 'All the best loaves have at least one dead mouse in them.'

'I went to see my dad the other day at his allotment, and he was trying to tell me something important, or at least something that was important to him, about the difference in outlook between himself and my mum, and about how he saw life in relation to this allotment. It seemed to be something about fighting where you stand, not trying to change the rules in your favour. Maybe I didn't fully understand, but that's what I think he was saying.'

You heave the dough in one mass into a coarse earthenware bowl which you cover with a moist linen cloth, then set it to rest on a shelf close to the range.

'You're lucky to have your dad to talk to. I hardly remember mine. He died in the First World War, when I was still a little girl. He left me his piano – that one that's in the other room. I even tried to learn to play it, as a sort of memorial to him – 'cos his body was never actually found. I think it was the piano as much as anything that attracted Eric to me: my husband, that is – was. We got married in a rush when it was obvious war was about to be declared. Then he went and got himself killed in the Battle of Britain.'

'He flew a Spitfire?'

'Hurricane, actually. He wasn't strictly one of the Long-haired Boys. Sergeant pilot. It was all a bit gentlemen-and-players in those days. He'd been an apprentice in a factory making agricultural machinery. But he had the gift for it. And he did write a few poems, too; but he was always too shy to show them to me. Said he'd show me them after the war – when things had cooled, as he put it. I never found out what had happened to them. They weren't among his effects when they sent them back to me, and they weren't in the forefront of my mind at that moment; and by the time I remembered and asked about them, it was too late.'

Can it really be true? Can you really have been born before the First World War? But wait a minute: this is all ten years ago, isn't it? And you must have been in your mid-thirties then. So it's perfectly possible. For someone of my generation, the First World War is almost as remote as the crusades. Yet Clegg fought in it, and he hasn't even reached retiring age. One forgets, because he doesn't have much to say; but only the other day something prompted him to start telling us about an incident when he was wounded, bundled from the front line on a stretcher during a bombardment, every slither and bump jarring the shrapnel in him, seeing the edges of the trenches above him outlined against the Very flares and thinking in his delirium they were the lips of his grave. And then your husband, writing what I imagine were poems of sensitive valour in the halcyon year of his death, never to know the outcome of his sacrifice or even whether future generations might regard it as folly. After all, the CP was still calling it a bosses' war. 'Weren't very lucky with your menfolk, were you?'

You shake your head.

'Tell me, as a would-be pianist: what sort of music would a socialist play to celebrate a Labour election victory?'

'What on earth makes you ask me that? Let's see... Something by Chopin – one of his bouncier pieces?'

'Will you play one for me?'

'Tomorrow, perhaps – at least, I'll try my best. We can't leave this room for the moment.'

'Why not?'

'The slightest draught, and the dough will collapse. See – it's rising nicely.'

I gaze at your tough, scarred hands clasped on the yellow oilcloth table-covering. The light is beginning to fail, and you draw the paraffin lamp towards you. Tweaking the ring that controls the wick, you light a match over the tall glass funnel. A blue flame potters across the webbing, seems about to subside into darkness then gushes to a bright orange. Soon the lamp is casting a steady, tawny glow over the two of us; and, as you withdraw your arm, I glimpse up your short sleeve a luscious, luxurious, lascivious thicket of tightly curled hair. Tonight, in bed, I shall long for you as only a ten-year-old can.

Yes, in this lethargic, rats'-fluff land
Your eyes are the wings of the hawk,
Among the trampled weeks of spring
The green and velvet iris of the storm,
Your smile the sound of distant thunder.

At present the jokes are all on me; but in this instance I have no difficulty joining in the hilarity. Indeed, it would be diffi-cult not to see the funny side of my antics as I slice up cardboard tubes of different diameters, not excluding toilet-roll centres, and gum them together in an attempt to see exactly how the light would fall where in fact the light never does fall: on the insides of cast brass valve casings. It's an odd job, this one. A recently established ad agency, Chuck Chesterfield Alliances – the 'Alliances' being meant to signal that they can draw upon a wide range of specialist talent beyond the ambit of their permanent staff – have taken on a commission which is a little outside their usual field as well: a set of brochures for some new-fangled hydraulic control equipment. So they came to us for help; and I was muggins. Even my old paintbox has been called into service: black and dented, each colour sauced with some other colour, the crimson worn down to the tin. Used to be Dad's, actually; but it's only when I accidentally knock it onto the floor that I notice, gummed to the underside, an old luggage label printed in faded red which bears the inscription, 'From Auntie Enid with love, Xmas 1917.' The space for 'Destination' remains blank.

Frank Rillington says, 'You could get a job on a kids' television programme.'

Ron Cottle says, 'Royal Academy, mate. Flog it to the Royal Academy.'

Bill Newcombe says, 'Make sure you get credited for your artwork. Want to see your name in print, don't you?'

'Hmm – yes, I suppose I do.'

But when I get back from a meeting at the agency – minor revision of the layout proposals in response to revised brief from clients consequent upon preview of the dummies, everybody required for their input, team effort and all that – the atmosphere in the big office has changed: no badinage, no localised flurries of laughter. I raise a questioning eyebrow at Bill.

'It's Bob Bobson,' he says. 'He's in with the Old Man. Been in for rather a long time.'

I've just resumed tinkering with my mock-up when Bob comes in through the swing doors. I glance up at him, uncomfortably conscious that everyone else is also glancing up at him. Not a murmur. No cheery 'How'd it go, then?' We're waiting to take our cue from him; but he simply goes to his board, takes a few personal items from his shelf, wraps his pens and compasses in a washleather, puts everything in a brown paper bag and saunters back with it to the door. There he pauses for a fraction of a second, as if composing himself, then turns and treats us all to a broad grin. 'Bye, folks – it's been nice knowing you all!' And, not waiting for a reply, ignoring our incoherent murmurs of solicitude, he opens the doors with a flourish and strides out so that they crash and rattle into silence behind him.

'So that's it. He's got the tin tack.'

'Never thought that would happen.'

'Mind you, he was a bit of a lazy sod, wasn't he.'

'Never saw him do a stroke, to be honest...'

Past tense already. I ask if this has ever happened before, and the older colleagues shake their heads. Then Clegg, to my surprise, growls: 'Bastard bosses!'

'Oh come on, though,' – this is Cottle at his primmest – 'you've got to let the officers give the orders, else where would we all be?' And I catch Stallworthy, former Major Stallworthy, giving him a glance of what I can only interpret as loathing.

Who was it who said, a moment ago, that he'd never have thought it could happen? No more would I. I've been living in my own little paradise here; and it's a shock to realise it. All right, I've always known it's a commercial firm, locked into the world of business. Maybe it's something to do with the ethos of consultants being somewhat above the fray, somehow on a more elevated plane than contractors with their rough-and-tumble and competitive tendering. Then again, maybe it's not that at all, but simply my own experience of this as a relaxed place to be, a place of tolerance where you could chat about anything from holidays abroad to Henry Moore, from National Service to Christianity, safe haven for human detritus of all varieties, rag tag and bobtail... Another possibility, of course, is that it really wouldn't have happened until now: that things actually are changing: that what I once heard Stallworthy call 'post-war liberalism' – by which I think he meant a sort of mutual respect which he saw as having informed many aspects of social life – is on the wane, and that the wane has now reached our own little island of happiness.

Clegg is on his high horse. I missed the start of it, but he seems to be elaborating a point about authority in general: '...right in the knee, I got it. So I was invalided out, shipped back to Blighty – three cheers! – where they kept me five weeks in hospital – made a pretty good job of it, all things considered, though I still limp a bit – then a couple of months' convalescence, at which point the doc said I was fit to return to duty. So what did they do? Sent me straight back into the same fucking battle, that's what they did. Battle of the Somme. It was still going on – as if I'd only left yesterday, except none of my mates seemed to be around. Wonder why that was...' I may be wrong, but I have the impression it's the only thing he ever does talk about, drawing on it to illustrate any point he wants to make. Perhaps it's because everyone around him sees the Great War as a thing of history, and he knows we do, that his experience becomes dissociated from the general flow of life: like that total internal reflection you can get in a raindrop: as if he were trapped in a temporal short circuit. So how would you see it, Aunt Cassie, from your standpoint in a different generation?

Softly, almost inaudibly, someone is whistling *Lili Marlene* – unless I am imagining it, summoning it out of the disregarded background sonorities which reach us from the contingent world as if the signature of history survived in its steel and stonework or in the molecules of the air. My mind turns to that evening in the old office, when I was working late, and... And what? I'm not sure quite what happened, or even if anything did; but I came out of it knowing I wanted to write poetry, or thinking it was the right thing to do, or simply thinking it wasn't the wrong thing to do; or something. Anyway, it's a moment I always remember as having had tremendous importance for me; and I must ask myself now whether I don't have to question the validity of that. Yet how can an experience be invalid? Well, in a sense obviously it can't; but I can at least ask whether I didn't draw the wrong conclusions from it. So what conclusions did I draw? It was all to do with those cats and lupins, wasn't it – and with the absence of lines on a drawing being a representation of tiles on the wall of a chip shop where there was a bottle of vinegar and a sifter of salt, and... One conclusion you could reach about this would be that it was simply a middle-class indulgence: an experience empty of any true content, and therefore not transferable in the form of language to the benefit of others. That's almost certainly what Graham would have said, and conceivably he'd have been right. Another way of looking at it, though, might be to argue that the quality of that moment, its sense of grace, was

57

the subjective accompaniment of what was in fact a significant conjunction of elements amounting almost to an
insight, even if an insight I couldn't plot out and analyse: a
sort of aperture in the world. What I'm saying is: just
suppose that to capture the light flickering on the white tiles
of a chip shop, or on a blue clock on a station platform with
no numbers, just ticks, might be to pinpoint moments when
life opens up a space – or perhaps it's language that opens
up a space – for me, for you, for the proletariat, through
which the unexampled may enter? Looked at that way, it
becomes simply a question of how to harness such sense-
data under a benevolent sign – the spontaneous revelation
accompanied by the imprimatur of significance – so that it
may be both a lived thing and a thing primed for communication. I glance at the bent backs of my fellow workers –
weary oarsmen – and realise how preposterous that sounds.
Would I dare say it to them? Absolutely not. What ought I to
do, then? Withdraw my little stash of savings, leave the
company – I could even represent it as a protest against
Bob's dismissal – and take a course of some sort in English,
preparatory to bursting on the literary scene? I've probably
left it too late already. If you look at those mini-biographies
on the backs of Penguin books, you'll see that practically all
of the authors had their first books published when they
were twenty-six, which probably means they'd have to have
had them finished by the time they were twenty-five: which
doesn't leave me with much time if I've still got the trade to
learn. The truth is, I've no idea what the options really are.
Should I try to get a job on a local newspaper and work my
way up from that? One thing's for sure: if I decide to stay on
here, to fight where I stand, I'm going to have to take a more
realistic view of the place. 'Show where you stand by marching.' For example, I was thinking not so long ago that the
blokes here will talk about anything; but that's not strictly
true, is it? The other day I overheard Nick Galloway –
Galloway, like the cough syrup – telling a story about an
electric drill: 'I was trying to drill a hole in this metal

window-frame, see, so I grabbed hold of the frame with one hand and switched on the drill, and the bloody thing couldn't have been earthed properly, 'cause the current went straight through me and I was throbbing away like someone in the electric chair and my muscles were in spasm and I couldn't let go. Luckily, at that moment, the wife came back from shopping and saw what was happening and switched me off at the mains.' The wife. That's how they refer to their wives, almost invariably. Not by name, merely by function. Not even 'my' wife. They talk about sex, of course, endlessly; but they never talk about love. So that's one place you can plot the invisible barrier; and doubtless there are others I'm not aware of. Might one say, then, that one challenge for the working poet – I just stopped myself in time from thinking, 'the working class poet' – could be to infiltrate such experiences as love into the lexicon in a form of words which would avoid any threat to the prevailing taboos? 'No answer' was the stern reply – as Bob used to delight in saying whenever the opportunity presented itself.

> The busman cycling home from the terminus
> Smiles at the driver with significance only
> Of green reflections in the eyes of a cat.

So by some machinery I have to pick up on those lupins – pink and white and blue – cats' eyes, flasks of vinegar: to harness all those involuntary comings-together under – what was it I was saying a while back, or what I meant or hoped to mean by it? – a benevolent sign – that's right – conviction ungainsayable as the wax of a papal stamp. But how is one to reach the revolution through this? And even affirming it was my personal Damascus, why should anyone else be interested? No, no, that's not it. I'm sure there was something I told myself to remember.

Morbid reverie – in the sense in which one speaks of a 'morbid' growth – interrupted by Stallworthy. It's time to set off. Dad has never grown lupins. Chrysanths and sweet peas and marigolds, yes, but never lupins.

A rain-swept, asphalt lot with a car or two parked in it and plentiful puddles: more puddle than dry land, at a cursory estimate – like the surface of the Earth. We splash towards the cluster of buildings: some old, renovated, a school or a flour mill, fronted by others single-storey, in post-Festival style, paint already peeling. I expect to see stains on the ceilings and probably moss beginning to colonise the inside edges of of the window frames; and sure enough, there are. Two meagre shrubs flank the reception hatch.

'Ah yes. Just take a seat. Someone will be down in a minute.'

Three of them appear: middle management. One, scarcely older than I am, is holding all the folders. The handshakes are without cordiality. I've been wondering why Stallworthy was insistent on bringing me along on this visit; and it occurs to me now that perhaps having a junior in tow is part of the game, a declaration of status in which you have to match up to your counterparts. They seem to be taking us a long way round, doubtless planning to impress us with an unscheduled tour of the factory. We march through the sheet metal shop. Windows high up, broken, through which pigeons flutter. The operatives watch us pass as alligators might watch a punt drift by, wondering if it was worth the trouble. Then it's the main machine room, a cacophony of humming and screeching and grinding, presses and stamping machines so packed together that one is almost surprised not to see overhead leather belt drives whipping and slapping like demented washerwomen. Alongside a bank of capstan lathes a wiry, scrag-end little man – Welsh by the look of him – is collecting the swarf into a central bin with his bare hands. For God's sake, is this place beyond the jurisdiction of the factory acts?

We arrive at a room on the mezzanine with a wide internal window giving onto the works floor below; and we all seat ourselves on spindly chairs around a kidney-shaped table. The paper-work is distributed, and I scan it with what I hope will pass for keen intelligence. From the tone and manner of the contractors' representatives I recognise – I suppose I ought to have foreseen it – that they don't consider our supervision necessary. That's what this meeting is all about. They believe they know their jobs; and who am I to think otherwise? Page by stultifying page. Twenty bum-numbing minutes. Stallworthy is being imperturbable as usual. No, actually, he's being more imperturbable than usual. He's hamming it up:

'These estimates for outflow from the centrifugal pumps seem a mite optimistic.'

'Well, you've got the calcs in front of you.'

Stallworthy grunts. He's already turned his attention to the next sub-heading when I spot it:

'Hang on; hang on a moment. Seems here you've taken the circumference of a circle as $\pi R^2$ instead of $2\pi R$. That would rather inflate the figures, wouldn't it?'

The two older men peer disbelievingly at their documents, while the young one turns red as the People's Flag. It was obviously his doing. Stallworthy is trying hard, I think, not to catch my eye.

Of course, it's bollocks. It's not that the contractors can't tell an area from a circumference. It's a mistake anyone could have made, working in a hurry; and they'd have found it and corrected it soon enough. But they can't say that: not without seeming to resort to feeble excuses. And we're not going to let them off the hook, are we? Our company's got a commission riding on the contract.

So now we're seated in this cavernous, baronial place with smoky beams – real or reproduction, I wouldn't know – and dark-framed aquatints of shaggy cattle standing in water. Stallworthy has decided that victory deserves to be celebrated with a visit to a steak house. I've never imagined he had much of an opinion of me; but for the moment I'm in his good books, and I want to take the opportunity to try and draw him out a bit. Why, in particular? I don't know; it's somehow distantly related to Dad, to the experience of previous generations – its opacity, the difficulty of knowing how to engage with it. Talk, desultory to begin with, turns to the office; and I let fall an ambivalent remark about Cottle and his adherence to Queen's Regulations. Stallworthy takes the bait:

'Little berk! I can't for the life of me fathom what he's about. He's never been in the war – I mean, not on active service. Too young. So who knows how he'd shape up? He might acquit himself well; he might not. You can never tell. But all this spit and polish – what's it for? It's just toytown stuff. Nothing to do with being under fire. You don't even risk getting seasick in one of those bricks-and-mortar establishments they call HMS this, that or the other. Yet it's all the world to him. Obeying orders! Manages to make it sound as if obeying orders made him some sort of a maverick. An outsider because he's an insider: inside his safe little fantasy. I mean, it's not as if he was submitting to the discipline of a Stalinist cell, or what-have-you.'

'He wouldn't be telling us about it if he was.'

'Exactly. So there'd be no point in it as far as he was concerned. Only the other day – I think you were out at Chesterfield's – he started telling us all about Dunkirk, some compulsory talk he'd attended, queues of gallant little ships taking turns to pick up the queues of gallant little soldiers. I happened to remark that I'd been there at the time; but he wasn't discountenanced at all by that – went right on telling me what it was like.'

'What was it really like?'

'Really like? It was like one of those Lowry paintings, that's how I remember it: one of those paintings that's full of people, and the perspective is defined purely by the people getting smaller and smaller. The beaches, that is. Oh yes, and stuff burning. Smoke. Burning rubber. But really, how would I know? There was too much going on, too much to keep tabs on. I reckon you'd *have* to have not been there to know what it was like.'

Not wanting this conversation to slip out of my control, I improvise: 'I was reading somewhere recently about some Frog poet who sat on the beach correcting the proofs of his latest volume while he was waiting to be rescued.'

'Well, maybe there's a reason we have to resort to French for the expression *sang froid*.'

I'm not getting there. What I'm thinking is, supposing it wasn't just my dad, the specifics of what happened to him: suppose it was more general than that? I remember my Uncle Albert, and launch into his story:

'Uncle of mine, he'd been at Dunkirk too. Bright chap, he was, with a bit of an education – branch manager for one of the big insurance firms before the war. And every so often they'd offer to put him forward for a commission, but he always refused. "Why's that? Do you have a low opinion of your officers?" "No sir. Personal reasons, sir." They could never get any more out of him, 'cos he knew he'd be in the soup if he told them the truth. But the truth was that, as I say, he'd been at Dunkirk, and he'd seen all the officers scrimmaging to be first on the boats and leaving it to the NCOs to take charge of the men. He could never forgive them for that.'

'Hmm. Can't say I witnessed actual cowardice; mutton-headedness, yes; but I suppose it depended on where you were standing and which way you were facing at the time.'

'Oh I'm sorry,' – realising I've probably dropped a clanger – 'I didn't mean to imply... I mean, I know you were an officer...'

'Not at that time, I wasn't. Not until later, when the Sandhurst mob had all either got themselves safe postings back at HQ or else got themselves shot to pieces by being more interested in having their trousers correctly pressed than in keeping an eye out for the enemy. That was what was special about Monty. He may have made a balls-up of Arnhem, but he did have a realistic sense of what mattered and what didn't.'

'Is it true he kept a photo of Rommel in his command trailer in order to figure out what he might be thinking, what he might be going to do next?'

'It's true about the photo. But if you ask me, it was basically a myth: a myth that was put about to cover for the fact that we'd cracked the Enigma code, and Monty knew perfectly well what Rommel was going to do next. Being a mystical lot, the Germans may have fallen for it. In fact most of us fell for it at the time. But it was one of those things like bowls of grated carrot in the pilots' messes – help them see in the dark, and all that.'

'So when it comes down to it, all the stories...' We're right on the verge of what I really want to know; yet I'm far from sure how to phrase it. 'Look, the war: all of us saw some of it, even us kids, but nobody saw all of it; we've all heard stories, we've all seen the propaganda films of the time, and there's a general overall sense of what happened in those years, and – but – all the stories are now being replaced by different stories, which are sometimes more heroic, sometimes less, but it's never quite the same as it was before and yet it's still supposed to describe the same thing. I mean, isn't there any truth at all, even to what we've experienced personally?'

'The truth's the way you put it together. That's no different from how it always is. The war's just a particularly striking instance. People start projecting their own needs onto it – people like our friend Cottle – even while questions start being asked about its conduct, and secret reports start being revealed, and so forth. And it won't stop. It'll be an ever-expanding argument as theories disintegrate and re-form: the pattern of complex doubts and mythologies, like a big flower opening, a slow explosion.'

'So Cottle's navy, for example: all those things he tells us about: is he making it all up?'

'I dare say everything's happened exactly as he says it happened. I don't think for a moment he's fibbing. But he makes it serve his purposes. So in a deeper sense, yes, I'd say he's making it all up.'

    The ladder lies along the stairs
    With an air of recumbence
    This saddened haunt:
    Faint universe where one comes out
    Blinking

Doubting of doubt.

'If you're chocker with being a draughtsman, and there's other things you'd like to try, I'd say give it a go. What do you stand to lose? You've only got one life, haven't you.'

I sort of knew, even before I confided in him, that Bill Newcombe wouldn't see it as a problem. If that's what you want, do it. Why do I find it so difficult to explain? I try to say that it's about not wanting to feel that I'm ratting out, that writing is about clarifying our perceptions, on behalf both of ourselves and of other people; that our verbal reconstructions of life will be of no value if we've turned our back on it: that I need to experience life as other people do. Bill laughs:

'If life's going well, you get on with it. If it's going badly, you put up with it. But no-one with his head screwed on would set out to experience it.'

There's another thing nagging at my mind. Ever since that incident at the factory, when I effectively booted that young man in the goolies – after all, I could easily have waited till after the meeting, then quietly taken him aside and pointed out his error – I've been asking myself: Is this the sort of bastard I want to be? And is this the sort of bastard I'm going to have to get used to being if I want to be accepted as a mature employee of this company?

That aside, there's the question of whether I'm right about the relation of writing to experience. Sometimes it seems to me that you don't need experience at all in order to write, because it's all there, already present in the language: all the experience of the human race, stored, fossilised, encrypted, compacted. All the poet has to do is tune in to it, chip away at it: learn how to free its meanings from the immemorial marl.

Over and over I go, rehearsing the same arguments. They don't change. But it looks as if the time of decision may have come, and come sooner than I ever expected. Chuck Chesterfield, phoning to invite me for lunch to acknowledge the successful completion of the brochures – not the sort of gesture we learn to expect in our normal line of business –

added the remark:

'And perhaps we could have a little chat about your future.'

'My future?'

'Well, I remember that old bird Brightwell said something to me about you having aspirations in the literary line.'

Mr Brightwell, of all people. He obviously pays a good deal more attention to what's going on around him than most of us quite realise. So here I am, punctual as ever, outside the Chinese restaurant in Glasshouse Street: hefty stone torsos with arms sliced off, bronze loincloths with tassels and bronze turbans supporting the entablature, if that's what you call it, over their stern and savagely bearded heads: scarcely the style you'd associate with Ming porcelain. Upstairs, too, where the restaurant is, there's a solemnity in the regular distribution of square tables with starched white cloths which hints rather at an Edwardian gentlemen's club or even – though there are naturally no book-shelves – some place of advanced learning. I've never eaten Chinese before; but Chesterfield advises me that a chop suey, a chow mein and fried spring rolls form an acceptable combination. We're pretty well finished, and on to the green tea, before he gets around to asking just what my objectives in life are. It's a question I find difficult to answer in spite of the thought I've been giving to it, and especially difficult to answer without feeling pompous; but I try to outline for him the fascination I find in the idea of bringing poetic method to bear upon normal, everyday living: the apparent gap between the two, my curiosity as to how that gap might be closed or at least narrowed.

'Sort of poetry for the masses, eh?'

'Well, I'm not sure. I've never met a mass...' He raises an eyebrow, and I quickly move to patch over what I fear may have seemed a facetious remark: 'I mean, the question of whom the poetry's addressed to, or who'll read it, is another one again – a further stage of the debate, if you like. For the moment I'm only thinking about the relation between method and subject-matter: working life as a subject for verse. What sort of verse would that have to be? Would existing popular forms serve as a basis? That kind of thing.'

'Hmm. But do you ever read your poems to your workmates?'

'No. I'd be too embarrassed.'

'Bad sign, bad sign.'

'Yes. When you put it like that, it does seem to cast a certain doubt over the project. But I've been inclined to assume it's only because the stuff I'm writing isn't yet good enough. And of course there's always a problem about performing in front of people you actually know, people who have a prior impression of you or who've already cast you in your role in the office drama.'

'That's all true enough. But what it makes me wonder is how essential the working context really is to you. Could be that it's not much more than a romantic and, dare I say, a political attachment – ? And maybe it's even getting under your feet a bit.'

'I can't deny the possibility. Not even to myself. But... Well, the other day I was listening to the radio, and I heard this woman say that a woman shouldn't have children if she wants to be a writer; and I thought, There's something wrong with that. If a woman decides to relinquish an essential element in her experience in order to write about her experience, then the writing will surely be compromised.'

'Emily Dickinson didn't have any children.'

'That's not quite the point, though. I'm not saying a woman *has* to have children before she can be a writer; simply that to give up on children *in order* to be a writer is a questionable move. And I think – though I haven't quite settled the matter in my own mind – that I'd feel the same about giving up my job as a draughtsman.'

'OK. Well just let me throw a thought in your direction. You might find you could resolve your difficulties by taking a job with us. We'd employ you first of all as a technical illustrator – more or less the sort of thing you did for us on those brochures – but you'd soon find yourself with opportunities to write copy for this or that, and if you proved yourself talented in that direction – well, the field's wide open. It's scarcely what you'd call literature; but it's closer than you'll get in your present employment. Chance to hone your talents, and so forth. Why not?' Stumblingly I begin to thank him for his offer, but he silences me in the same benevolent gesture with which he takes the bill and reaches for his wallet. Our crumpled napkins huddle by our rice-grain cups. 'We're the future, you know. The future is one hundred percent advertising.'

I laugh at what I assume to be his exaggeration, and add: 'But you'll still need people like us to supply the goods for you to advertise.'

'Up to a point. But only up to a point. From our perspective, the product is only one element in the campaign. And we look forward to a time, not so far from now, when products will be designed solely to slot in to a pre-formulated sales strategy. In other words, the image – the dream, if you like – may actually come first. At that point, I won't need to be defensive about our relation to literature. We'll have outstripped literature in terms of creativity.' He smiles as we make for the door. 'Anyhow, think a little about what I said. Give me a call if you're interested.'

Men in black with tears in their eyes
Bowler hats
Amid the floundering intensity of midday
Infatuation leaps at the throat
Useless
Falls away like a shot dog

Cycling back from Dad's allotment, I catch successive glimpses of the setting sun, a blown glass globe cooling to an ever-darker red, netted in the trees' branches. I wish I were coming home to your turnip, parsnip and broccoli soup, full of wartime nourishment. You examine your palm calloused from the plough, your hair tumbling grey around your shoulders, then turn upon me a quizzical stare: 'Don't you think you may be taking this big decision of yours a little too seriously? It's not Antigone, you know.'

'No. But it is my life – my only life. If I get it wrong...'

'Hmm. I'm not sure there is such a thing as getting it wrong. Life, I mean. What would a wrong life look like?'

# THE WORKS

He was still thinking about it as he climbed the steps from the Underground into the sunlight at his daily destination, an hour-and-a-half's journey from home with three changes of transport. He was still thinking about it. The really creepy thing was that they had looked almost identical: two old men with grey stubble and the stoops. But one had been wearing a uniform and the other not. Sid Rawsthorne handed in his ticket, sampled a lungful of the relatively unfouled air of the North Circular and embarked upon the final ten minutes' walk to the factory.

They could have been twins from the look of them, but one kitted up on a shoddy railway outfit – no telling what – and the other wrapped in a mac, sitting on a low wall with a bundle of manky newspapers. The wall, presumably, was government property – there must have been some pettifogging legality which counted as a reason – and the geezer in the railway gear was browbeating the other one, telling him to scarper or he'd call the law: pulling rank, for God's sake, because of the uniform. No other distinguishing features, your Honour. I should have belted him one.

As he neared the factory gates, Sid saw Mr Harper's typist, who liked to be called a secretary, approaching from the opposite direction. Right and left wheeling, they turned into the gates together and up the gravel path between the rose beds towards the stucco '30s frontage to what was really no more than a conglomeration of tin shacks. Her enormous false eyelashes, achieved by gumming two normal pairs together, would have gathered dust by the end of the day. He'd noticed it last Friday as he queued past her desk for his wagepacket.

'Morning, Mr Rawsthorne. You're nice and early today.'

Festering schoolmarm! What gives her the right to compliment me? Sid smiled: 'I always like to turn up on the

early side. Makes me feel I'm choosing my own hours, like –
not a slave to the clock.'

He'd spoken those words many a time to different people
– tapping between the cells – you a rebel too? – and once in
a blue moon it elicited a grunt of comprehension. Today,
however, only the blank stare of someone indissolubly
wedded to the system, from this day forward, forsaking all
others, in sickness or... Sod 'em all, Mrs Weston. A fitting
start to another day of the cold shoulder.

Sid punched his card and lodged it in the rack, stashed his
jacket in the locker, shrugged on his overalls and made his
way to the sheet metal shop, where he sat down for a fag
while waiting for the dot of eight-thirty. They weren't going
to get anything out of Sid for nothing. Yes, I should have
belted him one. 'Cos it wasn't respect for his age that
stopped me. Just cowardice. Plain bloody cowardice.

The others arrived – three of them. And, at once, what had
been plain peace-and-quiet changed into silence. Not that the
others didn't talk among themselves. They did. And they
pitched their voices at such a level that Sid could just about
overhear them, and therefore felt like an eavesdropper. The
subtlety of man! Work – that's the only answer. Get on with it.

Ventilation trunking for an air terminal. Three-foot-six-
inches by two-foot-nine-inches in six-foot sections. Not even
any bends. Boredom. Still, far be it from me to ask for the
difficult stuff, drawn up by junior draughtsmen who've
passed all their exams and never met a sheet of galvanised in
their lives. Plan and elevation. 'What do you mean, it won't
go together like that?' Just like it is on the drawing, bending
two ways at once. But it's no use telling them – they can't see
it. Have to redesign it yourself half the time, and you don't
get paid for your helpfulness. Wish Jimmy was here.

Half way through the morning, it being payday, the shop
steward came round and received Sid's dues as if exacting
penance for the misdemeanour of his continued existence.
Addresses me as 'Rawsthorne'. All right, that's the name on
my card. I can't prove he's being deliberately offensive. Like

I said – subtlety. In fact, of course, the firm was not fully organised. That was part of the trouble. And they were paying Sid under the odds – though he knew he wasn't the only one. But at thirty-eight... He'd got the message when he first came for the job. 'We're not very union-minded here, ' the works manager had said, the threat looming through the casualness like a periscope through a mist. But Sid had kept quiet and calculated the housekeeping. *I can't give you anything but...* What with the kids.

*Soviet-land, so dear to every toiler,*
*Peace and progress found themselves on thee.*
*There's no other land the whole world over*
*Where man walks the earth so proud and free*
                                        *– tiddle-di-dee.*

The canteen was also the recreation room, which is to say that it was fitted out with a ping-pong table and a darts board. All at one end were the wooden benches at slatted tables through which cutlery could easily drop and which looked as if they had spent a long time out in the open. Sid approached them, steering well clear of the darts, carrying his lunch on one of those fibreglass trays which could spring up unexpectedly in the middle and slop your tea. But you could collect your tea later, if you liked. Your pudding, however, you had to collect with your first course: so that, unless you were an exceptionally quick eater, it got cold. Breast of mutton stew with baked beans, and treacle pudding with custard. Sid liked the treacle pudding, and had once said so to Madge behind the counter – Madge the mash, as Taffy called her – in an attempt to be friendly. Madge had smiled dutifully, but had clearly not been pleased, almost as if she'd been offended at the suggestion that questions of taste could enter into it at all.

Sid selected his position carefully, at a bare patch of table. Let others sit near him if they wished. Perhaps Taffy would come today, Taffy of the Brylcreemed hair and nutcracker jaw who cleared up the swarf in the turning shop with his knobbly bare hands – 'Give me leather gloves for it once, they did, but it tore them to ribbons.'

Behind Sid, and to his left, his three colleagues sat hunched over the crossword they had begun in the tea break, their voices just audible:

'It's 'cause Ron in't here, that's why it's taking us so long.'

'He's good at 'em, is Ron.'

'Yeah. He cheats, though.'

'How d'you mean, cheats? How can you cheat at crosswords?'

'He gets the paper on his way in, dumps it before he gets here, thinks about the clues all morning. By the time we get started, he's ready. Crafty with it, though. Just drops them in one at a time, like, as if he'd just thought of 'em.'

Taffy didn't seem to care who was in favour and who wasn't. But he didn't always eat in the canteen. Probably went down the pub. Or the bookies, more like. Chatty, yet not what you'd call matey. A strange character. Sid was about to add some pepper to his stew when he saw Wally, the van driver, approaching. Wally always shook enough pepper onto his own grub for Sid to get all he needed with the fall-out. Whenever there were baked beans, Wally would say, 'Shirttail dirtiers,' and laugh. There was something wrong with his right eye – possibly a budding cataract.

Wally sat down, nodded towards the beans, laughed and said, 'Shirt tail dirtiers.' He showered pepper onto his stew, Sid reaped the benefit and they ate in silence. Three tables across, the wizened man with the polished pate and the hooked red hooter, whom Sid had christened Mr Punch, was rattling on as usual in that maddening, high-pitched voice of his. I should have belted him one. Wally was the only person in the works, except for Taffy, who ever spoke to Sid outside the requirements of the job. Perhaps, as van driver, he was not even aware of the situation. Sid was aware of it, though. Oh yes. Taffy had, either from humanity or from malice – he probably wouldn't recognise the distinction – explained it all to Sid on his third day here:

'I suppose you must have noticed a certain – how to say – *chill* in the atmosphere? Know what it's all about, don't you? Well no, I suppose they wouldn't have told you, now, would they? Got nothing to do with your rate of pay, boy. They're not that union-minded here. Besides, they were getting less than you are. Who? The two they chucked out, that's who. Little over a month ago. "Superfluous to requirements" – that was the phrase they used: "superfluous to requirements." Indolent pair of buggers they were, too. But with them taking you on, like, and so soon after – well, it's bound to look a bit suspicious, isn't it? I mean, that's the way people think. Shower of bloody Baptists, if you ask me.'

Then, without apparent concern for Sid's reaction, his fork squeaking on the aluminium plate as he tried to impale a morsel of mutton, he had continued: 'See that? No teeth. Not a tooth in my head – look. They give me false ones, the National Health, but I couldn't get on with 'em – slithering around – useless, they were. But I manage all right – nice juicy steak, anything – just with my gums. Only one thing I can't eat, and that's apples.'

Sid returned to the table with his cup of tea – 'With or without?' – 'With, please.' Words murmured around him, ragged and pointless as clouds. Darts plopped solemnly into the board.

'A young fellow from here may pick a rhyme: L, two letters E, three letters K...'

'... gorgeous pair of Bristols...'

'... went out with the Clem Attlee brigade, but then he got himself into...'

Somewhere a radio was scratching out *Slow Boat to China* – one of those trannies that seem to have been programmed entirely with deservedly forgotten songs. Like in the old place. I remember Jimmy once saying, 'Listen to the distortion on that sound,' and me saying, 'Nobody seems to mind,' and him saying, 'That's just the point. Nobody does mind. And you know why? It's 'cause they're not actually interested in the music as such. It's just the *idea* of the music. See what I mean? It's what Plato was on about. Ideas. Look at this stuff we're eating. If we stopped to taste it, we'd complain. But it's the idea of food, just like it's the idea of music. A world made up of a few simple ideas, that's what we're living in: the idea of food, the idea of sex, the idea of brotherhood...'

'The idea of money.'

'No. Money *is* only an idea.'

'Not a bad one, though, sometimes.'

And as for brotherhood... a half-blind van-driver with one sentence of conversation and a bloody Welsh lunatic who tries to chomp apples with his bare gums and rolls the management's phrases around his tongue as if they were Sophocles. Even dreamed about him last night. And me feeling guilty towards the Union – Unity is Strength – and this load of shysters hating my guts for something I can't do anything about. *There's no other land the whole world over...* Two young lads were chatting between strokes over the ping-pong:

'Not stopping here, I can tell you.'

'What you going to do, then?'

'Get a job as a draughtsman.'

'Draughtsman? Pull the other one!'

'People do.'

'Got to get your Ordinary National.'

'So – I'll get it.'

'Dog's dinner's chance!'

'They start you off easy. Don't need no GCEs.'

'Right. My bird's brother was telling me. Start with fractions, end of the second year you're on calculus.'

'Look, knock it off, will you – you're perverting the course of my play...'

Sid often wondered what had become of Jimmy – Jimmy Sexton, that was his name – who'd been too near retirement to find a new job when the old firm was bought out, last heard of scraping by on his redundancy. Jimmy and his *New Statesman* competitions! Still, it broke the monotony, him chuntering on. Won it three times, too. Or so he said.

'...get these collars, see – insecticidal – stops 'em migrating up to the head at night-time...'

'Snowball in hell's chance, sonny. It's your upbringing.'

As you stood up, you could see through the window; and Sid got a shuftie of the contract gardener dead-heading roses in one of the plots alongside the main entrance. Must be one of the saddest jobs in the world, dead-heading roses on the North Circular. Mr Punch was still holding forth upon the care and maintenance of the Airedale And why not? Should I despise the bloke just because he likes dogs? Would I be seeing all these people as caricatures if they hadn't shut me out from their society? I mean, even Jimmy was a bit of a caricature if you wanted to see him in that light. Educated bugger in his way. It's just that his way wasn't anybody else's. Still, they have shut me out, and that's that. So grin and bear it, as Dad would have said. *I'm going to celebrate, because I'm feeling great...* Only one more half day, and there's another week gone. *I'm the guy who found the lost cause.*

Say good night to them all, just to brazen it out. A few gruff responses. At least they've the grace to look embarrassed. But how long are they going to keep it up? Another day? Another year? Always? It's bad enough being bored silly without people behaving like this. I've got nothing against any of them. But they treat me as an enemy, so I start looking for reasons to dislike them. I try not to. But what's the difference? All the good will in the world won't change their attitude. So – as I so often have reason to remark – sod them.

On the ten-minute trek back to the tube station, Sid found his mind again haunted by the image of the two interchangeable old derelicts, the one with a uniform bullying the one without. He couldn't feel angry any more, but he was still haunted by it. Just the *idea* of the uniform: that was all that had mattered.

At the ticket office in the middle of the hall there was quite a queue, and Sid shuffled forward with more than his usual impatience. The moment he reached the window, with his right money ready, the man turned away to deal with someone at the other side – the side for season tickets. Sid drummed his fingers on the sill. Ten seconds. A bulky grey flannel shadow. Fifteen seconds. Why couldn't he have dealt with this queue first? Twenty seconds. An argument about the expiry date of a ticket. Half a minute. Sid leaned into the hatch and saw the button with his fare marked on it. Putting down his money, he reached in and pressed. There was a loud whirring, and the ticket swept into his waiting hand. As he walked away there was a shout behind him: 'Here, you! What the hell d'you think you're doing!' Will he follow me? With an effort, Sid managed to maintain his pace, neither speeding up nor showing hesitation. 'You – come back here!' Don't turn round, or he'll recognise you tomorrow. Pretend you think he means someone else. Now down the steps. You can take them a bit faster without it looking like panic. But he's not following anyway. Perhaps he's afraid the queue would get stroppy if he left his post – though in fact they'd probably back him up. Nobody likes a rebel. Makes them feel inferior.

Sid strolled along the platform with a spring in his step which brought back to mind the first time a girl had said to him, 'OK, see you again tomorrow.'

Nobody loves you when you're down and out. Just get out there and screw 'em. It's better to be a bastard. D'you hear me? It's better to be a bastard.

# THREE

Gottlieb – *pow!* – of Chicago – *pow!* – which passeth all
understanding – *diddle-diddle-splat!* – *chokka-chokka* – beer
slops onto the pane – *chokka-chokka-chokka* – it's how long
you can keep it shuttling without – *prang!* – see that? – the
old double action, ball from the tip of one flipper to the
centre of the other and away – *thudder, thudder* – back into
the whirligig, rigmarole, rodomontade, middle fingers
twitching, Aces High in pyrotechnic lights on the back-
glass, gangster in snap-brim fedora, chick in the foreground
niftily slipping the ace of spades from the welt of her stocking – *jigger-jigger-jigger* – cigarette dangling from his lip, hers
too – wonder how they kiss – it's how long you can keep it
shuttling with a calculated tremble, seeing as if by
Egyptology the hidden pendulum shaking in the ring – if it
touches, the whole thing goes dead and TILT is displayed;
but – *jigger-jigger* – gone – *slap* – *CRACK!* – a free game
already, and I'm still on my first ball, wasn't even paying
attention to the score-count – *kerchugga-kerchugga* – again
bouncing between two capstans and keeping it below the
threshold of cut-off, intuitively acting against its resonance
like someone in a B-movie, The Man with the X-ray Eyes –
then trundle and drop as it rolls between the tips of my flip-
pers; but it's early days yet, I've four more to go, so I adopt
a louche attitude, strike the spring-plunger with my palm
and we're off again: the smack of cards from a croupier's
spatula, ace of diamonds, tight leather skirt, a girl's best
friend, *ker-chink; chink; chink-chink-chink-CRACK!* – never
happen again – can't – law of averages – aware, peripherally,
as people begin to congregate around me, cigarette smoke
caressing me like phosgene, of mirror-backed mahogany
shelves crowded with Christmas-coloured potions and
potations and potent syrups, glittery glass painted with
cornucopia and Bacchanalia, beer-pumps like truncheons –

CRACK! – someone stands me a fresh pint but I can't look up to see who it was – *ker-chugger* – *ker-diddle* – *ping-splat-ping* – the centre of attention now, not a sound beyond the sounds I'm making – at one with the machine, as the cliché has it – shrill bottles juddering, sympathetic vibration – remember at school, under the lid of each desk, a pinned sheet of paper representing – so it was tacitly accepted – the dashboard of a Spitfire: altimeter, speedometer, fuel gauge, artificial horizon; our feet on the desk strut for banking and turning, *wheeeaaaauugh*, the joystick a cricket bat the domed top of whose handle served as the thumb-trigger for our cannons, *pah-pah-pah*! – the 109s going down like nine-pins – *CRACK!* – *ker-prang, ker-diddle, diddle, trundle, trundle,* drop... And it's all over. Spontaneous applause engulfs me, almost lifting me off the ground. Eleven free games. No-one's ever seen the like of it. I smile, pick up my beer and say, 'Have those on me.' I'd be a fool to try and match my own performance. Fluke, obviously; yet you can't help feeling ennobled by it.

Moving away from the crush in search of some lonely spot befitting my now mythic status, however temporary, I notice two girls from the local library whose glasses are nearly empty, and casually ask if I can get them the same again. I leave my beer on their table as I go to the counter for their re-fills; and when I return I take a seat facing them. It seems quite the natural thing to do; yet I wouldn't have dared do it if I hadn't been high on success. They, I now realise, were not watching my game, having been sitting all the time on their horse-brown faux-leather banquette. But, for all that, the prevailing elation seems to have predisposed them in my favour. The older of the two, late twenties at a guess, whose hair tumbles around her face in seemingly undisciplined chunks, takes a sip of her Campari before fixing me with a quizzical and unabashed stare:

'Well, now, I hardly expected to find our old-style autodidact frittering away his time at the pin-tables.'

'Your what?' I glance at her companion, who giggles. 'I

see. I'm firmly established as one of life's harmless eccentrics, am I?'

'We didn't accuse you of being harmless,' the younger one says.

The older one says, 'Perish the thought!'

Feeling I may be getting into deep water here, I decide that simple truth is my best recourse: 'I suppose you've been noticing the sort of books I borrow. Funny thing: it never crosses your mind you may be being judged by a librarian on your choice of books.'

'We're just part of the machinery?' the older one says.

'Yes.' Well, I'm buggered if I'm going to flatter her by telling her she doesn't look remotely like any machinery I've ever known. But I say it with a smile, and she smiles too:

'There aren't that many men of your age – if you'll forgive the presumption – who take out Conrad, Arnold, Powys... not on quite such a regular basis, at any rate. It's mainly either students swotting for their exams or elderly folk re-visiting the books that stirred them in their youth. That's all I meant.'

'The fact of the matter is, I've been trying to catch up a bit. When I first went out to work – I was fifteen – I was determined I was going to educate myself. I remember buying *The Years* to read during my lunch breaks. I think I got about a third of the way into it. Too much studying to do; and then, later on, too much hard graft. Recently I've found myself with a bit more time to spare: so I've been devoting it methodically to pinball. Does that clear up the mystery?'

They laugh; but I realise I've touched on something I haven't been wanting to think about: that my pinball days are over. I can never go back to the table again without the over-whelming certainty of failure. Andrea used to come with me to the pub until she got fed up with what she called my descent into the seventh circle of obsession. But I'm not at all sure how things stand with Andrea now – either from her point of view or from mine. A shaft of late sunlight pierces the stained glass of a nearby partition, briefly reanimating its mediaeval pretensions while lancing the lavender folds of ciga-rette smoke which hang across the width of the room. Following some aimless chat about the scribes of the early twentieth century, the younger of the girls says she has to nip to the loo. Left with the older one, I find I'm fixing her with one of those looks which holds too long to be dismissed by either of us as casual or insignificant. A smile flickers around her mouth, and it's clear she's waiting for me to make the first move. Adopting a jaunty, mock-adolescent tone – after all, there's no accepted way for a man of my years to behave in this situation – I say, 'Come to the pictures with me sometime, then?'

She rummages in her shoulder-bag for a notebook, tears off a page and scribbles her name and a phone number. 'Give me a buzz when you think you can squeeze me in between English lit and the pinball championships and the gruellings of overwork, OK?' She hands it to me just in time to assume a bored expression as her companion returns; and they leave together.

Her name is Glynis.


Year in, year out; year in, year out: the same old conversation, spiky with inconsequence. Still, things do happen once in a while. Like when the firm found itself so big with success that it decided to split into two sections, the domestic and the maritime. I opted for the maritime; and that meant a three-month refresher course at the polytechnic – a welcome break from routine. So now we occupy separate premises, an airy office with eight boards arranged face-to face; and I find myself once again, after a break of several years, working alongside Bill Newcombe. Nick Galloway, in the far corner, has meanwhile settled, seemingly for good, into his role as man with wife problems – a role he plays to perfection. It was a while before anybody spotted that Mr Brightwell was no longer present in either building. He'd taken the re-structuring as an opportunity to retire. Funny: you'd have expected a big farewell, Award for a Lifetime's Achievement, or some-such. Instead, as one of the lads put it, he just disappeared in a puff of pipesmoke. Poor old soul – identified with his pipe in perpetuity.

It was going to the polytechnic that brought me into contact with Andrea. Her hospital was on my way from the Underground. She'd recently been made up to Ward Sister, and was still finding it something of a struggle. She used to take a rest before and after her shifts – sandwich and a quick drag – on a bench in the square opposite the main gates; and I got to passing the time of day with her, and eventually to having my lunch alongside her in preference to staying indoors in the canteen if the weather was half-way decent. Funny thing, though: she always sat facing the hospital, never with her back to it. I never went into the building, of course. But I can imagine it well enough: linoleum the colour of milky coffee, walls the colour of artificial cream – *very* artificial cream – and an inescapable smell of volatile substances. Oh, and a scattering of abstract paintings to show we're no longer in the era of Florence Nightingale or that realism is no longer deemed mandatory for the sick. Am I right? Getting close? She'll never talk about it. Never would.

The conversation seems to have turned to the Unions – all about how Head Offices nowadays have their own agendas, their own interests, treat the membership as pawns in their game, etc. Somebody, slapping a fake London accent on top of his real one in the cause of comedy, announces, 'Out of step with their grass roots, brother!' Thus, as so often happens, a serious debate is capped and neutralised with a witticism. A jostle of opinions, no more. I find myself taking less and less part in it. Anyhow, there's work to be done.

Andrea is of the stripped pine persuasion: dinky spice racks, mugs fire engine red, kitchen knives with rivetted handles bought as a set, a Le Creuset frying pan you couldn't lift if you were at all prone to arthritis; framed Victorian play-bills with slab-serif fonts on bottle green or French mustard paper: *Positively the Last Week but One!* There's always a touch of magic about entering someone else's living space: the accumulation of her possessions, and not necessarily the ones she's consciously chosen to represent herself; the sense that this is where chance and her predisposition have brought her, to a place so different from that to which my life has brought me: postcards wedged in the mirror from places I've never been or never even heard of. Perhaps, in spite of everything, I may yet cheat destiny by coming to share this as if it were my own. Yes, there's all of that. But what actually drew me to her in the first place? I think it was the grey hair, grey hair for which she seemed too young. Perhaps it made me think of yours. But in her case it's chemically-assisted, though discreetly so. She told me. Once she noticed her hair prematurely greying in places, she decided to dye the lot and have done with it: a token of her new station in life. Thinking of hair, I've always been partial to nuzzling a woman's bush. But in Andrea's case it takes a long time to tease any odour from her follicles. Must be the result of all that draconian hygiene: no place for your fragrance of onion and loam.

So what do you think, Cassie? No answer. 'No answer' was the stern reply. Where's that come from? You're surely not annoyed that I address you as Cassie? I can hardly go on calling you Auntie now that our ages are much of a muchness – though admittedly with half my mind I still see you through the eyes of childhood: dawdling home from school – the school-room with the map on the wall where the British Empire was displayed in chalky red and Austria-Hungary in drab gamboge and where on good days Miss Snapdragon would read aloud from the gigantic book of folktales but on bad ones Miss Snavernake would cane you, not across the palms but across the fingers, for stumbling over 'When fear cometh as desolation and their destruction cometh as the whirlwind...' or for flicking rabbit-droppings at Myrtle Staines – I'd stuffed my pockets full of them – straggling home towards the ridge where thunder frowned at us, where rainbows beckoned us, past the secret hollow where, it was whispered, little Millie Cunningham could always be persuaded to squat among the hot foxgloves and do a piddle in front of favoured boys, clusters of us sharing our daydreams of her as eagerly as if they'd been a bag of sticky bull's-eyes – home in our mud-laden boots to the promise of suet pudding boiled in a rag and topped with marmalade, to a cold-water bath in the zinc tub before the open fire, my arms all goose-pimpled in the russet glimmer, your grey-streaked hair stroking my bare shoulders.

'...ever thought of leaving her, have you?' They're trying to get Galloway going. It's not difficult.

'What's this, then, Nick? Your wife doesn't understand you – is that it?'

'On the contrary. She understands me very well. In fact she understands me so well that I'm beginning to worry whether there's anything left of me beyond what she understands.' And then, after a pause which Frankie Howerd couldn't have bettered: 'But it's the spam pizza that really gets me down.'

It's easy when you can make a joke of it. But what if you can't? Then it's revealed as somehow both profound and meaningless, as if it were nothing but a diagram or an automaton – something with no human substratum – calling on fragments of recollection and endlessly reconstituting them in experimental arrays. What am I trying to say? It's the thing that should be the most intimate, the most satisfying. That's what the books all tell us. It's when we're making love. And there's always a point, close to completion, when she shuts her eyes – Andrea, that is – Andrea shuts her eyes. They say all women do. Perhaps it's a signal of some deeper malfunction in our relationship that I should have become fixated on this. But, whatever the truth, at that moment, when she takes herself off into her garden of inscrutable delights and leaves me to labour to my climax alone, I feel more utterly abandoned than at any other moment in my life. Is that normal? A more conventional way of looking at it might be to say that she has, for a few brief seconds, granted me total and absolute possession of her. But the residuum of my teenage socialism rebels against such a thought. In any case, that's not how it feels. It is more as if Andrea had transformed herself into a doll; but inside this doll was the person who had made the doll and was still controlling it, cynical and even vengeful when anyone should presume to question the autonomy of the doll, its total introversion, its identity with its hidden factor.

There is a clang as Cassie hangs the tin tub back on its hook in the scullery. I've dried myself and dressed by the time she comes back to lean on the door frame gazing at me.

'It's impossible to give anyone useful advice about such things,' she says. 'All I can suggest is this: if you're going to hurt someone, hurt them once.'

'You mean don't keep vacillating? Don't keep bringing her back for more rejection?'

The last time I sat with her on that bench facing the hospital, things were pretty tense between us for reasons I could not quite fathom. When she said it was time for her to get back to work, I moved to kiss her; but she pulled away.

'There are people dying in there,' she said.

'I know. I just thought you might welcome a little life-affirmation.'

She looked at me with complete contempt, then gathered her things and left. All right, it was a pretty feeble riposte; but did I really deserve such a slap-down? After all, her own remark was a bit odd, when you think about it. Might she not, as a senior nurse, have been expected to stress the fact that people were being saved from death in there? It's possible they'd lost a patient on her ward. As I say, she'd never talk about those things. As for Nick Galloway, I'm bound to confess to a degree of sympathy for him, largely because he's the only other one of us who doesn't drive a car – and comes in for a good deal of mockery on account of it. But I get no sense of that sympathy being reciprocated.

'Miles away, weren't you?' Bill Newcombe is smiling at me.

'Sorry.'

'I was asking whether you were still beavering away at the old poetry.'

'Nah. Haven't touched it for yonks.'

'Mm. Pity.'

'Yes – I suppose you could say that.'

'Took up too much time, eh?'

'Well, that was certainly part of it.'

But it wasn't all of it. Loss of confidence was the main thing; or you might prefer to call it the ebbing of youthful arrogance: the feeling I was being a bit of a git, taking myself altogether too seriously. I remember once, when I was assiduously correcting the grammar on one of our all-purpose cut-and-paste specifications or forms of tender, hoping to make it a touch more comprehensible, one of the chaps – it may actually have been Bill – said to me, 'What are you up to there? You're not supposed to be writing a novel, you know.' And of course he was right. It's a matter of time-saving. You don't want to have to re-think the phraseology for every job that comes up, do you? The degraded language serves its purpose, just as the degraded language of politics serves its purpose – for politicians, at any rate. Why question the language we live by if we don't mean to question ourselves? Besides, looking back now on that stuff I used to write, I see that it was founded on two principles: firstly the attempt to capture the raw moment of feeling, as if the words which popped into my head to the accompaniment of a certain experience were the absolutely right and proper ones for the expression of that experience and to tamper with them in the least would be to scupper it; and secondly to allow words to take over, to take their own course, build their own castles, whether found in life's dustbins or generated from my own fevered brain. And it didn't occur to me for one instant that those two principles were mutually contradictory. As for the working classes, Cole Porter and Kipling measure up nicely. End of chapter.

My footsteps boom on the boards like clods onto a coffin; and, where the board is springy, puffs of dust expire from the gaps. Twists of fluff tumble softly across my field of vision – the sort of fluff that used to gather under old, high bedsteads and which the Scots, someone once told me, call *oose*. Now who could it have been told me that? Downy feathers from age-stiffened, split pillows I threw out days ago drift through doorways as if unable to settle. Where the carpet has been removed, the tufts of underfelt still clinging around the more intractable tacks give the floor the look of an animal afflicted with mange. It had to be done, though. I couldn't stand it any longer.

The cane chair creaks as I sit in this arbitrary patch of sunlight – arbitrary because the room is now so featureless – to sew a button back on my shirt. Such things as this I've kept, things that may be useful: Mum's old book of needles, suede-bound with washleather 'pages' for bodkins, sharps, carpet sharps and thins, plus one of those flat jobs, scarcely to be called a needle, which I think was for threading elastic – can't see myself having much use for that actually. And I'm keeping some of the ornaments, too, for sentiment's sake: things I identify with Mum and Dad and with my childhood. So long as Dad was alive, it seemed natural enough to hang on to Mum's possessions. They were doing no harm, occupying the cupboards they'd always occupied, out of sight and out of mind for the most part. But once he'd gone, I began to feel I was living in a repository of holy relics. So now there's only my bedroom and the kitchen left looking as they did less than a month ago, the living room reduced to two chairs and a coffee table for the telly. Haven't quite decided what to do next. Get the place redecorated, obviously, while it's nice and empty. That'll be useful for if I want to sell it. Or I could let off a part of it unfurnished. Even if I wanted to let it furnished, I'd still have to fit it out with up-to-date gear; it wouldn't have done as it was. So it was the right course of action either way. Suppose I'll have to get down to the allotment and retrieve Dad's tools and what-have-you – let the Committee know he's passed on. Nothing of any great note has come to light in the clear-out – except, perhaps, for that suit. Right at the back of the wardrobe: navy blue, scarcely worn by the look of it; and it had a medal ribbon on the lapel, wine red with five thin, pale blue stripes. What would that be? I could look it up at the reference library. It may not have been Dad's at all. Still, I'm glad my parents kept up the tradition of lining drawers with newspapers. One, less than ten years old – relatively recent as such things go – I may even have put it there myself in belated devotion to Mum's standards of housecare – carried a story about branch lines fallen victim to Beeching's axe; and they included yours, the one that passed through Ryehill. So there you are, Cassie, my exemplary phantom aunt, no longer even accessible by train, trapped in the wicker cage of your widow-hood, your grave of heroes.

The shed smells of cobweb and creosote, but somehow caressingly, without threat. Outside the light is brown – the brown of a procession of penitents intoning a lugubrious anthem. The wind's low baritone occasionally buffets the walls. I've lashed the fork to the frame of my bicycle, and rolled the hand-tools tightly into a sack. It remains only to investigate the big square biscuit tin, his name indented on the lid with what was probably a steel scriber. The lid rasps open and I inhale a snuff of dried husks. It's mainly a store for seed packets: some still sealed, some slit and then tightly folded and secured with rubber bands, others, where presumably the rubber has perished, spilling their contents all over the place. But there are other things too. Here, nestling in a lucky dip of chaff and nasturtium corms, are old envelopes containing official notification of employment and salary – Comyn Ching, a curt note regretting his decision to terminate – relatively anodyne communications from the Inland Revenue querying this or that – receipts for his rental of the allotment at a rate of £1 – 3s – 6d per five-rod plot per annum – and, among all this flaky paper, his Merchant Navy discharge book: ragged, disintegrating, each voyage reduced to a scramble of rubber stamps, incomprehensible abbrevia-tions and indecipherable signatures, and, through the fog, the muted tolling of Very good, Very good, Very good in the column for 'Character'. Did Dad keep this thing protected in some waterproof wrap during all those hours in the sea? Or are they retained at the office of the shipping line until a sailor's safe return? So much I don't know about Dad's life: not just the big things, but little things it would never have occurred to me to ask about. A large envelope bearing the trademark of a fertiliser company contains some clippings from journals or magazines:

Now and then, whether in an individual relationship or in a commercial venture, we glimpse the fleeting outlines of a possible society behind the real society – sometimes, indeed, so tantalisingly clear and whole that, despairing of rational argument with those blind to the possibilities, we are inclined to say, "A child could see it!".

That one's on glossy paper, perhaps some in-house publication of Mum's John Lewis Partnership, conceivably even a contribution of her own. The next, clearly from a different source, has a more homiletic flavour:

The only wisdom in life is to bear uncomplaining those pains that come not from the nature of life, nor from the iniquities or inequities of society, but from the pursuit of paths one has freely chosen. For as life proceeds, such account for the major portion of our sorrows.

Written on a scrap of paper in a handwriting I don't recognise, certainly not Dad's or Mum's, is:

Imagine a schoolchild asking a question of such startling innocence as, "What is an acceptably structured thought?"

and that is stapled to a page which looks as if it had been torn from a book of fiction – page 179, in fact:

What he wished (or fantasised the wish of, since he never acted upon it) was to walk that park, to bathe in recollections softening to the skin, then return by that once automatic, now scarcely remembered route to the room where long ago, briefly, he had been his own man, where the undemanding proximity of others, the presence of meaningful interaction behind partition walls, had provided an ambience in which he too might act meaningfully but without their direct involvement or the need for their approval.

At the very bottom of the tin lies a shallow blue box. I open it and lift out a silver disc with the embossed profile of King George VI suspended on a dark red ribbon with narrow blue stripes. On the reverse is a design of St George slaying the dragon. It is the George Medal. I gaze at it for a long moment. The box shuts with a clop: the sound of a single horse's footstep – a clop without a clip.

I drag from the shed the green-painted, backless kitchen chair, which I shall leave here when I go as a blessing upon the next tenant. You can see the polished patch on the doorframe where Dad used to rest his back; and I place the chair in position and sit, trying to occupy exactly his space and his shape, though he was somewhat smaller than I am. His twisted snippets of foil – bird scarers – still twinkle on their stretched taut strings. Beyond them is a row of canes each topped by an upturned milk bottle which glints leadenly in the dull light. Close to my feet the chives are flowering: frail mauve globes. Dad would never have allowed that. 'He believes in you, you know,' Mum once said to me. It was a belief all the more demanding for being unvoiced. So he was awarded the George Medal. Must have been for some act of bravery at the time his ship was torpedoed – I assume. Never said a word about it. Neither did Mum, though she must have known – must have known about the ribbon on that suit in the wardrobe, surely. I wonder what it was he did. Maybe there's some way of finding out – some record kept somewhere like Somerset House or the Maritime Museum. What would it mean, though? I mean, what would it tell me about him if he didn't think it worth telling? That vicar, or parson, or whatever the hell they call them these days, the one who officiated at Dad's funeral, having presumably found the distant cousins more forthcoming than I was as research sources for his eulogy, said that as a result of his terrible experiences Dad had become progressively less able to deal with life. I imagine that's how most people saw it. But still it came as a shock to hear such glib phraseology employed to cover such complexities. What complexities? Well, I have the evidence now, even if I didn't then. You don't go cutting quotes out of newspapers – quotes about individual responsibility, quotes about the structure of society – if you're not still engaging with life on some level. In any case, are we expected to believe that someone would hold on for so long in the freezing water only to let go, give up, once they got him back to dry land? All the same, I have to admit he hasn't made it easy: hasn't left me with anything I can easily grasp to continue his presence. Those cuttings probably make sense only in the context of some wider debate, a debate which was going on in his mind but to which I have no access. Once, long ago, looking around the allotment, he said, 'This'll do me;' and then with a sort of earnestness he asked if I'd understood him. I think I said yes. I'm pretty sure I said yes. But of course I hadn't really – or at least, I don't think I had. And that imposes on me a sort of duty to go on trying, difficult as it may be. One thing I'm sure of, especially having seen the contents of that tin: I'm sure he wasn't saying it was better to have no hopes – simply watch your garden grow, as they put it in the musical of *Candide*. You've got to look to the density of his experience, attend to the particulars, not be in too much of a hurry to make an abstraction out of it. I think he meant something more like, 'You have to be careful not to tear the fabric of your being.'

Still, you have to stop thinking after a while. The past globulates, disappears into a phosphorescent glow, is no longer what it once was, is transformed into columns of noughts and crosses, into folklore, refuses comfort. Selfhood is a fragile state; but it's only at moments like this that it comes home to you. I try to smooth my hair over my bald patch, then remember I don't yet have a bald patch. For an instant I have mistaken myself for my father.

We're in a curiously depleted flat. I'm married to Glynis, and we have a daughter of about five. We tell her to go into the living room, where she'll be able to watch the parade through the window. She goes, then comes back crying. We go to see why. The window is slightly open at the bottom, and a sleety rain is blowing in, wetting the floor and the hems of the net curtains. On the window ledge outside, which must once have been a balcony but has no railings now, a wooden chair faces the street. Then we notice there is someone concealed behind the faded cerise drapes with their tasselled cord. It is our daughter aged fourteen or fifteen. She doesn't raise her eyes, but says very seriously, as if it were a grudge long nurtured, 'Mum, you said there was a bus went from here to Clapham Junction.'

A comment on the evanescence of childhood? When I recount this dream to Glynis, she says, 'If we have a daughter, we'll call her Morwen.'

'And if we have a son?'

'Then it's your choice. You can call him whatever you like.'

Considering we've never yet made love, let alone considered the possibility of marriage or offspring, this conversation takes me a little by surprise.

Dirt, I was once told, is simply matter in the wrong place. No doubt people can be tentatively categorised by what matter they have where. In Glynis's flat, which is a pretty ample one, reading matter predominates. The floor of the corridor is lined with copies of *Ambit*, *Stand*, *The London Magazine*, so that one has to move down it in slightly sidelong fashion. There are currants in the cutlery box; and the lampshades – old-style dark green enamel ones, which seem to remind me of somewhere, my school I'd imagine – are thick with dust. The large living-cum-bedroom contains one of those yellow steel bins with a slanting lid which you see at the roadside full of salt or grit for winter, but which here serves as a repository for old newspapers.

'Where on earth did you get that?'

'My ex-boyfriend. He was in Highways Maintenance.'

High on the walls, unframed and a trifle tatty, are posters for major retrospectives of Bonnard, Epstein, Léger, plus one in German for Käthe Kollwitz; also, unsurprisingly, Soft Machine at UFO with Boyle projections.

'He was the one who turned me on to Bonnard,' she says, following my gaze.

'Who was?'

'My highwayman boyfriend. Used to like having me in the bath.'

'Can't say I've ever tried that.'

'I wouldn't. It's too bumpy on the elbows.'

One leg of her bed is propped on a thick volume which – I twist my head to see – turns out to be *A Glastonbury Romance*. I ask Glynis if she's read it.

'Yes – donkey's years ago.'

'Is it good?'

'Depends on what you want. You know Powys, and that's a full-blown example: everything developed far beyond what you'd think possible – characters all larger than life, and still getting larger and stranger long after everything seems to have been said about them. I'm never quite sure whether the effort's worth it.'

'Yours or his?'

'Both.'

'I know what you mean; but I think that's what keeps me coming back to him: trying to decide whether the world, whether life, can really be as extravagant as he wants us to believe it can be. Can I borrow that?'

'No. I need it to prop up the bed. There's more than one use for literature. Feel...' She sits down hard on the edge. 'It's quite stable.'

It's the first time I've been here. For the past few weeks, avoiding by tacit consent a return to the Pope Joan, scene of our meeting and of the climax of my pinball career, we've been shyly introducing each other to our cherished worlds:

she taking me for afternoon tea at Maison Bertaud, where the lace curtains ought to give out upon a trellis of roses but in fact overlook the squalid traffic of a Soho street, or for a quiet beer at the dilapidated Anchor pub from whose windows, it is said, Christopher Wren watched St Paul's taking shape block by quarried block bedded in straw and blown on hefty, overburdened barques from far-off Dorset; myself taking her to a tiny Italian bistro whose red check tablecloths we covet and whose rough red wine we treat almost proprietorially, as if we'd trodden it with our own empurpled feet, and which she says tastes of old barn-yards. You, Cassie, would probably approve of that. It's so easy to forget: to forget, and therefore to be amazed afresh that a new woman should have her own distinctive way of deciding when to cross the road, her own way of deciding when to speak and when to remain silent, her own way of choosing where and when she wishes to be touched and at what point to return a risky intimacy with an equally risky one of her own. What do they signify, these differences? 'They don't mean a thing,' you say; and I say, 'I could almost believe you were jealous;' and you say, 'Me – jealous of the living?' But still I'm not sure what it was about Andrea. Some buried memory of someone I knew at primary school – a slightly older girl I had a crush on? – not one of the blatantly juicy ones the boys used to talk heatedly about but one whose image I kept private, a secret from everybody: and now, finally, a secret from myself? Whatever the memory may have been, it has disintegrated into shreds. Someone disappears round a corner; someone slides into a seat behind a desk; briefly the wind catches her greying hair.

Now, Glynis wearing nothing under her orange-striped beach robe, myself nothing under my casually-donned trousers and sweater – we couldn't be making it more obvious that each expects the other to want to come back to bed, but there's something pleasantly conspiratorial in the fact that neither alludes to it – she's preparing coffee in an electric mill. Alongside the kitchen door, lovingly mounted in a small, once-gilt frame, is a reproduction of a Picasso – blue period – arguably a wee bit over-emphatic in its representation of poverty. I'm about to ask about it, but then don't. There really does seem to be a density about Glynis's life which, much as I enjoy encroaching upon it, and being invited to encroach upon it, I feel should be kept sacrosanct. Maybe this picture is connected with her bath-time highwayman; maybe it goes back farther to some long concluded or perhaps still dormant affair. I'd rather not know. I shall never know everything about Glynis; but the sense of continuum between what I know and what I don't know is an essential component of her appeal. It's as if she were a world in her own entirety.

Green: mottled and hollowed and dancing in the sunlight. The surface of the pond is scummy, almost fluorescent with its topping of malign algae. Beneath, in the deeps – and who knows how deep it may be? – lurk, trembling as the water trembles, the asdic shadows of forgotten fish. Peacocks brush the paved patio with sidelong sweeps of their tails which they occasionally raise in display with the racket of a defective Venetian blind. There is a clamour of eager voices. One knows that London parks used to be cropped by sheep before the invention of the lawnmower; but in this case it's difficult to imagine it. No great tracts of grassland. You'd say this park had everything a park should have; yet everything here seems somehow to be an *attempt* at something. The wooded walk is an attempt at a forest. The rose garden with its strangely named varieties – Ave atque Vale, Colonel Crowbotham, Laudanum Delight – is an attempt at an Edwardian country retreat. The shrubbery in which lewd statues sulk in varying stages of disrepair is an attempt at – I'm not sure exactly what – a child's dream of adulthood, possibly. Maybe that's why Andrea and I came here so often, regarded it almost as 'our' park: the sense of something trying to be something but never quite getting there: an echo of ourselves. Is that why I've come back today? Saturday, as often happens, is a working day for Glynis. I'd certainly have fought shy of bringing her here. But

I'm scarcely expecting to see Andrea – indeed, I probably wouldn't have come if I'd thought she might. So what is it – bitter-sweet sentiment? An attempt to summon ghosts in order to lay them? Just that I couldn't think of anywhere else to go on a Saturday afternoon? Or am I trying to prove to myself that a place is simply a place, that I'm untroubled by her breaking with me? 'Her breaking with me'? Now there's an interesting slip! I've been taking it for granted that I broke with her – even grappling dutifully with guilt on account of it. But that last farewell of hers, the contempt in her voice: did she believe – as I've chosen to imagine – that she could hold on to me only by showing her lack of need for me, whether temporary or permanent; or had she at last concluded that her world would be the better for my absence from it? Did she feel at last ready to embrace fully her new rank as Ward Sister; in which case, will she approach her next lover without the compulsion to scrub her intimate parts with Grandma's Lye Soap?

Emerging from a tunnel of warring clematis, I reach the lawn where a cluster of late-flowering hippies sit under the hawthorn playing bamboo flutes, strumming the odd acoustic guitar while keeping an indulgent eye on a wandering toddler, or reading the *Duino Elegies*. As I glance at this little group with envy – envy, primarily, for their resistance to the onward march of history, which is to say of fashion, which tells us such behaviour is old hat – I'm reminded of an incident which occurred several years ago. God, how long would it be? I must have been in my late twenties or early thirties, but it was still the era when students wore long, collegiate scarves; and I was in a café watching two or three of them talking in that animated way they have, and for a moment I felt an enormous longing to be one of their group, to share the breeziness and the freedom which, having never been to university, I had never experienced at first hand and of which those scarves, flung carelessly over the shoulder, seemed the most heart-breakingly potent symbol. Then, pulling myself together, I recognised such freedom for the fraud it is. Well, not fraud quite; but if freedom consists in the ability to make choices, these students' freedom consisted only in not having made them yet. In other words, to exercise freedom – at least in the limited sense in which I was envying it – was to obliterate it. Youth was a Siren call to shipwreck. True freedom meant sticking by the choices you had already made and striving to fulfil them. Maybe that was why – or partly why, I'm not sure – I elected to stay in engineering rather than chance my arm in the world of literature. Potent as it is, all that really remains of that memory is the scarves the youngsters were wearing, identified – though scarcely to anyone outside the colleges concerned – by the colours of their stripes. And did that, too, contribute to the appeal of the moment: the promise of a mode of identification so local as to identify us to no-one but ourselves? Who's to say there may not be some such quality of the hermetic at the root of all benign recollection? Just think: one might be able to postulate a working description of memory – 'description', that is, as one speaks of 'describing' an arc – in some kind of symbolically logical, or logically symbolic, system.

A notice, pointing to a low building whose entrance is down a few steps, so that its roof seems to slope up almost from ground level, says Mechanical Drawing. Presumably once a storage place for wine or for ice or for gardening implements, wallflowers nestling against suncrumbled brick, this is a series of rooms recently refurbished as an exhibition space. The title is, as I guessed, intentionally ambiguous. There are spirals pirouetted onto an Archimedean cradle; designs shakily enlarged from foreign postage stamps with a child's pantograph, which is displayed alongside for our amusement; landscapes translated into alphanumeric sequences and printed out on sprocketed paper by an IBM; threatening imagery collaged from boiler manufacturers' catalogues, a bit like Paolozzi but without his take-it-or-leave-itness: then, in the final chamber, something which seems wholly familiar: hand-tinted machine drawings framed behind glass. The familiarity, in fact, is uncomfortable, provocative. It extends not simply to the balance of fine and bold outlining but to the hand-executed capitals of the legend. And abruptly I look at the accompanying leaflet and see that yes, these are the works of Alice Cave. I peer at them for some time. What led the organisers of the exhibition to categorise her drawings in particular as art? Did she submit them as such? Is she claiming some extraordinary merit for them; or is their lack of individuality precisely the point? Then I begin to notice the oddities. There is a universal coupling which – you only see if you look carefully – would not function as a coupling at all. There is a pedestal for a swivel bearing which, for all the precision of its detailing, could not actually exist in real space. Then there is the matter of the codings for materials: single diagonals for cast iron, double for steel, alternating continuous and broken diagonals for brass, and so forth. I've a memory of travelling by bus up Ludgate Hill one evening when I was studying for my exams and testing myself on these conventions and feeling absurdly proud that I was probably the only person on that bus who was conversant with them. Here they are being consciously – knowing Alice's past expertise, I'm in no doubt about it – consciously flouted. Thus we have a connecting rod made of lead with cast iron bearings; and here, most bizarrely of all, a valve casing cast entirely of water. The oddest thing, I realise, is that scarcely any of the people who visit the exhibition will have any idea what is going on in these pictures. Alice is claiming the right to the esoteric in art: almost as if it were a private conversation. A private conversation with *me*. That's what's so unnerving. It's as if I were looking over her shoulder at her tracing of one of my drawings, and, without my ever noticing it, she had included some absurdity, something which would debar the drawing from ever being used for its intended purpose.

I've just sat down with my coffee and Danish on a ricketty metal chair at a ricketty metal table. People are passing to and fro along a path a few yards away. And suddenly I see her. I'm sure it's her. Her feet are bare, and she's wearing an ankle-length linen dress with a pattern from a William

Morris wallpaper, and her hair's done in an Afro – though a rather sparse Afro, you can see sunlight through it – but I'm sure it's her, all the same. The man at her side is burly and has a T-shirt with the motto, 'Stockhausen is the Fonz of all Wisdom'. I raise my coffee cup in both hands to my lips and avert my eyes as she glances in my direction with a hesitant half-recognition, then continues out of sight. Meanwhile a dark, shaggy German Shepherd has veered in my direction and pauses before me, peering at my pastry and allowing its tail the suggestion of a wag. It occurs to me that the melancholy of dogs, their bitter, unquenchable melancholy, lies in their stopping just short of complexity. Though dogs do differ in personality, there is a certain level at which they may all be said to behave alike: which is another way of saying that irony is beyond them. Scorning my analysis, the German Shepherd makes off, miffed.

She's got some wonderful books, has Glynis. Browsing while she showers, I come across this catalogue of Léger drawings from an exhibition held in Paris in 1933. Flints, trousers, roots, beef and mutton haunches, a handkerchief, a lock... It's as if he were searching for the simplest common language: the least ornate, least culturally pre-determined, set of visual equivalences: a vocabulary which would hold good for all these diverse objects and yet serve to distinguish them. Thus the beef and the handkerchief differ little, the lock greatly. The shoulder of mutton relates both to flints and to roots; and so on. Very disciplined; and, in some way I can't quite put a finger on, very brave. Absurdly, I almost wish my face could be represented in this fashion. She emerges to reach for a towel, water trickling from her hair and her pubis.

We're strolling along the Embankment holding hands like a couple of teenagers.

'We should take a holiday together,' she says.

'Good idea. I dare say we could synchronise our entitlements by at least a week.'

'What do you usually do?'

'Eh?'

'For holidays.'

'Oh – various things. I took a trip to Paris once; but normally I stay here. Not driving a car, I tend to pick a central spot from which I can take plenty of interesting walks. I like rambling. Even took a short course once – night-class – in hill walking.'

'You took lessons in walking?'

'Compass. Weather. How not to fall over cliffs in the fog.'

'You seem to like evening classes.'

'Well, yes, it does become a sort of an addiction after all the years of study you have to put in in my sort of a job – that's if you want to get anywhere.'

'Ah, self-advancement!'

'Well, OK – but the work gets more interesting, less routine.'

'So that's really all you do with your evenings – classes and homework?'

'Not entirely, not in the summer; and not so much these days. I used to go to the pub quite a lot with my mates – played a lot of pinball, you may remember.'

'Did you give that up because of me – because you thought it wasn't my scene?'

'Yes and no, I suppose.' The thought flits across my mind that maybe she wasn't so indifferent to my triumph as I've been assuming. 'Look, why the interrogation?'

'It's not an interrogation. I just want to get to know you – find out who it really is I seem to have got myself entangled with. You wouldn't want to think I didn't take any interest in you, would you? Right then, books. What sort of books do you read?'

'You know what books I read. You stamp them for me as part of your professional duties.'

'Early-twentieth-century English literature for purposes of self-education. Check. Anything else? Hard-bitten police procedurals? Bodice-rippers? Sword and sorcery?'

'Not really. Basically I read the stuff everybody else is

reading, so I can keep my end up in conversation at the office: James Baldwin, Günter Grass, those autobiographical tomes by Simone de Beauvoir. Actually I've been meaning to ask you if you can suggest anything to broaden my scope.'

'Well, there's someone called Ursula Le Guin, if you're not averse to women; or, if poetry appeals, Hans Magnus Enzensberger has brought out a historical sequence of cantos called *Mausoleum*; and then there's Julien Gracq in France – though he hasn't been translated yet. Otherwise, there's always Philip K Dick.'

'Thanks.'

'Now films. What films do you go to see?'

'The obvious ones – Bergman, Buñuel, Kurosawa... And you?'

'Oh, I don't know – anything that's got Fred Astaire and Ginger Rogers in it.'

I believe her: it's not meant as an interrogation. I ought to be learning more and more about her too; but instead I seem to be learning less and less about myself. I mean, the more I list myself, list my preferences, the more I seem to diminish. With Glynis, I feel certain, you could choose any three of her possessions at random – or, for that matter, any three of her thoughts, her sensory percepts – and they'd generate a vibrant sense of her being. With me, however much I proffer in the way of self-sampling, I seem only the more fatally to stutter away into emptiness.

We pile into the brick-red 2CV with enough luggage for a few days' break and head off for the North, hoping the car will be up to it.

'What made you get one of these?'

'It reminded me of an Anderson shelter.'

'They'd probably repossess it if they knew. Don't forget, the point of advertising isn't simply to make you buy the product; it's to make you buy it *for their reasons*. But anyway, you're too young to remember Anderson shelters. You weren't born.'

'Not during the war, no. But my grandparents ran a dairy

in Shoreditch. Lots of Welsh people did. They were actually referred to as Welsh dairies.'

'Yes. I'd forgotten that.'

'Well anyway, they'd got themselves an Anderson shelter in 1939, and once the war was over they realised it would make a perfect cold store for the butter and things, stop them going off. Because in those days nobody had freezers. So I do remember the shelter. But then of course dairies disappeared as supermarkets came in, and all the Welsh people seem to have evaporated – or perhaps curdled. Another thing I remember is that every dairy, my grandparents' included, had two ceramic storks in the window, one at either side. About three feet high, they were, a white one with a fish in its beak and a black one with a frog in its beak – or it may have been the other way round.'

'Are there such things as black storks?'

'I don't know. I used to wonder. But the other thing I wonder is what happened to them. All those storks. I've never once seen one of them in an antique shop – never. So where are they all now?'

'I used to ask the same about my grandparents' lustres. No home was complete without a pair – one either end of the mantelpiece. Maybe they've got a landfill tip all to themselves – tens of thousands of them.'

'A stratum of crushed glass. Cracking and fracturing and glissading beneath your feet.'

'Glissading?'

'Yes – like icicles. Spectral icicles.'

'Isolated icicles. Isinglass icicles.'

'Isosceles icicles...'

'Trickling like tricycles.'

'Quite: imprisoned prisms...'

There's something oddly un-English about these North Riding towns. A church, black and white with box pews, a draughtsboard of moral simplicities rectangular in its rectitude, a three-tier pulpit still operational. Next a gothic cathedral, spick and inevitably span as if built yesterday, its cargo of supine marble bishops failing to disguise the repet-itiveness of the cold columns: a repetitiveness which is that of authoritarian architecture everywhere, and reveals this not as a charming relic but as a repository of power. On the other hand, a ruined abbey with a French name is oppres-sive in the sheer *quantity* of its stones, which defy interpretation. Entrance-ways are blocked. Column bases give no hint of how they could have been bridged by arches. Where was inside and where out? What seems a cistern is labelled 'library'. Where was floor level? How did light get in? How was the wind repelled? A gurgling of pigeons in hollow spaces; a whirr of wings. Yet the place is denied its character as a ruin by the sleek-mown grass and the insis-tence on explanation – which turns out self-defeating. Never mind, this is a holiday. There is a gorge dropping savagely to the sea to whose vertiginous sides a village clings where we round out a delicious meal with creamed plums marinated – or should that be 'marinaded'? – in Kirsch. A rivulet, purling and gurgling, contributes to a waterfall – which in these parts is called a 'force'. Force. The word even makes you see the thing differently: registering the effort as it erodes the stone and stirs some buried memory, deep as the cleft it has cut, of water clattering and cataracting down tilting wooden chutes, some mechanism. Then on to a museum built of honey-coloured local limestone, full of local finds. Pride of place goes to a bronze age burial recon-structed amid a sprinkling of sand in a glass or perspex box. It is a child's burial; and the bones, frail as a turkey's, are clean as if sucked bare by a wolf in a fairy story seated at a deal table. The child, with only one or two milk teeth, lies curled as if asleep; and beside it are a few jet beads and a tiny carved bear. I'm about to make some comment about the antiquity of the use of jet for jewellery; but as I turn towards Glynis I see the sorrow in her eyes. She says:

'This is all it ever became. Yet somebody cared that it had died. Somebody cared enough to put those trinkets in its grave with it.'

And she is right. There is no circumstance remaining here: no skin colour, no evidence of creed or status. All that remains is the compassion. And it took Glynis to point this out to me. I know, from this moment, that she is the only person I shall ever love – and it is a love which owes nothing to any calculation about whether or not we may be suited to each other or are likely to be happy together.

Less than a fortnight later, she tells me she is pregnant.


'At first you only tell your closest friends; then, afraid it may be getting noticeable, you spread the word casually to your general acquaintances; then finally it dawns on you that you don't need to tell people – it's too obvious to be a secret any more.'

She slips on a pavement-light, greasy in the drizzle, and I clutch her arm protectively. 'Only a couple of weeks to go. You must be feeling a bit like a marathon runner approaching the finishing line. I hope you're ready for all the crowds and the applause and the flashbulbs as you complete the last lap of the stadium.'

'Nature's got it timed very well. I've been carrying this thing long enough. I've had my fill of bovine placidity. All I want now is to get bloody rid of it. After that – so everyone tells me – it'll be a different world.'

The sky is clearing as we enter our local Indian at the bottom of the hill. It's pretty basic. None of your red flock wallpaper. Rather the way I'd imagine the student canteen in an Indian university – benches and trestle tables and a limited menu changed daily. But we're used to it; and it's not too far to walk.

'Funny how things become part of normality,' I say. 'It doesn't seem so long since there weren't any Indian restaurants. Chinese food was the height of exoticism. Freddy Mills used to have a place on the Charing Cross Road.'

'Freddy Mills? I thought he was a boxer.'

'He was a boxer.'

'You ought to learn to drive.'

'I've never thought it was worth it, living in London.'

'You could drive me to hospital. I'd have thought, being an engineer...'

'An engineer's the last person who'd trust his life to a machine.'

'Are you serious?'

'When am I ever serious?' There's something about her manner, a restlessness, that's putting me on edge, edging me into a sort of tiresome brittle jollity which I dislike in myself, but don't seem able to arrest.

'I don't think I could squeeze in behind the wheel of the 2CV now,' she says; and then, after a moment's silence: 'I think my waters have broken. You'd better get the bill.'

We've scarcely finished our first course; but I go up to the counter to pay, before the waiter can approach us at our table, muttering something about being short of time and leaving a guiltily exorbitant tip. The proprietor gives me a warm smile, not realising that these regular customers of his will probably be too embarrassed ever to come back. Glynis is trying unobtrusively to wipe the bench underneath her with the long cloak she's taken to wearing recently – perhaps this is why. 'I think I've mopped up the worst of it,' she says.

'Don't worry,' I say. 'Let's just go.' Absurdly, we wait till we're out of sight round the corner before hailing a cab. The cabbie, sizing up the situation at once when we ask him to take us to the hospital, chucks us some old newspapers to put on the seat. This'll mean another sizeable tip, I suppose.

The early evening is drawing to an end. Trying to make conversation – how strange that I should be trying to make conversation with my most intimate companion – I say, without thinking: 'That's what my Aunt Cassandra would call a streaky bacon sky.'

'I didn't know you had an Aunt Cassandra,' Glynis says.

'Well, she's not a real aunt.'

'An aunt by marriage, you mean? Or one of those ancient family friends we always had to call Auntie when we were children?'

'No, actually. Not even that. I mean she's never existed at all.'

'Well, well, you never cease to surprise me. I knew little boys had imaginary friends; but I didn't know grown men kept imaginary aunts to talk to.'

The hospital is built like a fortress; but the people on the desk are full of smiles. 'Ah, a nadgers ahead of schedule, are we? Never mind, just take a seat there and we'll have you fixed up with a bed in a jiffy – or two jiffies at the most.'

Glynis asks me to go home and bring some things she'll need – meant to pack a bag, but left it too late – night-dress, soap and towel, toothbrush – oh, and clean clothes for when she comes out – won't want to wear the things she came in with: 'Use that rucksack that's in the cupboard under the stairs – or no, perhaps that zipper bag, the green one – that should be about right for size. Better bring me a book – I don't know how long I'll be here for. And you can take this cloak away with you. Be sure and burn it before I get back.'

By the time I return with her things, they've got her installed somewhere. I'm sent up to her floor with the bag, and give it to the duty nurse. It's probably too late for me to see Glynis, but she says she'll find out. The nurse disappears through some swing doors, and I settle myself on a windowsill on the landing. Time passes. Nothing happens. Hospital staff, passing up and down the stairs, glance at me with curiosity. At last – I've left my watch behind, but it must be nearly eleven – another nurse emerges through the swing doors and, seeing me, asks if I'm waiting for anyone in particular. I give her Glynis's name, saying obviously it must be too late now to visit her, but I'd sort of like to know what's happening – how she is – the baby... Oh, she says, Glynis has been asleep for hours. They're expecting her to go into labour soon, but meanwhile she's getting a good rest. Yes, of course, there are people ready to help her as soon as the contractions begin. It's a maternity unit. No they don't foresee any particular difficulties...

There's nothing for me to do but go home. Next morning

I force myself to wait till 10.00 before phoning, and am told that Glynis gave birth to a healthy six-and-a-half pound baby girl a little over half an hour ago, there are no apparent complications, she's sleeping now, recovering, ought to be in fit condition to see me this afternoon, visiting is 2.00pm till 4.00 – no exceptions can be made.

Traffic is diverted for a burst water main – bus driver seemingly rattled by the angry swarm of black-on-yellow arrows – and I'm five minutes late arriving. Glynis is in a small ward – only six beds – and people are already clustering round the others with cooings and sympathetic murmurings and sheaves of flowers. Shit, you're supposed to bring flowers, aren't you! When I reach Glynis's bed she is dabbing her eyes with a tissue:

'I didn't think anyone was coming to visit me.'

'What?'

'Well, you know – unmarried mother and all that.'

'Darling, are you completely bonkers? Did you seriously think – ?'

'Oh take no notice.' She laughs weakly. 'I'm just over-wrought.'

The doors at the far end open and, in oddly ceremonious fashion, a file of little iron cots are wheeled in, each to be positioned at the foot of one of the women's beds where she cannot reach it without help.

'Fast asleep,' the nurse whispers, leaving us alone again.

I go to take a peep, but can see only a mop of curly black hair amid the swaddle of white blanket.

'You can pick her up if you like,' Glynis says.

'Are you sure they won't mind?'

'I don't give a damn if they mind. She's our baby.'

So I pick her up – very gingerly – and, feeling the faint rhythm of her breathing, leaning over her concealed head as if I were the celebrant in some druidically-approved ritual, pronounce the name, 'Morwen'.

'I like that name,' Glynis says. 'Is that what you think we should call her?'

# HIGHWAY CODE

... all his insufferable naval lingo like brass buttons in an aunt's tin box embossed with anchors and ornamental cordage dhobi for laundry furlough for holidays liberty boat for taxi home God knows whether it's still current outside his outfit or even inside it just seeped into him like embalming fluid Ken Stuttle RNVR neck sore from the electric clippers and so keen to keep a straight back his arse wags like a duck's and his goolies'll be on active service today all right hot summer's day bit of all right how the sun shines through their dresses but you've got to catch them at the critical moment moving from shade into light so it's not just Ken Stuttle if I'm honest about it only he's more vociferous more coarse as if privacy of thought were somehow reprehensible or plain unsharing but who wants to share that guy's soiled fantasies up there already he'll be there already with his Prussian punctuality swapping queasy anecdotes with Poddington and trying to make Wilf Ormwood rise with cracks about his lateness but no response there and our pinko poet perhaps sensing vulner-ability always on the dot the heat already drumming from the forecourt but mustn't let the raillery get through to me or at least not let him see if it has fatal if he starts on about motor-ing not that its any secret but maybe one evening the wife a bit the worse loose-tongued who knows if only she'd given me a second chance but said I'd scratched the wing and scared hell out of her into the bargain so that was the end of it Stuttle bawling his ditties roll up roll up see the house of mysteries ladies pay a penny and get tickled in the dark with Poddington leering perhaps resents the presumption of this pipsqueak on his war service Libya with Wavell and anyhow seems to have the sense to see it's all a load of bilge when there isn't a war on but still plays it for laughs Ken Stuttle being immune to subtlety or else doesn't care and glad enough of a ready ally if only by silence in the game of derision a ready nucleus in the game of ganging-up everyone's been hurt some time must have been though some show it worse than others only Wilf Ormwood seems impervious I've seen Stuttle reduced to all appearances of despair and a note of hysteria trying to needle him and our very own mute inglorious Mayokovsky gazing into space as usual blank as a sheet never been shot at penning his posies composing his odes never seen action any sort of action I wouldn't imagine just thinks he can understand the world by pure brainwork and Stuttle seems to respect or up to a point God knows but hey-ho on with the job re-vamping the risk analysis programme in the light of fresh data starting with zero and ending with infinity but between those it's up for graphs so into the typing pool collapsing into giggles and Lou Lilac can't possibly be her real name smoothing down her skirt pretends they've been comparing knickers but I don't believe it just a ploy to embarrass me and it succeeds even though I know it's a ploy 'cos there's no prescribed etiquette Ken Stuttle'd probably say give us a squint then and maybe they would all testing the limits and somehow I've always felt reinforcing the ultimate barrier with all this small-talk 'cos how could you ever the closer you get the curve goes exponential shoots off to infinity the limiting value never reached yet I must be wrong after all some do or say they do and it's probably true at least some of them say you need a secretary

Braking distance at 30 miles an hour?
Seventy-five feet.
And at 50?
A hundred and seventy-five.
Good. That's in what?
Dry weather.

say you need a secretary weekend conference take my advice choose yourself a lumpy one sod the looks the plainer the hungrier mantelpiece and fire and all cats grey in the dark but preferably a wheatfield nice summer's day September moonlight's better than excessive tips to nudging bellboys commissionaires dozing hall-porters just pull up in a B-road wander along the hedge for a bit then crawl that's the thing to remember crawl the thing to remember when you're shagging in a wheatfield is never stand up and sus out the height and for Christ's sake don't smoke but you need a car and knows damn well I can't so I peel the tab from a pack of Gauloises all that's left metaphorically of that holiday twelve years ago and shake up a fag in sign of manhood Poddington smirking maybe he knows maybe he doesn't I tried for fuck's sake I tried even after I faced up to it again and again and maybe I'd have won through if only Vera all right she saved me from death by electrocution but what the hell you'd do that for a dog my own bloody fault I never denied it so make a joke of it but no sense of humour Wilf Ormwood chuckling to himself and I know why I asked him one day it's this cartoon he saw in Punch years back with just a notice board saying it is forbidden to throw stones at this notice board

What if you turn a corner and see an amber light, then?
Prepare to stop.
Stop, mate, that's all – just stop. Never mind the 'prepare to'.

to throw stones at this notice-board so Ken Stuttle shrugs and gives up and goes on about being a Gunnery Instructor means you can drill officers and it obviously means a lot to him to be able to yell at his superiors though you wouldn't guess it to see the way he behaves with old man Vernon arse-hole-crawling he'd call it if he caught anyone else and never hear the last of it three bags full sir yes all cockiness but a little glassy-eyed as if in constant umbrage at some slight not quite formulated always on the brink of utterance and why join anyway if he doesn't like the discipline but somehow manages to present a para-military set-up as a haven of individualistic liberty and perhaps in some way for him it is with six-gun salvoes to baby bunting and piping the scrambled egg aboard a three-storey block everyone calls HMS in defiance of sense-data but that's where Poddington parts company up from the ranks with ghoulish glee about public school twats from the OTCs riding knight errant varsity scarves rippling in the slip-stream strafed from the hatches first week out of Alex as the armoured convoys see-saw inharmoniously over dunes shimmery as chip-fat and endless as a recurring decimal and the battened-down working class shuddering and bumping deafened on their fretted iron seats awaiting their inheritance onward to Huddersfield Tech on a demob grant and into the company when it was still undermanned or he wouldn't have made it now neither would I for that matter honours or nothing these days and not even in basic research God help 'em just like the services Queen's Regulations listen to me lad you're paid for a twenty-four hour day and sleep's not a right it's a privilege you spastic syphilitic ponce what are you a spastic syphilitic ponce sir but none of the comradeship just first to publish squalid brain-pickings all right not quite the wake to reveille only leisure a quick wank to a copy of Health and Efficiency but not far short by all accounts and each fighting his lonely Stalingrad to the last round of ammo last stick of kindling last grain of thawing salt so buck the system by sitting tight and what's the alternative would Vera think better of me didn't even like the present I gave her because sometimes I think as I look at her and I sit in our silence which is the only thing we seem to agree on I think perhaps I've just given up perhaps she's waiting for a gesture perhaps unlikely as it may seem in this morgue of truce one gesture might serve to reverse the turn of the spiral and even if I don't love her now the spiral might turn and gather angular momentum and we'd be kinder and kinder to each other in response to each other's kindness and maybe in the end you'd recover some love we both might so I gave you that stained glass pendant on the gold chain and you said how lovely you'd have to buy something to wear it with which was your way of saying I'd misjudged your colour sense just say you need a

secretary Euro-shindig confab with end-users management
don't give a damn wouldn't risk a mutiny all sons of Adam
when all said and done but what's the use no jalopy no tart as
Ken Stuttle puts in with admirable unsuperfluousness even

> Sequence of checks on first entering the vehicle?
> Check doors including passenger's are properly shut.
> Check position of rear-view mirror. Handbrake on.
> Gears in neutral. That's four. Er...

unsuperfluousness even for him and anyway what am I
dreaming of secretaries shagging in wheatfields a bit old in
the tooth if it hadn't been for Kim unbelievable Kim
Calderdale looked at me without the obligatory mockery
went with her once or twice to the sandwich bar Ken Stuttle
bellowing get your prophylactic from the medical orderly
and it was like suddenly being without a headache you'd had
so long you'd forgotten just her normality just her frankness
just her wrist arched as she stirred her coffee then back to the
sniggers and hope you haven't caught a dose lad only way to
deal with him's be more offensive than he was about to be so
he can't cap you without going over the top but it's a tricky
business judging how much'll propitiate their lust for vulgar-
ity because if you overdo it miscalculate he'll reverse on you
with a tut-tut what a boorish fellow trying to impress but this
time I win by accepting the role playing it for tedium you
don't often win so he lights up a fag to a call of queenie
queenie make smoke Mayakovsky smug as they come duff
foghorn you'll cop it with lung cancer one of these days and
Poddington muttering d'you think anybody'd waste money
on them if they didn't know that a really scary remark and
not quite in character the character he shows us but nobody
picks it up 'cause the conversation's tailed off conversations
having their own contours you could probably determine by
dimensional analysis the minimum of fixed variables to plot
it against time perhaps population or more likely density of
distribution and of course insecurity how could I have over-

looked insecurity old man Vernon a whole new generation of microprocessors old man Vernon clipping his fingernails into that great pink bubbly glass ashtray latent heat of champagne liquefaction and picks up a paring between stubby digits and says a chip that size could do your job mine too so try to keep my end up whizz-kidding but can it make things happen and he looks morose drops the clipping turns suddenly bitter says have you in the dole-queue sonny that's what it can make happen and no use dreaming of a truck-driver's free as the open woebegone waifs in high-slit skirts who'll grope you for a spin on the jukebox and a lift to Carlisle no second chance no jalopy

A sense of theft masking itself in a treasonable weakness.
A reluctance suppressed, saliva swallowed drily. The removal of a key-ring from a handbag. Jingling.

second chance no jalopy no tart Kim said it was true the girls pooled notes on the hirsute endowments of upper-to-middle management and Lou Lilac who had most to reveal was keeping it all tabulated Kim Calderdale who clued me in blushing slightly so I wished I hadn't asked gone now gone a kid to look after took a night-cleaning job for the hours sod the money be with the kid don't blame her haven't seen her since no jalopy so I flick up another Gauloise in memory of a forgotten moment perhaps not mine either perhaps out of a film or God knows what try to make the best of things which all depends on the efficiency of your endorphin receptors old dear in the tobacco kiosk about how honest as the day is long in her day wouldn't do the boss down by a brass farthing not in her day they wouldn't but how do you tell her all that pride she's an accomplice in her own exploitation self-righteous as Ken Stuttle telling us we're defrauding the consortium by getting in ten minutes late bumptious little jerk and anyway she's probably time-warped into the war too lost a loved one pitting our puny Samaritans and Wallabies against the impregnable Manfreds of the Wehrmacht looming in phalanx from the swirl of sand at first like an illusion due to the lens effect of thermal stratification superimposition of mirage upon its source but no they really are twenty-two feet high not counting the radio aerial and hermetically sealed with synthetic rubber from Dortmund and have crawled across the Med on the sea bottom shouldering aside the rotted elephant ribs of triremes in a silent cloud of churned silt and twinkling shoals to emerge shaking their turrets free of water globulating on their duck-oiled plates to leave only a residue of small-fry floundering in the gun breeches and materialising behind the British lines at Mirsa Metruh but what the fuck it's all very well daydreaming Rockfist Rogan Lost Commandoes just like the kid I always was but what's the use to man nor beast I'm here and it's now not Gusty Gale no Truth About Wilson wouldn't help anyone even if I wrote it myself not that I haven't sometimes considered it adventure or romance or perhaps pornography just to utilise my own most lurid Lou Lilac in a wheatfield thighs sticky with black and yellow husks of wasps swamped in her carnivorous secretions but don't suppose they pay too well so it's hail to the Nelson the Rodney Renown we can't hail the Hood 'cos the bugger's gone down and where does that leave us now it's the driving but always something used to blame my troubles with Dorothy on the contradictions of capitalism God knows how I arrived at that but eventually it was getting silly manning the barricades and where the hell's everyone else oh they're back jumping the queue for promotion sorry didn't know it was your place well it's my place now recruited callow in the euphoria of our glorious red allies attending a few meetings of withering correctitude and points of order I now call upon Comrade X to be followed by Hedy Lamarr and a fleet of tanks for the memory but somewhere like the other week-end at lunch with the Bradshaws the phone ringing and Bob saying hello saying yes saying why not come for supper what about Wednesday and it struck me I'd never ask someone to supper without checking with Vera it's up to you but don't expect me to cook for them not that I couldn't myself but I'd feel a bit of a prat if she decided to go out or worse still said they're your friends you can feed them in your study and if I said but I always join in when you invite friends she'd say no-one's forcing you and the truth is she's got control of the car that's what it

A plan perfected to the last detail and so long nurtured as to have assumed a quality of the fated rather than the willed may, for this very reason, at the moment when the chance for its implementation arises, present itself as an act rather of blind impetuosity than of calculation. A compact kept which is a compact with no other but with dreams.

control of the car that's what it boils down to like everything else with Kim Calderdale irretrievably gone irretrievably gone and what the hell did it amount to I ask you three hurried lunches at a crowded counter and a sense of doors opening on fresh perspectives beatitudes possibilities not to be dulled by actuality a companionship without map a love not founded on preconceptions or predictable charades opening gambits learned by rote and tactics forged in differ-ent wars under different flags for different spoils but no it's just another defeat another cowardice another ignominy to be endured with grace so it's back to the bawdry of the typing pool where they know the score and there's nothing anyone can expect from each other but more of the same and a new victim called Jansson on secondment from our sister-enterprise in the States inevitably Yank Jansson supplying Ken Stuttle with a whole new repertoire on the theme of yanking off oh see her toss a penny up catch it in her arse-hole turn a double somersault and catch it in her cunt and he doesn't know how to take it his defences aren't geared for low-level attack digests of information on new systems to maintain strict accuracy imply novelty while revealing nothing of possible use to competitors and the odd jibe so oblique no-one's quite sure whether it's a jibe or not and no-one's sure who's winning if anybody is or if there's even a war on then someone asks casually where he was born and

Ken Stuttle seeming impatient to consolidate his hegemony launches into a great spiel about how he wasn't born his mother shat him out after an enema for tapeworm and elaborating a whole sub-plot about the mother's intestinal condition not done with overt viciousness oh no just matey join in and laugh but this time no-one laughs no-one joins his gang an uneasy silence and then unnervingly I catch his eye and glimpse not discomfiture but triumph

> Not, mercifully, the retching aroma of the leather of old taxi-cabs recalling childhood travel sickness and twisted barley-sugar sticks like the brass rods of merry-go-round horses, but clean webbing, odourless plastic, spray-gunned metal of high gloss.

not discomfiture but triumph real boiling lunatic triumph and for the first time I realise he's not interested in the hegemony not interested in the ganging-up not even interested in winning all he wants is to be out there in front where no-one'll follow him out beyond the pale out beyond the walls meshed in dithering searchlights which iris in on him as he scampers away that's all folks with a V-sign over the shoulder a nose-thumbing gargoyled goblin but it's not the end it's never the end as a Messerschmitt rips past perforating the brown glass in a neat diagonal fold here rataplan on the petrol drums fire belching saplings shrivelling on the concrete sward and between lift-gear and tank-housing behold a small group heads bowed bell-bottomed and dispirited as the boatswain culls from his small call a pibroch plangent with lamentation and old Vernon's mortal remains are lowered in a painter's cradle of the deep till lost to view like many brave souls in the mangle and pound of traffic the asphyxiation of exhaust the exhaustion of hope the hope of resurrection to a better world if only anyone could tell us what that might conceivably be like just imagine I tried asking Wilf Ormwood straight how he managed to keep his rag under all provocation our CPO Stuttle's a fool he said has to keep the war going by artificial respiration just so's he

116

can cast himself as the wiseacre cocking snooks at authority when really he's only acting in the margin authority permits its faithful like all of us really but he'll never find out 'cos his authority doesn't exist he's had to invent it a fantasy restraint to shore up a fantasy liberty and a fantasy delusory liberty at that so no wonder he Charlie Chaplins away into the gloaming like me in my Party days affirming his freedom by an appeal to discipline just as we justified discipline by an appeal to freedom a symmetry a mathematician would doubtless call exquisite and Wilf Ormwood's eyeing me quizzically then he says it's a question of optimism

> Gloom of the car port, dazzle through the door raised as a visor. A summoning of courage in the spirit of a narodnik pacing his garret steeling himself to roll a bomb all spluttering under the festive carriage of the Czar.

of optimism and I say sustaining it and he says no avoiding it it's a trap just think of old people I used to ask myself why old people were so calm and then I realised it's 'cause they've nothing to look forward to spend our lives looking forward but they've seen through the sham the future's a rip-off the only time's now our reward regardless so here's me trying to make the present yield its bounty out for a meal with Vera quibbles about the venue and can we afford it and can't make this time what about that it's not as if I were used to you asking me out I dare say you mean well just thoughtless not that she'll actually reject my treat just hedge it with sufferance to curb my satisfaction beats the spam pizza if nothing else and then for a moment when her mind was averted I found myself looking at a white-glazed stoneware jar with the label Moutarde Meaux Pommery aromatisé au vinaigre fin centred on the check tablecloth with red and blue anemones real not plastic and for some reason perhaps memory forgotten perhaps not but for some reason a sense of wellbeing an indefinable sense of wellbeing and what does it matter if I can't drive a car it's no more discreditable than not being able to play the piano and I remember another sense of wellbeing fifteen-odd years ago that's one hell of a wait between epiphanies out on the towpath late one summer evening and the sky over the brewery pure jade with a gash of vermilion like the sleeve of a Tudor gown and a tired bee was mumbling in a thicket of dog-rose and I knew I was shielded knew nothing could harm me knew for certain at that moment nothing could ever harm me all I had to do was call to mind that moment if I ever doubted and sure enough for a week or so it worked and then gradually without my really noticing it stopped working and all I was left with was the memory of a sense of wellbeing without the wellbeing to go with it and what's the point of these flowers if I don't know the connection with my true possibilities or whether there truly is one and OK optimism's just looking forward to death but can we put it behind us so easily 'cause old people aren't calm for Christsake they're weary their joints are jammed arteries throttled and spend half of what's left of their energy trying not to let the pain show so's not to spoil the grandchildren's holidays

> The key in the chrome cartridge turning, so easily, a cough and a purr, so little resistance, the sweet simplicity with which the last taboo confesses its insubstantiality, its impermanent-as-thistledown frailty, all in the mind. A real world is out there for the taking. Depression of the clutch like a trodden bloom and the oiled slide of the gear-stick into first notch. The raising of toes inside the shoe – as he was taught – gives smoothly imperceptible access to power: to real power.

the grandchildren's holidays so if that's the only answer to Stuttlery then stow it the war's long over and peace will never come but the permanent present's a rip-off too just a trick with words effective in its way but a trick with words a stentorian shout of stand by your beds and who needs a mystical present with this crowd repeating themselves day in day out Yank Jansson tells the story of a friend back home who dosed himself with speed before his finals history of technology I think it was and he wrote like a demon three hours non-stop yes three hours non-stop and he thought he must have scored 90 percent maybe 95 and then when the results came through he'd scored nil how the hell can you score nil just in quantity alone and he's so incredulous he makes inquiries and they're not supposed to tell you but in his case they did and it turned out true enough he'd been writing for three hours non-stop but he'd neglected to move his hand across the page three hours in one position worn a hole through nine sheets of paper a blue clotty hole and Mayakovsky looking decidedly disconcerted perhaps wondering if that's all he's ever done with all his damned scribbling make holes in paper mightn't he as well top himself for all the use he is and Poddington hunched over his calcs Houyhnhnm face pasty with patience smirking as if the whole world's his private joke never ceasing to confirm his extrapolations nobody's mug and probably deserves to be in R & D with the brains he's got but says he'd rather be a king among cabbages than a cabbage among kings actually had the moxie to say that in front of us all in that mouth-full-of-Yorkshire-pudding forthright manner another word for rudeness but no-one dared challenge him 'cos everyone knew it was bloody true his Mam making him buckle down to homework after the rissoles and peas yet the fact remains he smokes yes carries on smoking can't make it today without paper qualifications amazing the contradictions you can be blind to when you share the normality that breeds them calls them cancer-sticks but still smokes them no more of your LLC evening classes up by the bootstraps Charlie's a late starter WEA and universal literacy sod that for a game of soldiers they're back in the saddle scarves like pennons no more serfs gazetted in the hour of need full powers restored in perpetuity for the rugger-mugger all sweat and balls and raucous bonhomie of the blue-blooded who won't be riding the turrets not this time learned that lesson seated at the consoles tickling the terminals extemporising sequences for posthumous second strike yes I did say posthumous and Stuttle's

# FOUR

I sold the house in the end. Well, there didn't seem much point. Echoes of empty cupboards, hollowness within emptiness, emptiness echoing with absences. For a while I rather liked it. It seemed to chime with some essential solitude. Trains rumbling past in the night. But then I began to find such feelings artificial – when I became conscious of them, I suppose that was. Actually there hadn't been much point even while Dad was alive; but I wasn't prepared to badger him into shifting to somewhere smaller, which he'd never have learned to regard as home, just so's I could have the convenience of a pad nearer the centre. Anyhow, we maintained a sort of human presence for each other even if we never said much. So even after he'd gone I hung on for a year or two – though by that time I'd half moved in with Andrea. Still, it was reassuring to know I'd half not. But when Morwen was born, naturally, things changed. I wanted to be with her and Glynis. This flat's quite big enough for the three of us – comfortably so – so long as there are only the three of us. But what I didn't foresee was the consequence of moving into a space which someone else had already established as their territory. Maybe it's that, or maybe it's not. Maybe it's something more specific to the dynamic between the two of us. Whatever it is, I can't escape the feeling that my status has become confused with that of a domestic animal, at best aspiring to the dignity of a large dog, at worst a hamster running its wire treadmill at dead of night, eyes red in the torchbeam. Perhaps I say animal only to stop myself saying something more demeaning – servant. Animals inspire a measure of affection, don't they. And really it isn't that bad. In fact it isn't bad at all, it's me being paranoid – or it probably is. Only something in her manner sometimes, not all the time: the way she'll sometimes say, 'You'll have to do such-and such' rather than, 'D'you think you might...' No, it's me – been my own master for too long. It's stupidity to start sowing seeds of doubt in one's own mind.

Certainly there's nothing to match the delight of watching a child learn: the grasp of concepts and grammar in a constant race with the discovery of fresh things to name and to describe. Morwen went through a phase – I dare say there's a term for it in the literature – before she was able to talk properly, when she would chatter nineteen-to-the-dozen without producing a single recognisable word; and it struck me that, for this brief and wonderful period, she must have thought she'd cracked it: that she was doing what she'd seen adults doing, and had only to produce a torrent of sounds to have mastered the art of communication. One afternoon, on the way to the park, when I was carrying her in the sling on my back, she launched into this excited chatter. As I turned round, Glynis laughed and said, 'She's seen the moon;' and sure enough, her gaze was fixed in an ecstasy of discovery upon that pale near-circle almost invisible in the pale sky; and it was impossible to resist the feeling that I was seeing it for the first time too.

Anyhow, it so happened that I couldn't have chosen a better time to put the house on the market. The district which throughout my parents' lives had been decidedly down-at-heel was suddenly on the up-and-up. The money I got for it was enough to pay off Glynis's mortgage and still leave us with a fair bit to spare. In my view this was no bad thing. The situation at work has been looking more and more precarious: decline in production, especially on the maritime side; reduced need for our services; early warning of possible layoffs and redundancies. Not that I think my own job's under threat – yet – but having a little stashed away does make me less jumpy. Glynis, taking the unarguable position that you only live once, has been leaning heavily – leaning on *me* heavily, that means – towards the idea of an extended foreign trip, preferably, as I understand it, to somewhere remote and inhospitable. Dissent on this question has been simmering for at least two years, myself being cast more and more irrevocably into the role of stuffy old buffer. Now, however, I'm caught off-balance by a complete change of tack. Glynis is saying that she wants to join the women's camp at Greenham Common:

'Only for one year.'

'Only for one year?'

'Yes.'

Shortly before Christmas she went up with some friends – I wasn't allowed – to join in the action they called Embrace the Base, where they all held hands in a nine-mile ring around the area where they're going to house the Cruise missiles. I hadn't thought for a moment they'd get enough women to do it; but they did. I could tell it had made a great impression on Glynis. She came back with several rolls of photographs she'd taken – though for some reason she hasn't got around to having them processed yet. But this – the idea of going for a year – is a different matter altogether.

'So what about Morwen? What'll happen to her?'

'I'll take her with me if you don't want to look after her.'

'I didn't say I... No, you're damn well not taking her with you. All right, I haven't seen it with my own eyes, I admit, but I know well enough it's no Girl Guides' camp. More like the battle of the Somme, more like a mud-bath. The Council are constantly trying to evict the protestors, usually in the middle of the night. You're perfectly well aware... I mean, I'm not illiterate. I read the papers. Only a few days ago some of the women managed to get through the fence, and the police dragged them out again over a stretch of razor wire. OK, you're an adult. You can take those sort of risks if you want to. You know what you're letting yourself in for. But there's no way I'm going to have Morwen exposed to all that...'

'All right. If you think you can cope.'

'And anyway' – and I hear myself sounding like the sort of people who get invited to take part in debates on television, whom I despise as much as Glynis does – 'she has to go to school.'

'I said all right. I suppose we'll have to think about hiring a child-minder for while you're out at work.'

'You mean have someone minding Morwen while I'm working for the money to pay her to do it? Not sure I wouldn't prefer to spend the time with Morwen myself.' Somehow it irritates me that Glynis should want a part in addressing problems occasioned by her absence. And all at once I realise that, in considering these problems, I'm allowing the main issue to go by default. 'But hang on a minute. What's made you suddenly decide you want ditch us in order to spend a year at Greenham?' The wrong question; because I know the answer. But it's too late.

'It was that action I went on with Cindy and Barbara. I know you thought it was going to be a flop, though you were kind enough not to say so. But actually I thought so too. It just seemed to be one of those things I couldn't decently turn my back on, otherwise I'd have to hold myself responsible for ensuring that it *had* been a flop. But obviously thousands of people must have acted on the same reasoning; and, for that very reason, it wasn't a flop – it was a tremendous success. You know that. I can't believe you don't feel the rightness of it too, however vicariously.'

'Obviously I feel it. But feelings can mislead us. Look how many people felt the rightness of Adolf – all those rapturous crowds...'

'Honestly! I can't believe you said that.'

'All right, I withdraw the reference to Adolf. But the fact remains, group action generates its own momentum, its own sense of purpose, its own sense of fulfilment. And what are you actually demonstrating for with all this enormous dedication?'

'You don't have to be sarcastic.'

'I'm not being sarcastic. It does take enormous dedication for so many people to abandon their homes and comforts for months on end – far more than for a token strike or a big rally in Hyde Park. But again, for what? What are your demands? It's not even a protest against war as such. It's simply a protest against a particular weapon being deployed in a particular place.'

'This particular weapon happens to represent a significant

escalation of...'

'I know. You don't have to explain the technicalities to me. I know perfectly well what it represents. But I still say it's a detail. War preparations also follow their own logic; and war is a product of tensions within a global system.'

'Wonderful! So you think we should destroy the system – get rid of capitalism and everything will be all right? Well I'll let you into a secret. There are millions upon millions of people who'd be only too glad to be rid of capitalism. But how's it supposed to happen, eh? Arise ye starvelings from your slumbers! But how much longer are we supposed to wait?' With an uncomfortable déjà vu, I see myself occupying the position of my old mate Graham in his revolutionary purism; and Glynis is performing my role a good deal more trenchantly than I think I ever managed it: 'Actually, I think a protest against war "as such" would be pretty meaningless. People really would have the right to say, "What are your demands? What are your policies?" I think you do have to fix on specifics, start with a detail. But maybe it's a detail on which a lot hangs, in that the authorities can't give way – and, above all, can't be seen to give way – without reversing some essential aspect of their policy. Once one thing goes into reverse, then who knows what else may? And if it doesn't, then public pressure can be intensified – or it can if you're sufficiently imaginative to keep the thing bubbling. Do you think 30,000 women would have turned up on a wet Sunday just before Christmas if they'd been told it was a demo against war in general? I'll go further. Perhaps the fact that 30,000 women turned up was ultimately more important than the proximate issue of Cruise missiles.'

I notice in passing that, in a reversal of normal process, what began as an argument has elevated itself into a discussion. 'So why does it have to be women? There were men there to start with, weren't there? Why did they chuck them out?'

'So it could legitimately be called a women's camp.'

'That seems like putting the cart before the horse, doesn't it?'

'What do you mean?'

'Well, just so you can call it something. I mean, can't a thing just be what it is?'

'In a perfect world, possibly. But an element of PR comes into this. Women against war has a ring to it.'

'But do you believe it? Look, Glynis, I really want to know your answer to this. There's only the two of us in this room. Never mind for a moment the attitudes you may want to adopt for the benefit of your friends, or even the ideology you may want to rub off on Morwen. By and large I value the things you value and oppose the things you oppose. So why do things have to be expressed in terms of masculine and feminine? Do you believe there's some essential difference between men and women – that women are fundamentally more peaceable, or more something-or-other?'

'No, of course I don't. But a difference doesn't have to be essential to be important.'

'You mean it could be nurture rather than nature?'

'I wasn't even thinking in those terms. The difference may be merely stereotypical, a local cultural myth. That doesn't stop it from resonating, from relating fruitfully with other myths and with luck generating something quite new – some symbolic nexus of meanings which simply wasn't present before. Ask yourself: why has CND become moribund? Because the nuclear threat has gone away? No: because you can't go on for ever saying the same things in the same ways. They're still true; but truth gets tired. Ways of saying things fall out of fashion.'

In another time-shift I find myself back with Chuck Chesterfield in that Chinese restaurant with its grey granite eunuchs or Mamelukes, and I say, 'That sounds like adman-speak.'

'Call it that if you like. I call it poetry.'

'And that sounds like a misuse of language.'

'Would you rather have a misuse of language or Cruise missiles? All right, maybe that's a glib answer. But the point I'm trying to make is that whether it's poetry or advertising is merely a matter of the purpose to which it's put. What's important is its core truth.'

'And you think advertising generates core truths?'

'Yes – though they don't necessarily have anything to do with the product. New linkages. New junctions. I suppose what I'm saying is that it's not so much a question of telling the truth as of creating a new one.'

'Aha – so we have advertising according to Karl Marx!'

Glynis looks suddenly tired, and I regret that last quip. 'Sorry,' I say. 'I know you're being serious.'

She smiles. 'Well, I assume Karl Marx was too – at least some of the time.'

Oddly enough, although we've been disagreeing, I feel this conversation has brought us closer together than we've been for some months. I'm even beginning to think that a year at Greenham for Glynis might do our relationship the world of good – and certainly that any attempt on my part to discourage her could only lead to catastrophe – when she takes me by the hands and says, 'There's one thing I want to say to you, at the risk of sounding pompous. Love isn't two people looking into each other's eyes. It's two people standing side by side looking in the same direction.' I suppress an intrusive image of a Soviet poster, or maybe it's some colossal statue, of a man with a hammer and a woman with a sickle striding forward together into the glorious sunrise. But then, immediately, I suppress the suppression. Those icons meant something. They meant something in their day; and even now, after all that's happened, countless people still see them as embodying what they understand by humanity. And what about that drawing of Stalin by Picasso? It may have been an attempt to capture the innocence of Stalin – which would explain why it didn't work. Glynis adds, 'If you're still not sure what I mean, get those photographs I took processed sometime.'

I open my mouth to state my fare to the conductor. I open it only slightly. Even so, I shouldn't have. The icy air knifes in to set up a maddening throbbing in this lower left molar. The temperature differential between the inside and outside of my mouth can't be that great, for God's sake. It's not as if it were mid-winter. At least, at last, it's time for my appointment, which I made four days ago thinking it couldn't possibly get worse in four days but it has got worse. I try ignoring it. Fat chance! I try methodical relaxation from the toenails upwards. I try concentrating on my breathing. I try shutting my eyes and trying to listen to the ambient sound as if it were music. I try telling myself pain is as much a part of life as joy, and that if we embrace the one we must in all consistency embrace the other. It still bloody hurts. Way back in my teens, I remember, I had my first tooth removed. And it struck me then that this was the first milestone of my decline, first step in my inexorable march to the exit. Why so? Presumably because teeth are serial, they can be counted, there is a finite number of them. Think of a sheep's jaw you find, dried up, rattling like an abacus. The teeth are loose with shrinkage, but still they don't fall out, and it's obvious they've been held in place by wedging and by the gums. That's why it's called gum. So they're just pegs, they do a job, but why do they need to have a blood supply and nerves that can hurt you? Why can't they be inert matter like your toenails or your hair? Your hair doesn't hurt you, does it? A flash of pain as the bus jolts over a pothole. I used to do useful things on the bus. Not waste a moment. Life too short. Now I simply daydream, haven't been able to read on the bus since I've worn glasses, too juddery, the focus becomes unstable; are they more juddery than they used to be or is it me? Not that there are the useful things to do any more, or nothing that seems to matter so much. I assume it's the same for everyone. You work your balls off to get your qualifications, assurance of a decent living, then, when you've secured all that, you look around and you think, OK, what's this job all about, why am I doing it? Mid-life crisis is the word. Or, if you want to be really silly, male menopause. Did people have it before there was a word for it, or am I simply fulfilling a scenario mapped out for us by the rent-a-shrinks of the tabloid press? How much of life is generated by the language we use – or consent to? And, while we're at it, what follows the mid-life crisis? They never tell you. More bloody toothache, that's what.

It's as well I hadn't reached this stage of agony when I had my tête-à-tête with the Old Man. Actually he's only a year or two older than myself, being the son of the man who was the Old Man when I was a young man. Anyhow, with some unease I put my case to him, explaining that my wife had been called away by family commitments which might prove quite long-term – I'm careful whom I tell what she's really doing, though of course I daren't try to keep it from the parents of Morwen's school friends – and I was therefore wondering if it might not be possible to come to some, er, more flexible arrangement with regard to my employment although, needless to say, I should hate to see my links severed with a company to whose generosity in the past I... flannel, flannel, flannel. In other words, I didn't want to burn my boats. His response was unexpectedly sympathetic:

'Well, obviously, I'm not conversant with the precise ramifications of your... domestically, I mean; but I have to say I think you may be acting quite perciapiently in making such an approach at such a time. The truth is, I'm sure it's no secret... in the present economic climate... To be frank, I'm not sure Father was entirely wise in choosing the moment he did to set up a separate maritime branch. That said... you know as well as I do, the future for shipbuilding in this country, or for any major engineering... Well, roads of course, and bridges; but that's scarcely our specialism. Perhaps we should have diversified into civil or structural – not too late, possibly – but then on top of everything there's this computer business, CAD they're calling it – you heard of it? – Computer Aided Design: anybody's guess how it'll affect us, but there's no doubt at all that it will. And it's quicker and slicker, needs fewer people... Shocking how progress nowadays seems to be measured solely by the

129

number of people it can put out of work. But then I suppose it always was – the power loom, and so forth... Anyhow, as I say, what with one thing and another, in the short term at least, it's been looking as if we're going to have to draw in our horns a bit, let a few people go – ghastly euphemism, "let people go" – but you know what I mean. Not that in your case... clearly, as you're well aware, we're an old company, tend to cling to old-fashioned values, loyalty to people who've been loyal to us over the years. But as you're in this situation, as you describe it... Well, I see two options that might prove mutually satisfactory – indeed, might paradoxically help to secure your continued employability in the long run. One would be for you to take work on a job-by-job basis, hours up to you so long as the project's completed on time; the other – and the two aren't necessarily mutually exclusive – would be for you to freelance as our Outside Man, troubleshooter, quality inspector, call it what you will. We need someone who knows how we think; and old Randall, bless him, is well past pensionable age...'

So I came away with more or less the deal I wanted. I also came away with my P45. As to whether I can do Randall's job without his thumping North Country accent – well, that remains to be seen.

The dullness is spreading. My tongue tries to explore an empty, featureless cavern. Behind me, out of sight, with a discreet clinking, the nurse is laying out instruments on a tray which I know will be swung to my side at the last moment so that I have little time to ponder them – a movement like that of the trivet of Aunt Cassie's old range which as a child I like to swing, seeing how many revolutions I can get out of it. Some things, it occurs to me, have not changed in my lifetime; and the dentist's drill is one of them, with its spider-jointed arm, its motor encased in a chrome-banded black ball, its spin transmitted by lengths of string which look as if they should have Heath Robinson knots in them. Will they ever be computer-controlled? I've heard there are such things now as water-cooled bits, which don't hurt so much because they don't give off so much heat; but this one hasn't got them. Come to think of it, those tools the nurse is assembling don't differ in any essentials from the kit that was used when the dentist doubled as the blacksmith. And here he comes, smiling. He takes firm hold of my jaw and presses my face against his chest: in fact, against the biro in his breast pocket. It's not pain; it's a sort of dead wrenching; and the sound – or am I translating some other sensation into sound? – is the mournful creaking of oars in the rowlocks of a small boat on a big ocean. And then it stops. For a moment the dentist brandishes the bloody tooth as if displaying the severed head of a traitor for the contumely of the multitude, then drops it clattering down the chute. So who is the traitor? Me? 'You can rinse out now.' A maelstrom of blood and sugar-pig pink disinfectant. 'I wouldn't try eating for an hour or two if I were you.'

Next the office, where I'm to discuss the specifics of work and schedules with Ron Cottle, who's recently returned to the company in some sort of a managerial capacity. He's already got himself a reputation as a pain in the arse; but he greets me as if he hadn't seen me since we were on the North Atlantic convoys together. I remark that I've heard things are a bit slack.

'News to me, mate. Non-stop go in this department – non-stop go.'

He offers me a Senior Service, forgetting that I never smoked. In no time he's fixed me an appointment to check progress on the re-fitting of a research vessel in Liverpool. It'll mean a night away from home, but one or two of Morwen's friends' parents have said they'll have her to stay overnight when necessary. 'I'll do the best I can for you, old son, though I can't promise it'll always be your class of work. Rough with the smooth, and all that. Still, we can do with someone like you on the job. You wouldn't credit what they'll try to get away with these days, cutting corners all over the place, a penny here and a penny there.'

'Was always like that.'

'But the difference now is... I don't know, they're not even ashamed of it any more. Normal business practice – know what I mean? Haven't even the courtesy to grovel. Mind you, it's true in principle what you say. You never worked for a contractor's did you? I did. Straight out of school. And for weeks all I was given to do was thumb the specifications to make it look as if they'd been seriously studied, put the drawings face-down on the floor – honest, we really did that, walked over them – to get them looking grubby. Meanwhile the bosses would be on the blower to the bosses of the so-called competitor companies deciding who wanted the job and agreeing the price they'd quote for it.'

'I can't believe the consultants didn't know it was going on.'

'Of course they knew. But think about it. A firm like ours is supposed to accept the lowest tender provided they're sure the contractor's up to the job, can do it in a workmanlike manner for that price – right? That's how the system's set up. But at the same time, the consultant's fee is worked out as a percentage of the accepted tender, isn't it? So a company like ours – honest brokers, pillars of society – will try to get the quote as low as possible in the client's interest. But just how hard will they try to get it as low as possible when their own fee is tied to it? Still, as I say, a system like this depends on a modicum of honour among thieves. Now even that's disappearing.'

'So what's the solution?'

'I don't know. Bring back National Service.' But he's only joking. 'No, I truly don't know. I guess it's up to us golden oldies of the anti-fascist consensus to hold the fort as best we can against the rot of the republic.'

Hold the fort for Sankey's coming
Moody's cut his throat.
You can see the blood all running
Down his Sunday coat.

'Right on, squire. Couldn't have put it better myself.'

I make it down to the ground floor and out through the

swing doors, then unceremoniously expectorate a gob-full of gore into the gutter. Truth to tell, Cottle may have had a point about National Service. There used to be an attitude of 'We're all in the same boat' which people seemed to have brought back with them from the forces, but which you don't seem to get nowadays.

'He was fighting for a system which had offered him little but servitude.' In my dream Cassandra, her wooden-soled shoes heavy with clay, moves exhaustingly along the row pulling swedes and topping them with a hook-shaped knife forged of iron rather than steel, catching the grey of dusk only dimly. 'He'd drawn upon his mechanical talents to begin working free of it. If he'd lived, he'd as like as not have been one of the first to use tractors and combines, to tear up hedgerows with their bounty of birds' nests and wormholes in wet wood, to make a factory of a farm. The man I mourn is the man he was, not necessarily the man he was to be. Having killed for his country, who knows what he might have become? It's as well you never met him. If he were alive today, I doubt whether he'd still be composing verses or playing the piano.' I notice that a cut on her left thumb is swollen, the lips agape and blue as if about to start issuing their own résumés. Reluctant to endure the rant of a wound which, once in spate, might prove hard to stanch, I ask her to allow me to clean and dress it; but she takes no notice of me, not believing that I rightfully exist. I drift away, a vapour disturbed by the spade from where vegetation mulches black and sodden.

The hall doubles as a gym, and smells of plimsolls. Everyone is smiling. I've already grasped the cardinal fact that, if you're going to get anything out of these primary school theatricals, you have to settle for becoming something of a connoisseur of embarrassment. Mr Thirsk, the Head Teacher, greets me, obviously surprised, even a little disconcerted, by my arrival. The majority of the parents here are mothers, naturally.

'We'd understood you were off on a jaunt to wildest Hull,

or somewhere.'

I explain that I was – Manchester, in fact – but managed to re-schedule the appointment.

'Didn't want Morwen to feel I was letting her down.'

'Quite so. Parental support is of the greatest importance.' Mr Thirsk has evolved a manner, doubtless from years of dealing with infants, which might be described as firmly indulgent or indulgently firm; and he has obviously decided to simplify the confusion of life's relationships by applying this with adults as well. Being a very tall man, he has to look down on almost everybody; so I suppose the difference between an adult and a child is for him only one of degree, of how far down he has to look. Smiling, he adds: 'It was our Mr Fanshawe here who wrote the little piece that Morwen will be appearing in.' Mr Fanshawe, who shows a sort of agitated keenness even when at rest, says, 'Well actually I mustn't claim the credit. It was a friend of mine, Peter, who does scripts for TV soaps.'

The bell rings – a genuine brass playground bell, would you believe – and I take my place on one of the tip-up wooden chairs among these summer-dressed women, mostly younger than I am, who wear their parental status as lightly as their perfume. We start with *Sheep May Safely Graze* performed by three recorders, an electric guitar and a solitary drum. Then a little girl stands up to read a poem about the alps by someone whom I've never heard of and who may even, it occurs to me half way through, be the teacher herself modestly seeking to launch her poetic career on this most humble rung of the ladder of fame. Now it's the playlet from Morwen's class, which seems from the costumes to be set in the middle ages with Morwen as the mother of a peasant family. I find myself desperately hoping Morwen doesn't fluff her lines; and I realise I'm exactly the same as all these other parents, hoping to accrue credit from my child's perform-ance: so I start consciously hoping Morwen *will* fluff her lines, so I'll be able to say, 'Well, she's only a six-year-old after all;' but that's disloyal to Morwen, who obviously wants to play her part well; so... Morwen seems to be some kind of Joan of Arc figure, going off to the wars to fight the wicked Baron who's reducing the serfs to penury. There's some by-play with the father trying to sew and cook for the family, and making a hash of it. The kitchen range, outlined in marker pen on corrugated cardboard, doesn't quite ring true as mediaeval despite its long, ornate hinges. When were cast iron ranges introduced? In the Victorian period, at a guess. The hinges, which we take for granted, are debased Gothic Revival. You push the damper in... What was it? 'You push the damper in and you pull the damper out...' Memories of being taken to the panto by kindly uncles. Anyhow, the daughter's boyfriend has turned out to be the Baron's prodigal son in mufti, and he's set the Baron straight about one or two things, and Morwen is transported back home in full armour – aluminium-sprayed skateboard helmet, cuirass of turkey foil chased with small dints – to resume her matriarchal duties. Applause. The best thing on the bill, to be honest, is the grand finale: a crowd of children in straw boaters, battered bowlers and whatever headgear they could dredge out of the dressing-up chest singing *Where Did You Get That Hat?* with consummate gusto. The reason it works is that it's neither more nor less than it claims to be: a load of kids singing a daft song. And the atmosphere briefly relaxes as we all join in.

Dutifully smiling again, I take my springy plastic beaker of orange juice and a cup-cake with water-icing sprinkled with those multi-coloured – what? – I don't know what – from the cookery class. I ought to be complimenting some of the mums – the ones I know – on their children's perform-ances. Or would that seem out of place, too much like pretending this was a real theatre? I find myself faced by Mr Fanshawe. Mr Thirsk, though talking to someone nearby, seems to have half his attention on us.

'I hope you didn't feel we were sailing too close to the wind, old chap. No harm meant.'

No harm meant? Suddenly the penny drops. No wonder they seemed a bit uncomfortable when I showed up. The little play that had been written for Morwen and her schoolmates was meant to be a reflection on our home circumstances: absent mother, incompetent father, deprived child. Who was supposed to realise this – the other parents? Were the children informed as part of the rehearsal process? Or was it just a little joke between Fanshawe and his friend Peter – with Thirsk's blessing, evidently – at a loss for an idea for the end-of-term show? I can't ask anybody any of these questions – not without appearing petulant, and certainly not without the risk of making more people aware of it than may already be. Mr Thirsk has now eased his way as if casually to his colleague's side, perhaps thinking he may require his moral or even physical support. I'm about to shrug the whole thing off as graciously as possible when a question occurs to me:

'Whose idea was it that Morwen should play the mother?'

'Actually it was hers. We'd cast her as the daughter, but she was quite emphatic she wanted the role of the mother – wasn't she?'

Mr Thirsk nods sagely. 'Emphatic.'

'I find it very interesting...' A sharp young woman with her hair drawn back punitively tight edges forward to shake hands with me. 'We haven't met. I'm Dr Bracewell. I'm a psychotherapist. I maintain a sort of voluntary attachment to the school. I was saying, I find it very interesting that Morwen should have wanted to take the mother's role in that play. It's as if she hoped by some sort of sympathetic enact-ment, some sort of proxy behaviour, to bring back her own mother into the family – don't you think?'

'No.' I'm well aware it's not a good idea to antagonise psychologists. They can be dangerous when provoked. But this time it matters. 'What I think is that you're missing the simplest and most obvious explanation for Morwen's action.'

'Oh?'

'She's proud of her mother.'

'Well, I was just saying I thought it interesting...'

'And I'll tell you something else.' I turn up my smile of bland insincerity one more notch. 'I'm going to take her out for a meal tonight, and she can have anything she wants, no matter how unhealthy I think it is, and she can have the biggest ice-cream on the menu, even if it's drenched in cherry brandy and meant for parties of sixteen.'

Frosted knuckles of earth, somehow reminding me of Léger and his tumid tubers and rigid rags, crunch under our shoes as we follow Glynis in single file along a path that is scarcely a path, dried brown bramble catching at our clothing. Only the pines are still green – crisp and gloomy. Now and then we pass a woman, muffled to the eyebrows, silent as a sentinel, hands tucked up her sleeves. They cast us curious glances. Of course Glynis has told them we are coming; indeed, our wish to visit has probably been put to the vote; but still, we must make a strange sight straggling through the copse with our canisters of pre-cooked turkey and our dinner plates and our convivial bright parcels. Glynis halts, saying, 'Here we are.' We don't appear to be anywhere. But she leans down to pull aside a sheet of black plastic thrown seemingly at random over a hazel bush to reveal a dark interior space into which we can just about squeeze, leaving room for a Trangia stove and a cluster of candles on a tin lid in the middle. She lights the candles, and I can see that the branches of the hazel have been bent over and secured to the ground at their tips with meat skewers. Of course: this is one of the 'benders' she's talked about in her letters to us.

'I had to make a specially big one with you lot coming,' Glynis says. 'Welcome to my temporary abode.'

'How temporary?' I ask.

She glances at Morwen to make sure she's not paying too much attention, then says, 'We've had a few days' respite.'

'I'd somehow assumed you'd be by the main gate,' Iwan says as he enters.

Glynis laughs. 'The Yellow Gate? No, that's for the lifers. I think I'd have felt a bit presumptuous trying to join them.'

Morwen snuggles up close to her mum, who is starting to organise the food for heating on the Trangia where a kettle is already set to boil. Glynis's mum and dad – Blodwen, broad and tart as a Bramley apple, and Iwan, with the unmistakable sheep-dip despondency of the hill farmer – settle as best they can at the back while I sit opposite Glynis next to the opening. It would be too dark and too airless if we were to replace the flap. Blodwen is unable to make herself comfortable: 'I seem to be sitting on something hard, a branch or something.'

'Oh – my black cardigan!' Glynis says, and begins ferreting under the blanketing and the plastic ground-sheet until she finally pulls out a three-foot bolt-cutter.

'Black cardigan?'

'Shh! Local slang. What kept you, incidentally? I was kicking my heels for nearly an hour out there by the roadside.'

'That was my fault,' I say.

'Well, it was mine really,' Iwan chips in. 'Bloody fan-belt went. A mile or so outside Woodstock, it was. Luckily I found someone who said he'd fix it – didn't have one, but said he could cobble one together for me if I liked to come back on Boxing Day for it.'

'Over Christmas? That was pretty good of him.'

'It was mentioning you that did it. I told him I was down to visit my daughter at Greenham Common for Christmas Day, you see.'

'You took a chance there. Just as likely he'd have thrown you out on your ear.'

'I know. I know. Could have gone either way. But if I hadn't had some sort of a reason, something special, he wouldn't have seen why he should bother with us at all; so I decided I might as well take a gamble on him being sympathetic.'

'How many people are, do you think?' Blodwen asks.

'Sympathetic? My rough estimate would be twenty percent for us, eighty percent against. But the balance probably goes more against us as you get closer to the camp.'

'Nobody's neutral, then?'

'We don't meet the neutrals. So far as we're concerned, there are people who are good to us, and there are people who are bad to us – and that's it.'

'Anyway,' I say, 'your dad phoned me at the hotel late last night, and we went up first thing this morning to pick them up. That's why we were a bit late. We'll be dropping them back to Woodstock tomorrow.'

Glynis makes instant coffee. 'Sorry about the non-matching crockery,' she says, indicating the plastic mugs. 'These are all borrowed from people who were going home for Christmas.'

'Oh, so some of them have gone home, have they?' Iwan asks.

'Yes – some.'

'But you couldn't.'

'Dad... We decided we couldn't risk leaving the camp with fewer than seven people. I thought I'd explained. We drew lots. It wasn't that I didn't want to come home.'

'I'm glad we came here to have Christmas,' Morwen says. 'I like it here.'

Blodwen takes the opportunity to deflect the conversation from what is evidently a touchy area. 'You seem to manage all right for water.' Glynis lifts a sack to expose two four-gallon plastic water containers, one full, the other half empty. 'Lord – is that all for you? You could take a bath in that.'

'No, this is for everybody.'

'So you've wangled yourself privileged access to the water supplies, eh?' Iwan chuckles.

'Privileged? That's one way of putting it. It's actually my responsibility to get the water safely out of the way as soon as there's any trouble. I leave everything behind. It's Jill's responsibility to rescue survival bags... and so forth. It's all based on priorities. There's nothing the police or the vigilantes would like better than to puncture our water containers. So everyone knows exactly what it's their responsibility to save. There isn't time to think about it when it happens. Every so often we hold a meeting to discuss reallocation of priorities, or of responsibilities, or whatever.' She laughs. 'Those meetings usually last quite a long time.'

Gradually the conversation lightens. Christmas dinner is as enjoyable as you could expect under the circumstances – for Morwen, naturally, the discomforts are a bonus. Iwan has brought a half bottle of brandy, which we drink from the plastic cups, cradling them ostentatiously in our palms. We exchange presents. I give Glynis a copy of *Pig Earth*; but, suspecting that books don't remain private property for long in the camp, I add, under the pretext of it's being from Morwen as well, a cheery necklace of vermilion and turquoise ceramic beads. Glynis gives me a parallel text edition of Aragon's poems which she says she found in an Oxfam shop. She gives Morwen a woolly sweater which she's knitted for her. I didn't even know Glynis could knit. Schooldays. Squares for soldiers' blankets – knit one, purl one, knit one, purl one – who ever sewed them all together? And suddenly it's the Western Front, Christmas 1914: archaic scent of pine twigs crackling; voices, not far away, singing *Stille Nacht*.

'Shall we join the gang?' Glynis suggests. 'There are a few other visitors here as well: Stella's husband, Jennifer's parents, someone else's brother and sister, I think...'

Dusk is already falling. In a clearing there is a small fire. People greet us without fuss, as if they'd known us for years, smiling. Glynis has brought the tinsel with which the parcels were garnished, and is winding it round the branches of the trees where it will catch the flicker of the flames; and I notice that others have done likewise. Somehow, in this place, everyone seems to know what is to be done. We join in the singing of carols – the bias clearly being towards the less reli-giose ones, *The Drummer Boy* and suchlike. *We Shall Overcome* is taken up without demur; but there seems to be an avoidance of specifically feminist songs, perhaps because it is felt they might make the men uncomfortable. I notice that, while this is going on, there is always one woman absent, presumably on guard duty. As soon as one comes back, without anything being said, another goes. Such routines have become second nature to them. Finally, someone strikes up with *Calon Lân*. Those who know Welsh – which is to say Glynis and her parents, plus one other woman and a seemingly unrelated man – sing it, while the rest of us hum along. And it is over. People shake hands warmly before fading into the night.

'Mum, can I stay the night with you in your bender?'

'I'm sorry, love, but I wouldn't want you involved in an eviction.'

Blodwen says, 'They wouldn't, surely? Not over Christmas?'

'I wouldn't bank on it. In fact I think it's rather likely.'

Iwan says, 'So what time of day do they do it usually?'

'Mainly after we've just gone to sleep or before we've properly woken up in the morning. That's not woolly-headed inconsiderateness. The point is harassment – maximum harassment. That's why I think...'

Morwen has been trying to get a word in: 'What is an eviction?'

'There isn't time to explain now. Daddy will tell you.' Glynis glances at me, and I nod. I hoped Morwen wouldn't ask that; but I more or less knew she would. Well, she was going to have to be told sooner or later.

'Chicketty-wobble, chicketty-wobble, chicketty-wobble...' She's trying to synchronise with the car's noises, in particular the rattle of the top flap of the window on her side, where the clip has been broken for months – and you couldn't call it more than a clip – all part of the charm of the 2CV, with its tinny shark's gills and its minimal dashboard where the dials are crowded like food on an in-flight tray and its cast aluminium door handles that resemble molluscs of some sort and can't exert any leverage.

'Here, love – wrap this scarf around you if you're in a draught.'

I don't like these road conditions at all. The snow that fell in the night was no problem this morning: still powdery. But now it's compacted and freezing harder. It wasn't till lunchtime that we saw Iwan and Blodwen safely away with their new fanbelt. Iwan turned noticeably more belligerent on the journey back, Christmas and its good cheer over:

'All a bit of a middle-class indulgence, if you ask me. No real hardship.'

'I wouldn't exactly call it a colour supplement lifestyle.'

'Can always go back to their creature comforts, though, can't they? There's people down in the valleys, whole families of them, know all about what suffering means. They'd eat grass, as the saying goes, before they'd give in to the bosses. The '20s and '30s, I'm talking about. And the way things are looking, I wouldn't be at all surprised to see it happening all over again before long. Meanwhile, these girls' idea of a victory against the class enemy seems to be getting the Royal Mail to deliver their letters.'

I grunted, but didn't answer. Glynis would doubtless upbraid me for having no clearly articulated opinions of my own; but it always seems to me a sure road to sterility when people start disputing the value of each other's struggles.

'Besides,' he went on, 'the whole point was supposed to be to stop the Cruise missiles being delivered, wasn't it? So I assumed that once they had been delivered the demonstration would be wound up and everyone would go home; but now she's telling us that's all the more reason to stay on...'

'I know.' I preferred not to tell him, especially in Morwen's hearing, that Glynis had originally said she was only going to stay there for a year anyway.

While Iwan was talking to the garage mechanic, Blodwen said to me, 'You know he's always hoped Glynis would want to take over the farm. That's what's the matter with him, really.' It was phrased as a criticism of Iwan; but I knew perfectly well it was also meant as a criticism of me. They both feel I haven't kept their daughter on a short enough leash.

'Ricketty-chong, ricketty-chong, ricketty-diddle-diddle...' Yes. Gottlieb of Chicago. Even the spring-loaded hand-brake on this crate reminds me of the plunger on the old pin-table: press down to give it some top spin, up to give it bottom

142

spin, one side to send it hurtling up the gulley by rolling against the wall. Got to be damn careful – I've felt the car begin to drift a couple of times. I sometimes wonder if that wasn't the best thing that ever happened to me – that day I clocked up my eleven free games. Was it the day the chemistry of my brain changed for ever? Shall I remember it on my death-bed? I'll try to remember to try. It was also of course the day I met Glynis – met her properly, that is. Long ago, I formulated a principle about pin-table, or at least derived from my extensive experience of pin-table: When you're winning, it feels like skill; the corollary being that when you're losing it feels like luck – bad luck. Does that really account for everything? For the whole of life? For Glynis? The traffic has been building up ahead for some time on this narrow road, which you'd expect to be deserted; and now we've stopped completely. Way ahead I see one or two cars peeling off and executing three-point turns to come back in our direction. As one of them passes us, the driver mimes a circling movement with his index finger. I don't know what the obstruction is ahead, but he's obviously telling us there is one and there's no point in waiting for it to clear. I heed his advice, disengage ourselves from the column and head north again. At the start of this road, which I'd judged to be the quickest route to Oxford, I turn left and head westward, looking for another left turn.

'Dad, why don't you live at the camp with Mummy?'

'Because it's a women's camp.'

'You could start a men's camp.'

'Hmm. I suppose I could. But then what would become of you?'

'I'd start a children's camp.'

After what seems nearly half an hour, but can't be, here's a turning to the left: a small road, narrower than the one we were on before, unsignposted. There is a slight but persistent upward gradient; and soon, with a sickening slew, we hit the ice. I pump the brakes and change down – thank God it isn't an automatic – and get the wheels to engage. Frankly, it feels

143

like luck. Was that a freak patch, or is there more to come? I proceed more slowly, peering through the smeary windscreen. It might have helped if I'd learned to double de-clutch; but they never teach you that these days – say you don't need it with modern cars. And here's one in the left ditch, rescue crew already in attendance and trying to manoeuvre their Land Rover with its jib-crane and its winch into position. I think of shouting to ask what conditions are like farther on; but what's the point? We either reach civilisation, or we have to sleep in the car. Or we crash, of course. This time I spot the ice, and we cross it with the snakey motion of a skater, sinuous and sinusoidal. Was he right, that instructor? Was it skill or was it luck? Right out in front of me – little black kid. I slammed down my feet as I'd been taught – emergency stop – but there was nothing to slam them down on. He'd got there first. Better reflexes, I don't doubt; but also a slightly better angle from the passenger seat to see him as he slid out from between the parked cars right in front of my wheels. Only doing about fifteen miles an hour; but there's no way I could have missed him, no way I could have stopped in time. And I knew that. The instructor saw me trembling, took me into a café for a cup of strong tea, then made me get back in and carry on driving: gave me an extra half hour without extra charge, said I had to overcome my shock there and then or I'd give up for good. True enough. When I got home I went straight to the loo and threw up, then burst into tears and lay down for three hours. But was he right – I mean, right to encourage me to continue? Because I've never been able to get rid of the thought that it wasn't just the more advantageous angle, or even the better-tuned reflexes. If he hadn't stopped the car, I'd have killed that child, not a doubt about it; and I've no reason to think I'd perform any better today. All right, I got over my fear; but I remain, in my own eyes, a murderer. And here's another car ditched – no-one here this time – the front wing telescoped from some impact. Sand has been scattered over several square yards, but the tell-tale dark brown is seeping through in the middle.

'Why have they put sand down by that car, Dad?'

'Er... for traction. So the wheels would get a grip on the road.'

'Whose wheels?'

'Well, the ambulance, I'd imagine. They must have taken the people to hospital.'

I negotiate yet another stretch of ice without mishap. When you're winning... But it doesn't mean you'll always be winning. It doesn't mean anything. That's why I gave up pin-ball.

'I spy with my little eye – something beginning with S.'

'The sun.'

'No.'

'Er – er – er... I can't look around while I'm driving – sorry.'

'Give up, then?'

'Yes.'

'The sunset.'

'That's cheating. I said the sun, and the sun happens to be setting.'

'No it's not cheating. The sun and the sunset are different things.'

'Hmmm...' What I refrain from telling her is that I've been keeping an obsessive eye on the elevation of the sun, whose lower rim is now touching the ridge of the distant hills; because if the sun goes down before we've got off this treacherous road, so that I can't see what things are like ahead of us... I'm driving as fast as I dare, but that's pretty slowly. Yes, I gave up pin-table; but oughtn't I rather to have given up driving? It's a good deal more anti-social, after all. Lethal, in fact. And there's one thing that's even worse than the guilt – so bad that I seldom allow the memory of it to surface: the thought which crossed my mind as I lay on my bed after it had happened: that if I had killed that kiddie it would at least have settled my hash, decided things one way or the other. What things? Well, all those things that never can be decided in life, like whether it's skill or whether it's luck, whether my respectably-paid job reflects any credit on me, whether the years of office badinage left me a whit the wiser, whether my hard-won manhood added up to anything... and then there's Andrea and her impenetrable certainties... not to mention Stalin... and moreover, however, in a manner of speaking... And suddenly we're there: the road to Oxford; traffic moving steadily, no ice, lights at the distant round-about; and it won't be long before there are lights all the way.

'Tell me a story.'

'A story? Well now, let's see... All right. There was a long, narrow field on the slope of a hill – rather like the ones we were passing just before the sun went down – and there was a team ploughing, a team of two horses with a little boy leading them with a halter, trying to make sure they kept a straight path alongside the previous furrow, while his Aunt Cassandra, who was wiry and tough with grey-streaked hair gathered loosely at her neck, followed behind guiding the plough. It was very heavy work for Cassandra, but the little boy found it rather boring, and wanted to be out playing with his friends. So when they paused for a rest, he said to his aunt, "If we had a plough with two shares, we could do the work in half the time. Isn't there such a thing as a plough with two shares?" And his aunt said, "Yes, there is. But you need three horses to pull it. How are we going to afford another horse?"'

'Is that true?'

'What – that you need three horses to plough two furrows at once? Someone told me so once. I expect it depends on how strong the horses are. Still, for the purposes of this story, you needed three; and they only had two. OK? So the little boy thought to himself, "Old farmer Milgrew's got more horses than he can possibly need, and his son likes to gamble; so perhaps if I were to become really expert at throwing dice, I could challenge young Milgrew, let him win a few times, then persuade him to stake one of his father's horses." For hour after hour the little boy practised, until he could throw any number he wanted. Then he went round to Milgrew's farm and challenged his son to a game. The other boy accepted eagerly, and our little boy let him win his favourite brass button and his iron hoop and his push-cart with the old pram wheels. Then he said, "I want to play for one of your father's horses." "Against what?" the other boy said. Our boy hadn't given any thought to that in his excitement, but he realised that of course he'd have to stake something of comparable value, so he said, "Against one of my aunt's horses." At that point old Milgrew's voice boomed out from behind them: "Your aunt's horses aren't a patch on mine. They're scranny beasts. You'll have to stake both of them. And while we're at it, I've been watching you, and I see you always throw the dice yourself. To make things fair, I'm going to throw the dice, and whoever calls correctly wins. Are you ready?" The little boy had no choice. From now on, it would be pure luck. Old Milgrew shook the dice. The little boy called "Two" and Milgrew's son called "Five" – and it was five. The little boy was horrified. How was he going to explain to his aunt that he had gambled away both her horses? "Best of three?" he said weakly. "Very well," said old Milgrew, beginning to shake the dice again. At that point a blackbird alighted on the gatepost. It was a blackbird the little boy had put out food for on the windowsill all through the harsh winter. The blackbird caught the boy's eye, and gave four sharp whistles; and without thinking, the boy called "Four" while young Milgrew called "One". It was four. The next time the blackbird gave just two whistles, the boy called "Two", and it was a two. In triumph, the little boy led the beautiful bay horse back to his aunt's farm. "That's wonderful," said Aunt Cassandra. "Now we'll be able to do the ploughing in half the time, and you'll be able to spend the rest of the week at school." So, now, who do you think got the best of the...' Morwen has fallen asleep. It's hardly surprising. What am I doing telling my daughter a story like that, anyway, a story riddled with morals each more unsavoury than the last and all cancelling each other out – the sort of story they'd have told us at my village school?

What village school?

It's taken me all this time to get round to it. From three plump envelopes in garish seaside yellow and red they slither out glossily onto my desk-top: Glynis's snapshots from her first visit to Greenham. I was expecting crowds, bobble hats, a mêlée of muddy activity, defiant glances towards the camera. There are, indeed, some backs of heads visible; but every single one of these pictures is of an object: an object sewn or stapled to the wire. I recall, when we were there at Christmas, noticing a good deal of string, wool, binder twine threaded through the chain link fencing, as if some hive-mind Penelope had embarked upon a vast and hopeless attempt to obscure the realities of militarism behind a tapes-try of an order yet to be revealed. But these are distinct and separate objects, often in pristine condition. Many relate to childhood. There are gilt foil crowns of Christmas magi. There are teddy bears in abundance, some with luggage labels presumably identifying them by name. One page from an exercise book bears a text, just in focus, in a child's well-fed handwriting: *I dreamed that a H-Bomb obliterated Leeds.* There are articles of clothing, some hand-knitted. There are greetings cards from shiny places. There are articles of jewellery which one assumes to be of sentimental if not material value. Were these intended as gifts, then? An attempt at propitiation? Were they votive offerings such as one sees in Mediterranean churches left in the hope of mira-cles – sacrifices to the Minotaur? There is a crucifix and rosary. There are photographs of children – some of them school portraits taken against the regulation dark blue back-ground. There is a wedding dress. More startlingly, there is a pink dildo. Is this meant as a jeer? Is there an aesthetic of repudiation at work? I've heard that, in the best circles, to use a vibrator in the shape of a penis is considered complicit with patriarchy. Are all these objects saying, 'We don't want this any more – we return unto Caesar that which is Caesar's;' or are they saying, 'These represent the values we uphold against yours'? Oddly, they seem to be saying both at once.

Of course such objects mean one thing if your keep them in a drawer, another if you hang them on a wire. You may be throwing them away or you may be affirming their worth; or you may be testing how they hold their own against weapons of mass terror. I look again at the wedding dress, and this time I imagine the Doge of Venice marrying the State to the sea by casting a gold ring into the lagoon: a gesture of solemn statecraft. The last of the photos shows a tiny bottle with a tag on it which I have to get the magnifying glass to read. It says, *My Tears*. A vial of tears, then – a vale of tears? – a phial of tears. How, I wonder vaguely, did she collect them? I arrange the pictures in rows in front of me. The effect is powerful, unnerving even. There is, I notice, something almost spectral about the light – it's almost the sort of unnatural light you get at the onset of an eclipse. But there was no eclipse that day – the women, with their cosmic inclinations, would certainly have made plenty of it if there had been. Perhaps it's something to do with Glynis's cheap camera; or perhaps a storm was brewing up. I reach for the wedding dress, and set it alongside a dark spangled ball gown. Why does that seem to stir a memory? Of course – Glynis's white and black storks in her grandparents' dairy. I set children alongside heavily franked postcards, and the children seem to recede into history. I select a close-up of a wedding photograph – a guard of honour with bared swords, hubby proud in naval rig – and I pair it with the gathered tears. There seems nothing you can do with these images that doesn't provoke some resonance beyond the immediate. The discipline of meanings has, like the veil of the temple, been rent asunder. Yet the elements here are in some ways as few and as rudimentary as those harnessed to such luminous effect in 'Dover Beach'. And at once I understand how it is that the women of Greenham have been able, out of their runes and their spells and their gender stereotyping, to generate such a field of repulsion for the forces of evil as to have become the indisputable moral centre of Britain.

I sit back in my chair realising that I'm being told something of enormous importance. I have been vouchsafed a revelation of what poetry can do. Did I have an inkling? Back then, I mean. Just what, I wonder, swam under the surface of my consciousness – or it might be better simply to ask what implications were cast up regardless – as I strove to summon into being those youthful poems of mine? I recall that I agonised mightily over whether I should give up my career in order to write: which means at least that I took my efforts seriously. They're all somewhere at the bottom of this cabinet, if only I can find them. There was a sense, wasn't there, of there being a duty to life-as-given: a sense that to escape from the hurly-burly in order to write about it would be to cripple the writing. Wasn't that the gist? That, I'm pretty sure, is how I'd have expressed it politically; but perhaps politics wasn't quite at the head of the queue in the way I'd now interpret it; perhaps it was more a question of truth to the experience – any experience. I remember reading about a scheme for raising subventions from the intelligentsia to rescue Eliot from the drudgery of his banking job, and its occurring to me that without the drudgery we might never have had *The Waste Land*. And at the same time I was concerned, I recall, with truth to materials – which was a bit of a fetish in those days – the 'materials', in my case, being language. I'm a little confused; but then I was probably confused at the time as well. Is that possible? One's motives have to make some sense, don't they? Well, possibly not. Psychologists will say they make sense symbolically; but by that they simply mean in terms of their own particular patent systems. So is this what I really mean when I speak of 'settling my hash': a wiping clean of the grubby slate which seems to get grubbier with every year that passes? In a word, shame. Shame in the face of an outcome never brought into being – is that what I'm talking about? All I can say for certain is that, if I stuck to my job for the sake of my poetry, I ended up not writing any poetry, either to celebrate the job or to protest about it, either for my workmates' entertainment or for future and more enlightened or more fortunate generations, or even for the fabled desk drawer. So why? I simply lost heart, I suppose. Couldn't see where it was getting me. Certainly I hadn't produced anything remotely as eloquent as these Greenham photographs, made of the world and for the world's benefit; and I don't think I ever tried to get anything published – not very seriously, anyhow. And here it all is: top copies neat in a ring-binder, though the foolscap paper has that greying, passé look; carbons flimsy and scribbled over, some almost too faint to read. Funny to think Glynis doesn't know anything about all this. Now then...

Two hours of detached perusal: a sort of willed disinter-est, a mental reining-in of the spirit, of the hopes. And what's the verdict? Embarrassing – yet not quite so embarrassing as I'd expected. In fact I rather like some of them, especially when they exceed their capabilities. I like them when they're drunk with discovery and wrench words from familiar contexts to set them glowing like perverse jewels. I like them when I feel they've come from two opposing directions, a felt experience and a linguistic exuberance, and the two have met in the middle like two trains colliding. I like the sheer incomprehensible ranting where I tried to stir up magic by throwing anything and everything into the pot yet at the same time to nail the moment, the precise smell of a thought or a perception. The problem seems to have been that I was too blinded by the sorcery of composition to see when it didn't work. But then that little word 'work' conceals a whole universe of cultural assumptions – of contested cultural assumptions. And what about my present reaction? Is it any more than the pleasure of rediscovering a forgotten self, a forgotten state of subjectivity? There's no way of knowing. All I can say is that, as of now, I can see things I think are good and things I think are not so good in these poems; and I can see how a little adjustment here and there might help some of them; and I want to try, out of respect for my former efforts, yes, but also out of a desire to reclaim something, to reaffirm something, something which I dare say I did not formulate very well in the first place but which was not necessarily for that reason without merit. There's the creak of the door behind me. Morwen is standing there with her thumb in her mouth.

'What's up, love – can't you sleep?'

She shakes her head. 'Can I have a cup of tea?'

'Tea? You'll be awake all night if I give you tea. Would you like me to make you an Ovaltine?'

She nods. She follows me around as I make the Ovaltine for her, then sits on the arm of my chair as I return to the desk.

'Mind you don't spill it.'

'What are you doing?'

'I'm trying to put together a collection of poems.'

'Who wrote the poems?'

'I did. A long time ago.'

There is a long pause. 'What are you going to call it?'

'What – the collection?'

'Yes.'

'I was thinking of calling it "Snapshots in the Dark".'

'That's a silly name.'

'Oh, I don't know. You've heard the expression "a shot in the dark", haven't you? It's a bit like that with poems. You never quite know how a poem's going to come out till it has come out, you see.'

'You can't take snapshots in the dark.'

'Well...OK, what do you think I ought to call the collection?'

'Promise you will if I say.'

'Promise I will what?'

'Promise you'll call it what I say I think you should call it.'

'Er... all right then, I promise.'

'Treacle.'

'Treacle?'

'Yes. Treacle.'

'Very well. Treacle it shall be. Now off back to bed with you!'

# THE OUTSIDE MAN

Overcoat of Loden cloth, green as moss on an acid diet, pork-pie hat with a partridge feather: externals worth the extravagance, even if it did mean a keen walk in a keening wind across Piccadilly Square and over the oozy Irwell into Salford. First things first. Who would know he was scrimping on a taxi? On a low wall along Deansgate ran the now familiar slogan: *Away Rumpelstiltskin – Your Name Is World War III.*

Nothing, but nothing, made him feel this was a good place to be at eighteen hundred hours on a February Sunday with time on his hands. Nothing. Out there somewhere, behind the lace curtains not washed since last bank holiday, all God's chill'n would be thinking their thoughts and dreaming their dreams vainglorious or smutty, frayed at the edges, too long in the freezer. But there would be no place in their dreams for him. The loner. The man with the flat gun strapped high. Holster-leather mouldy with funk-juices.

'Sorry, Mr Ransome, we don't seem to have your booking.' Elsie's grizzled hair seemed still fixated in a '50s-style home perm. 'We can put you on the fourth floor, if that's all right with you. We usually like to put you on the third floor, don't we, where it's a bit more comfy, but the third floor's all booked up with some theatre people, 'cause we didn't have you booked in, you see, but we can put you on the fourth floor if that'd be all right...'

Not often used, the fourth floor. Smelt like a sacristy. No carpet. One vast and wheezy armchair and a three-ply wardrobe. A baize-topped card table alongside the bed and a full-length, free-standing, oval-framed mirror as used by dressmakers. Preparing to take a long wash, Jim Ransome marshalled his hair brush, clothes brush, tooth brush and shaving kit upon the shaky table, then draped his jacket on the hanger in the wardrobe. It would not be there for more than ten minutes; but it was details like that that made the difference. A moan of wind pulled at the newspaper which had been drawing-pinned over the open fireplace, and Jim's eye was caught by two photographs of a man jumping to his death from a Chicago skyscraper. In the first he was standing on a ledge beside the raised window. In the other – more fuzzy – he was in mid-air, dropping.

Presence of mind, that's what. Hard-hearted? Well, you had to be. At least someone had benefitted. And the guy had been immortalised in his last moments. What more could he want? No, you couldn't say the world wasn't sometimes generous – generous to anyone with the savvy to grab hold of his chances.

Well, tomorrow would tell. But for tonight Jim must enjoy his freedom. Refreshed, about to sally forth, hand already on the doorknob, he paused. He returned to slide his palm under the bedclothes. Yes, there it was: beneath the cotton sheet, the precautionary rubber one, slippery to lie on: protection for the mattress against commercial travellers whose boasts were bigger than their bladders. The newspaper crackled insolently as Jim left, closing the door behind him.

The twinkle of lights through frosted glass led only to the disappointments of bars drab and underpopulated. In any case, Jim didn't want to spend the whole evening boozing. But there wasn't a flick he wanted to see. No wrestling at the Free Trade Hall. And to huddle against the stingy radiator in his room, reading a paperback and perhaps nibbling crisps until he could reasonably go to bed, seemed – well, somehow unmanly. The only alternative was to tramp the streets and pretend, if not to have a purpose, not to mind.

Albert Square by moonlight. Awe-inspiring. The whole great, Gothic jousting-temple of Liberalism now bisected by darkness. But then Jim realised, with a momentary disorientation, that there was no moon in the sky. They were washing the Town Hall. That's right – actually washing it. And while half of it still loomed in all its black-massive implacability, the other half now gleamed white as a winding-sheet. 'Where there's muck there's brass,' people had always said. To wash the Town Hall could only indicate a failure of nerve.

And those Northern faces, grey as if precipitated from fog – even the flabby ones, like Gosthorpe's he'd confront in the morning – gaunt offspring of the marchers who'd tramped one breezy Saturday into Chesterfield, town of the corkscrew spire, and his mother saying, 'I'm all for what they're after, but that's just not the right way to set about it' – and that had been that. And Dad sitting alongside the stove, black-leaded but unlit, nursing the euphonium he could hardly get a note out of because his lip had gone: a failure or nerve that, too, in its way. The one thing he'd never hocked, though, despite its battered value. But then who knew where it had come from? Vague hints of an armistice march-past which had ended in intemperate horseplay. Childhood. The smell of rope mats in passageways, and the scrape of spoon against pan under a mountain of mash in better times. Amen.

Taciturn, he parked his carcass on a bar stool. The regulars glanced uneasily. They didn't want trouble. Neither did Jim; but the waiting made him edgy. Without the action, the world lost its tang. 'A bourbon on the rocks, Mister.'

'Half of special, please.' Doing it for the sake of doing it. What a sodding pain in the... Ah yes, that doctor. The old locum he'd seen when he went with a swelling of the testicle which turned out to be orchitis, the adult version of mumps, which folklore said could strike you impotent. 'Got a lot of this in the army. What do you do for a living?' And Jim had said, 'I'm an outside man for a firm of engineering consultants – sort of hired gun, you might say;' and the doctor had said, 'Well, I expect that's a bit of a pain in the balls to begin with, isn't it?' And Jim had felt unreasonably reassured. Not that he'd ever been sold on the enforced camaraderie of the nissen hut. Enamel skies with REME in Calabria, guarding the allied lines of communication against the fast-diminishing threat of a fascist resurgence in the south: that was what he preferred to remember – as he remembered now his first-ever visit to this city, comparing the Saturday-night crowds in their neon baptism with those who had ambled and chatted in the piazza when the heat abated, and trying to account for the sense of hostility and latent aggression in what were, after all, his own people. But there was no doubt the doctor's bluff manner had lessened the pain.

Pitting his tiddliness against the raw air, Ransome moseyed through circuitous streets between bulky buildings whose shadows were heavier than themselves – stone and concrete and granite, idiosyncratic and skew to the highways, cheek-by-jowling of old against new, conflicting styles, proportions and architectural orders, all saying look at me, see me, don't ignore me: monuments to the mercantile impermanence of paper money desperate to assert a stability against the wind which raked the flat landscape, entering the town at one end and leaving it, none the richer, at the other.

Then he heard the horses. Ghost horses in massed gallop. A frail, unearthly, echoing sound. Curious, he mounted a shallow flight of steps at the base of an office block and moved forward between the shuttered shops and the bereft shrubbery of a pedestrian patio. A surf of litter foamed around his ankles, then withdrew at the wind's discretion. Still in pursuit of the noise, which somehow made him think of the First World War and had now swollen almost to a howl, he turned off into a service alley which opened into a bare, square area between towering glass walls. There, in an endless updraught occasioned by some freak of aerodynamics, a cyclone of plastic coffee cups spiralled the perimeter, rising swiftly and then more slowly until reaching the height of the twelfth or thirteenth storey where, still denied egress, they swerved towards the centre and tumbled down the funnel of the mounting outer circuits to achieve a brief respite in the middle of the tarmac before being snatched outward to begin again. Nonplussed, Jim stood watching this insane rotation and allowed his mind to elaborate fantasies in which generations of twinky office workers would toss their coffee cups from windows straight into the vortex until a solid pillar of whisking plastic would rise a thousand feet from this spot, leaning, teetering, swaying precariously like a Chinaman twirling plates on sticks, yet never toppling into the inanimate pile of garbage which it truly was.

It began to grate on his nerves. Time-to-go time, fans. Even the paperbacks couldn't get much mileage out of legwork. Never mind. One day – one day in a seamy office with the rent unpaid and the waiting so long that this time it might just be for ever – one day he'd sit down and tell it like it was, every goddam corn and bunion of it.

And so, back to the pub where he was staying. Boddington's Beers – The Lubrication of Civilisation. One more pint to finish with. His feet were aching now, and he was glad to sink into the slashed and re-stitched upholstery at a corner table where he could watch the minimal activity of the bar parlour unfolding for his boredom. In theory it was just about closing time; but some of the bar-flies placing fresh orders didn't look like residents – certainly not the acting troupe Elsie had said had booked the whole third floor. Then his eye was caught by a pale flicker of legs descending the staircase with its Hongkong-red banisters. The woman, perhaps in her late forties and very much done up for an evening out, was followed by a man – a somewhat over-age tearaway in an electric blue blazer – just finishing combing his quiff. They seemed uncertain whether to make their entrance brazen or furtive; and the fact that no-one was taking a blind bit of notice probably made it more difficult rather than less. Her hair had been bleached and then re-tinted gold and lacquered, so that it took on the glint of anodised aluminium – a pretty good match for the ashtrays, in fact. The man ordered a vermouth for his doxy and a scotch for himself. He seemed to have settled for the defi-antly conspiratorial – 'What we do is our own sodding business' – a sort of muted swagger. So there she sat on her tall stool in her off-the-shoulder dress and her black net fichu and her spiky, opal-framed spectacles, rubbing her little white thighs together and obviously fancying a drop more; but her beau was into post-coital self-congratulation mode now, and wasn't likely to oblige.

In all his years of road-showing his hard-won talents, Jim Ransome had never laid a broad in an hotel room – though he'd never have admitted as much to Joyce, his wife, for fear of losing her respect. As it was, he'd lost her altogether; but that was the luck of the game. In plain fact, despite the number of times he'd seen it happen, he'd never been confident he could pull it off without being overwhelmed by its grotesquerie. What did you actually say to a woman, when it came down to it? 'Let's go upstairs and have a quick whiff of stale ale and leaking gas, and listen to that dipso in the braces spewing his ring up in the bog across the corridor'? Too fastidious for his own good, that was Jim's trouble. Everybody told him that. Sure, sure, there was a seething great city waiting for him outside this dump. The world his oyster on 20 dollars a day plus expenses, and no divorce. The eleven-o'clock-shadowed face gazed back at him through the spray of bullrushes and the waterlilies where etched nymphs cavorted, toe-dipping and pure. He'd quizzed that phizog for more years than he cared to remember; but the answer had always been the same: Forget it!

Perhaps he ought to saunter over and join the group standing slightly off from the bar – there was a certain way of standing which said you were ready to be bought a round – with a view to replenishing his stock of blue jokes, as essential an item in his equipment as his swing hygrometer and his foxy look. But he couldn't be bothered. Soon the coppers would start dropping in for their nightcaps. Call it a day, pal.

*'Now, children, I'd like someone to tell me a story with a moral. Anybody...?'*

*'Please Miss, please Miss...'*

*'Yes – Sally...?'*

*'Well, Miss, the other day I saw an old lady trying to cross the road, Miss, so I helped her across the road, Miss, and she gave me sixpence.'*

*'I see. And the moral, Sally?'*

'Virtue gets rewarded, Miss.'

'Yes. Very good. Another story, anybody?'

'Please Miss, please Miss...'

'Mary.'

'Miss, the other day I saw an old lady trying to cross the road, so I helped her across, and she didn't give me nothing, Miss, but I felt all nice about it 'cos I'd helped her, Miss.'

'And the moral of that?'

'Virtue is its own reward.'

'That's very lovely indeed, Mary. Is there anyone else...?'

'Please Miss, please Miss...'

'Yes, Billy...'

'Well, Miss, you see, Miss, John Wayne was riding across the desert, Miss, on his horse, Miss, and these six Indians ambushed him and they come screaming over the hilltops from all directions waving their tomahawks, Miss, and John Wayne pulled out his revolver and bang-bang-bang, bang-bang-bang! – there they was, all lying in pools of blood, Miss, and he got off his horse and he took out his knife and he scalped the lot of 'em, and then he rode off again into the sunset – Miss.'

'I see, Billy. That's a very unusual story. And what might be the moral?'

'Don't fuck about with John Wayne.'

Up in his room, naked, Jim Ransome glowered at his image tip-tilted in the couturier's mirror, trying to raise an erection. No joy. Shrivelled as a dead mole. Anyhow, he'd do better to conserve his strength for Harry Gosthorpe. The lino, he noticed, felt oddly resilient; and he stooped to examine it. It was not lino at all, but a rectangle of carpeting, nap worn to nothing, compacted with the grease and grume of decades and shiny from the shuffling of countless feet and – for all he knew – the penitential knees of those who still said their prayers at bedtime. Jim was taken with the shivers. He slid into the cool embrace of the geriatric rubberware and lay listening to the crackle of newspaper over the dead grate. How had that chap managed without disarranging her hair?

He was asleep in a trice.

The tentative skittering of coffee cups on tarmac? A mouse crossing the floor like a pyjama button rolling? Warmth flooding across his loins. A child in hospital, for Christ's sake! He'd wet the bed.

Rolling over the edge like an Olympic high-jumper breaking his own record with a millimetre's clearance, landing on his feet, he wrenched back the top sheets and pinched up the rubber to arrest the pattering of urine onto the bare floor. Gently he heaved the bed away from the wall and swabbed up the puddle with his yesterday's shirt and underpants. Raising the window, with difficulty, an inch or two, he was able to wring them out without troubling to leave his room for the lavatory; and three journeys sufficed. Next he turned his attention to the bedding. Carefully disengaging the edges of the flabby rubber, folding it over so as not to disturb the golden fluid swimming within, he carried this too to the window and decanted it deftly out into the street. With something of a struggle he closed the window again – a loud and sudden thump, but it didn't matter now – and disposed the sheets for more efficient airing. To hell with the stench: he wasn't going to spend the night in an icy draught for anybody; and one more smell in this hole... He paused briefly to admire his handywork; then, swathed richly in blanket and eiderdown, he curled into the easy chair to enjoy the sleep of the just.

But Jim couldn't sleep. He had performed his mopping-up operation with a numbed efficiency; but now only the numbness remained. The chatter and crash of the newspaper in the unpredictable suctions of the flue began to irritate him. Was this, then, what he had come to? Was he truly so nervous of Harry Gosthorpe that the mere thought of the man could terrorise him into a second infancy? He enjoyed, after all, a nominal seniority: consultants' man trumps contractors' man... He remembered, with some distaste, that conversation back in the London office, a bunch of junior draughtsmen suggesting they adopt of the pronunciation 'vaulves' for 'valves' as a way of distinguishing themselves from the great unwashed. They'd only been larking, of course; but nonetheless... The irony, for Jim, was that his own standing among his office colleagues rested considerably upon his mastery of skills gained in the practical world – not only on a sense of what was physically possible and what wasn't, but on his ability to look at a drawing and say to some cocky young engineer, 'That rad's nowhere near big enough for a room wi' that much glass.' High time he gave up his wandering ways and settled for the peace and quiet of the drawing board. Joyce had always laughed at him: 'You and your great, grubby fingers.' Joyce had gone now, of course. Yet he still liked to think of himself, almost with pride, as too cack-handed and lumbering for the finer adjustments of the spring-bow pen. Not that the pride made much sense without Joyce to try it against. He remembered – why? – the night he'd been eating alone in the steak house and had laughed aloud at some cartoon in the paper, and had then felt uncomfortable because there was no point in laughing aloud without anyone to ask you what was so funny. No, he'd never make a draughtsman, even supposing he could get the qualifications you needed these days. So much of his life, in any case, depended upon his niftiness at turning the tables: resorting to a workman's wrinkles while standing on the bosses' dignity. Take that away from him, and he might falter. Yet what was he doing now if not falter? What sort of a figure was he cutting: wifeless, demoralised and trembling in a flat-ulent and likely flea-ridden chair? Was this, he wondered, to become a recurrent feature of his life, increasing in frequency with the advance of years? Of course, like most unpleasant things, it was probably a lot more common than anybody was going to admit. Still, be that as it might, he'd have to find somewhere else to stay next time. And the time after that? There was a word, he knew: enuresis. It helped a little; but not much – just saying it to yourself in a dark room. Words needed people to charge their magic. That old locum, the ex-MO, could probably have worked the miracle. He'd had the air of having witnessed so much suffering, and having lived so long in a world where it had had to be laughed off for want of analgesic, that he could have shepherded you through the gates of death itself without you pausing to take it too seriously. Pain in the balls – no more! Not the sort of cure, though, that you could share with the toffee-nosed junior design engineers or the senior partners, or with Joyce, or even with Harry Gosthorpe the way things stood. That fat bastard had been profiteering too long – and under Jim's nose. Tomorrow – today, that was – come what might, Jim was going to have to see that he got his comeuppance. Low between the dark roofs, the dawn sky was taking on the colours of tempered steel: pale straw to dark straw, pale green through blue to violet. Soon it would be time to clean his shoes – a perverse ritual, perhaps, before a day of slosh, but a question of principle. Ransome smiled tightly. He was a nothing, a nobody – less of a man, by most standards, than that slob in the blue blazer. But he stood for something. And that was all that mattered.

The thespians had obviously arrived in the early hours, and were crowding the breakfast room. They'd developed a tactic of resting one edge of their plates of bacon and eggs on a matchbox, so the fat ran to one side and they could eat from the other, and were giggling slyly over it. You could tell they weren't going to spend the day on the frozen wastes of a building site where they'd be glad of a bellyful of walrus blubber. Jim ate hurriedly. Must check out before Elsie turned her attention to the bedrooms.

The wind had dropped; and Ransome, stepping out briskly, soon began to feel sticky inside his big overcoat, though the cold still voraciously attacked the exposed areas of his skin. He'd not heard it raining in the night; yet the sidewalks were damp. It was as if the gritty moisture had transpired from the stones themselves. Arriving at the half-built hospital, he picked his way over the wet soil-casts of the Babylonian treads of tipper-trucks towards the hut, where, instead of knocking on the door, he rapped his knuckles against the copper radiator propped alongside it. The sonorous clang resonated with a memory, long-buried, of the pleasure of rapping the bell of his father's euphonium: the world returning upon itself with hallucinatory boldness, trying to speak.

'Fitter I were apprenticed with, when I were serving mi' time, he could tek a length of one-inch rod, and he could cut a Whitworth thread in it wi' a cold chisel so accurate you could screw a nut ower it. Just wi' a cold chisel. You don't gerr'em like that nowaday. Fitters? They're nowt but bloody assemblers.'

So Fatso had decided to soft-soap him with an appeal to the shared nostalgia of waning craftsmanship, standing there with his turn-ups in the muck by the splintered, blakey-bashed threshold of his refuge...

'Not that I envy t'young-uns much. Haven't got any of your own, have you, Jim.'

'No. Joyce always reckoned it was my fault we couldn't have any. But she wouldn't adopt one, all the same. Started on about the dirt and the mess and the inconvenience – as if it'd've been different having them through normal channels.'

'Aye, they're bloody inconsistent, women.'

But this wasn't going to wash with Jim Ransome – not this time. He'd be as pally as you liked, share in the ritual knocks at the opposite sex; but it wasn't going to stop him making a thorough inspection of the installation to date. He unzipped the drawings from his overnight bag. Gosthorpe watched with apparent indifference, and was already heaving his improbable avoirdupois back into the hut as he muttered to his side-kick: 'Alf – see to him, will you.'

A long walk with not much to show for it: checking pipe diameters at every junction and exit velocities from ventilation grilles, and finding nothing amiss. Finally Jim halted at a covered way to the new maternity block.

'I wouldn't mind having a look under there. Wouldn't mind at all.'

At a nod from Alf, two labourers who'd been filling in a drainage trench ducked under the transom of the still-unglazed partition to lift the access cover from over the pipe duct.

'Haven't got a wander-lead, have you?'

'Only a thirty-footer. That do?'

'It'll have to.'

'Can shove it in that socket there, look.'

Jim slung his coat over the aluminium frame of the partition. One of the labourers offered him the loan of his donkey jacket; and he accepted with gratitude. Everyone waited as he put it on; and then he lowered himself into the four-foot-six by three-foot-six crawlway and – dim bulb in one hand and sheaf of plans in the other – set off at an awkward stoop into the darkness.

Reaching the extremity of the lead, Jim Ransome realised he'd left his pencil flashlight in his overcoat. He felt in the pockets of the borrowed jacket, but found only a rumpled snot-rag. The duct ran for another hundred feet before the next branch – an eighteen inch one leading off to the left – shortly after which the various services split to their destinations in the new wing. The heat and stuffiness were becoming a torment: suffocating. Jim decided to continue. Wedging the flex carefully in a bracket, so that the light hung in mid air for maximum illumination, he edged forward again, touching his hand intermittently against the pipes for guidance. And then he found it. A bush. An abrupt and purposeless narrowing of the flow pipe from – as he gauged it with the crook of his thumb and forefinger – three inches to two-and-a-half. He waited for his eyes to adjust to the gloom, shielding them from the tiny glare away back down the tunnel – almost as if he needed not only to touch but to see this evidence before he could believe in it. Gosthorpe better hire himself a lawyer – and fast! Then he became aware of something else. A painted band of colour around the pipe. He pushed at it with his thumbnail. It seemed still malleable. And he felt certain that the colour underneath was different. But he could not be absolutely sure.

Gosthorpe's throne room was a mixture of office and stores. A pipe-cutter leaned against the plan chest, and the desk was littered with hemp grommets and assorted brass fittings to which, like new-laid eggs, their packing straw still stuck. Thunder-clouds of grimy thumbprint darkened what little paperwork was visible. Gosthorpe was seated on a high stool, back against the wall, his beer paunch barrelling onto his thighs; and it seemed as if only his being wedged between desk and plan chest secured him from slithering forward into a helpless heap. But his manner, despite the gravity of the charges levelled against him, was avuncular, even paternal:

'I'll tell you one thing, Jim: it's no joke for kids these days, no joke at all.' He was chewing tobacco as he talked. Not proper plug tobacco, but ordinary St Bruno slice. 'Charge hand of ours, he's got a lad, nineteen now, been on t'dole since the day he left school. I've tried all ways to get him fixed up. "Sorry, Mr Gosthorpe, we'd help you if we could." I've got my allocation.'

'Don't you think we ought to get back to the point, Harry?'

'It is the bloody point. It's what I'm trying to tell you. Phase three of this job's been postponed twice already, what with the economy. Who stands to gain from a firm like ours going down the pan – eh? If a firm like ours can't make a profit, what do you think'll happen? The governors cut down on cigars? A few more kids on the parish, that's all it'll mean.'

Seismic disturbances rippled Gosthorpe's grandeur. He burped. Ransome, unsure exactly what he needed for his advantage, tried to divert the conversation: 'There's a difference in my book between making a profit and downright malpractice.'

'Malpractice? What are y'on about, malpractice? That system'll work. It'll meet the design conditions. You know that as well as I do. You can tell just by looking at it. Well, won't it?'

'That's not what the drawings say.'

'Bloody drawings! Some half-hard prick of a draughtsman straight out o' Tec. I'm telling you that system'll work, and I'm telling you as you know it will an'all. Them charts the college kids use for sizing-up pipes: they mek a certain allowance, don't they, for accumulation of lime – for loss of diameter. Well you won't get any loss of diameter in these parts. Soft as a baby's bum, the water round here.'

It was still not the moment. Above the desk hung a calendar with a badly painted nude enveloped in what was supposed to be green gauze but looked more like an attack of aphids. For that matter, why go through the ordeal at all? He could simply have... Fatso spoke again:

'You lot are on a percentage, aren't you – percentage of the accepted tender.'

'Are you suggesting our people load the specifications just to push up the price?' One thing Jim was pretty confident about was that his bosses were on the level: a family of Quakers who sent back Christmas whisky to plant manufacturers because it could be construed as bribery, and because they didn't touch alcoholic beverages themselves – much to the chagrin of those that did.

'I'm saying as that's the way o' things, that's all – makes no matter who's running 'em. One of your lads over-sizes a pipe. Fair enough. And we, being sensible and experienced people, notice his cock-up and put it right. So the National Health Service saves a bit on its running costs in the ensuing years, and everybody's happy. Or they should be. But they're not. 'Cos the system doesn't allow you to come to me like a reasonable man and say, "Thanks for spotting our mistake, Harry. You may as well keep the change, and we'll just be satisfied with the extra percentage on the quoted figure" – does it?'

Somehow Ransome was not finding the openings. Of course, he could always call a halt to the whole business with, 'Well, I'm sorry, Harry, but I've got my job to do, you know;' but that was not what he was after. The men watched each other like two great cats, great sphinxes, tails whipping sluggardly, each waiting for the other to blink.

'Too young for the war, weren't you, Jim?'

'Served in Italy.'

'Aye, only just. Dunkirk, lad – Dunkirk.'

'I was old enough to read the papers.'

'Flotilla of gallant little boats? That's it. I were there. And I'll tell you: first we knew of any evacuation was when we looked around for t'officers and there weren't one to be seen. Not one. And where were they? Skidaddled, that's where. All aboard the Skylark. Of course, it all made sense. It allus does. They'd had it drummed into 'em at Sandhurst that an officer's life was X times as valuable to the nation as a private's life – I mean, just think of the public money spent on their training for a start – and therefore it was their beholden duty, in the taxpayers' interests, to...'

'Look, Harry...'

'Never mind "Look Harry". Just listen to me. I'm not boasting to you, son. I don't care a monkey's what you think of me; but I'm telling you. I were a sergeant, that's all. Nowt but a miserable bloody sergeant. But I got twenty-five men onto those boats – twenty-five men who'd have been dead if the sodding officers had had their way.'

'All right. But I don't see what you're...'

'Yes you do. I'm saying as scum allus rises to t'top. That's what I'm saying.'

There was a pause.

'I'm my own man, Harry, not theirs.'

Gosthorpe spat.

Ransome glanced at the floor. It was not covered with tobacco stains. Fatso had done it for effect. Like everyone else, he was acting – cultivating an image. Didn't give tuppence, probably, about those kids on the dole. It had to be now:

'I don't have to start quoting British Standard specifications for colour-coding of MS pipes to you, do I?'

Gosthorpe still gazed steadily at him, but was silent. Jim had won.

Either Jim Ransome's instrumentation was faulty, or he was suffering from critical caffeine depletion. But he wasn't complaining. Somewhere on that gradient between truth and falsehood which is the human habitat, a battle had been waged to its conclusion. Jim had been overdue for a boost to his credibility. Now he had capital. Young Geoff, at least – the Young Master, as Gosthorpe always called him, and who addressed his own father as JT ('Do you feel we ought to invoke the penalty clauses in this instance, JT?') – was never stinting in recognition of achievement. In hindsight Jim could identify – though it had not registered consciously at the time – the precise moment when the game had started playing into his hands. The look in the eye of that labourer, the one who'd lent him the donkey jacket, when he'd proposed exploring the pipe duct: the anticipatory triumph of a man who realises his gaffers are about to get clobbered. That was what had put him onto it; and, from there on in, it had merely been a matter of grabbing his opportunities. No, Jim Ransome wasn't complaining. His only worry now was to get back in time to catch the breadshop before it closed – the sort of thing Joyce would once have... But it wasn't for that that he most missed her. Nor even for 'the other'. It was for the small things, like deciding when to eat and what to watch on telly and what time to go to bed, instead of dithering on aimlessly till all hours, and even for telling him what a miserable, two-faced bastard he was. There had to be a way of putting it, though. All right, all that mattered in the end was what you'd achieved, and there was no future in brooding over the rights and wrongs of it; but nevertheless, there had to be a way of putting it, of telling it to yourself – like someone else saying it about you, so you could gauge yourself by it – a guidance plain as a pillar of smoke by day or a pillar of fire by night, or a pillar of a lifetime's coffee cups held together only by the wind. But you'd need to use the words that took you to their bosom. A pain in the balls. You and your great, grubby fingers. That way you'd be safe as a lullaby, all understood. Waiting for his train at Clapham Junction, Ransome stood gazing at the evening star and the crescent moon: a toenail paring and a diamond cufflink on a field of unsullied indigo: Astaire and Rogers at the Chesterfield Criterion, now gone to bingo and dust.

# FIVE

'Was Mum a hero?'

'Eh? What's brought that to the surface all of a sudden?'

'Well, we've got this teacher, Miss Gregson, she was talking about it and she said all the missiles being taken away had nothing to do with the women's protest. Most of their actions weren't even reported anyway. It was all a matter of big-time politics between America and Russia, and it would have happened no matter what.'

'In one sense that's true.'

'What do you mean, "in one sense"? It's either true or it isn't.'

'What I mean is that the women's protest may not have directly prompted the decision to remove the missiles – almost certainly didn't, in fact – but what's more difficult to know is whether the accumulated weight of public opinion may not have influenced the negotiators in one direction rather than another... I mean, the whole idea that removing nuclear weapons was to be considered a serious objective might not have entered their calculations without – well, who's to know?'

'You certainly don't seem to.'

'Oh come on, Morwen. The point is, how can anybody be certain...'

'Dad, why won't you ever give me a straight answer to anything I ask you?'

'Most questions don't have straight answers, that's why. No, don't go away. You asked me a question; so the least you can do is hear me out, even if you don't like what I'm trying to tell you: because there's another aspect to this altogether. Even if it's true, even if Mum and her friends made not one iota of difference to the course of history, does that mean they shouldn't have done what they did?' I pause. I hear myself sounding like a vulgar moralist. How can you express something simple without its coming across as simplistic? Nevertheless: 'What it comes down to is, can you imagine what a world would be like where nobody ever protested against things they saw as foul and intolerable? Would you want to live in such a world? That's what I'd like to ask your Miss Gregson.'

'Is that it? Can I go now?'

'Yes, you can go now.'

She slouches off to her room and slams the door. I can't hold it against her. For her, inevitably, I'm the custodian of her mother's memory. I still remember how upset she was when her school-friends, under the guise of sympathy, began to insinuate that Glynis's illness had been something she'd 'picked up' at the camp, perhaps as a result of the harsh conditions to which she'd deliberately exposed herself. Here, too, I think a teacher may have been the initiator. I had to explain to Morwen that cancer wasn't something you caught the way you catch 'flu. But even then I was a prey to uncertainties which I had to be careful to conceal.

The worst day of my life was when I heard from Jill, Glynis's closest associate at the camp. She'd gone into Newbury specially to phone me, to tell me she didn't believe Glynis was in a fit state to stay there:

'She may be envisaging some sort of a martyrdom; but it wouldn't be, really, would it? I mean, it's not like being trampled by a police horse, or anything like that, being injured in the struggle – simply not seeking medical help when one needs to... I think you ought to come for her pretty soon, if you possibly can. She won't want to go; but we'll help persuade her. She's always been so supportive of everybody else. There's nothing we wouldn't do for her, honestly, even if she takes it the wrong way...'

'How do you mean, "takes it the wrong way"?'

'Well, it's possible. I don't say she would, but it's possible she might see it as a betrayal – you know, her friends not wanting her when she's become a burden, and all that...'

'Has she become a burden?'

'Up to a point, obviously. I mean... It isn't that we don't want to help. As I say, we'd do anything. We love her. It's just...'

'It's all right; I understand. I'm not blaming you in the slightest. You're there for a purpose, and that purpose isn't ministering to the sick. I was just trying to get a sense of how bad things were.'

'They're bad. She's gone downhill a lot since you last saw her.'

And even that didn't prepare me for what I found when I got there next morning. I'd prevailed upon Morwen to stay in London with friends; and that turned out to have been the right decision. There'd been a dawn eviction so sudden and brutal that the women had been caught on the hop. When I arrived, people were rummaging through the undergrowth for their scattered and damaged possessions, while those that had been rescued were being redistributed from prams and supermarket trolleys. In the midst of all this, Glynis was seated, leaning against a tree, seemingly oblivious of anything but her own pain. In the event, it wasn't difficult to persuade her to come home. Jill and another friend packed her belongings into the car, and we said our farewells. She had been at Greenham for the best part of three years. She was to live another seven months and three days.

It still saddens me that this should have been the Glynis Morwen knew best, the Glynis she was old enough to retain as an image and to whom she still whispers in her sleep. Not that she didn't frequently show her former spirit, sometimes indeed for quite long stretches. But inevitably, as time went by, her chunky hair fell out and the skin hugged her skull ever more mercilessly. My last rounded recollection is of her propped up in bed – by now in hospital – waiting for her radio-therapy which would do no good, gazing stonily and silently ahead of her; and I wondered what was going through her still-living mind: whether she was engaged in all-consuming negotiation with her own suffering, or whether she was hearing again the mournful pre-dawn siren announcing an alert and knowing she must rouse herself to sit on the road to prevent the servicemen's nervous families entering the base, children's faces pressed ghostly against the glass, or to prevent the convoys leaving, and not knowing whether it was an exercise as usual or whether this time it was the real thing, in which case there would probably be no MoD police to haul her and her comrades out of the path but the missile launchers would drive straight over them. That is why I owe Morwen the duty of memory.

When Glynis died I wrote to Jill, c/o the camp; but my letter didn't reach her until after the funeral. Eventually she phoned me to say that the people at her Gate had been discussing it among themselves and wanted to hold some kind of a memorial ceremony for Glynis, and would I be interested in taking part and broadening the thing out to include her family and her friends from other areas of her life. We settled on a date six months after Glynis's death, and Jill and I organised it between us. We found a sympathetic vicar who let us use his church hall for nothing. There was a large oak cross over the platform; but we were allowed to cover that with white muslin which billowed out and sighed back at the slightest disturbance of the air like ectoplasm in a faked photograph. Ninety-six people came. The contingent from Glynis's village were a little surprised that it was not to be a religious gathering; but a male-voice septet sang *Myfanwy*, which from their point of view had the merit of flowing from the pen of the most considerable hymnographer since Charles Wesley. Good-humouredly the sisters retaliated with *You Can't Kill the Spirit*. Then they played a piece of music by someone called Charles Ives, *The Unanswered Question*, which someone from the camp said she'd been particularly fond of. I hadn't known; but then she'd often played music to herself on headphones, so as not to disturb me, when I'd brought a wodge of calculations home to work on, or even when I'd gone to bed. There was a lot of high, quiet stuff on the strings interrupted from time to time by rude brass phrases. I looked at the faces of the assembled people. Most looked blankly polite; but I noticed that one or two were smiling as if in wry recognition of some important truth. Next, Morwen read a poem she had written to the effect that her mother, of whom she had seen so little in life, was now completely with her in her mind – a poem which most of us found sadder than I think Morwen had meant it to be. It had been assumed that I would want to deliver a tribute to Glynis; and I worked at it for several evenings before finally giving up. How can you speak about someone who's meant so much to you? Landscape of an unresolved battle; wounds still smarting; abandoned colours drooping which no-one will come back to claim; a book put aside with a marker in it; sentences broken off; things not understood which once seemed understood, and perhaps understood which once seemed not: and for what? To end up only with a lopsided, unfinished portrait, a portrait of the soggy mess of one's own mind unmapped even by the recti-linear grids of archaeology? So instead I read some selected paragraphs from the closing section of *The Waves*, Glynis's favourite book. All right, they're about a man, so you might argue I was speaking implicitly about myself; but at that late point in life I think our experience becomes almost indistin-guishable – which I assume was how Woolf felt when she was writing it. It was one of the Greenham women – Rosalind I think was her name – who, in speaking of Glynis, made a remark which I managed to bury at the time but which kept demanding my attention until, a year or two later, I forced myself to confront it. She commended her for the bravery with which she had withstood her own pain out of commit-ment to the cause. How long had she been in pain, then? Was this merely a rhetorical flourish; or was there more here than I knew about? I even began to wonder whether Glynis had already known she was seriously ill before she made the deci-sion to go to Greenham. But by the time I allowed myself to entertain these thoughts it was far too late to seek out Rosalind and ask her. The camp at their gate had dispersed, and I did not even have an alternative address for Jill. Those are the doubts I have never revealed to Morwen.

The title of the book is on a bull's-blood red strap superimposed on an image of a grey, vermiculate root system in dry, friable, de-natured earth. The title is upside down, but I can read it. It is *Escape from Greenham*. I turn the book the other way up; but the title remains upside down. And it becomes apparent to me that I am dreaming.

At her commemoration I found myself somehow envying Glynis not only for her character and her humour and her comradeship; I found myself envying her also for being dead: for being complete in herself, for being beyond question, for having tied the final knot. After a while, though, I was able to persuade myself that once you are dead you start receding. Or withdrawing. Present only fitfully in the triangulations of a viewpoint; acting only on the mute screen of a restored or rediscovered film. There was nothing for it but to go on.

This thing is a monstrosity. They make them expressly to be thrown into skips: a bulky plastic box the colour and texture of boiled chicken skin, with a keyboard that rattles and the keys fall off. Everything about it manages to be at once both flimsy and self-gratified. As sculpture, you wouldn't give it house-room. As a mechanism it is an outrage, an insult to any sense of workmanship: a great, graceless hulk which dominates the entire surrounding space with its disproportion. And make no mistake, its shoddiness is deliberate. Deliberate and derisive. After all, it's not as if this were the 1940s. We live at a time when much intelligence and sensitivity is devoted to the design of domestic objects. But this is designed only to belittle us. It sits there taunting us with the assertion that the only reality worthy of the name is whatever may happen in its own soup of electrons and in the cheated spaces it condescends to display for us. It bullies us to disavow the tactile, to forget the days when we sat on hard forms and dipped our nibs into porcelain inkwells – another item, like the lustres, now vanished in their millions. Yet I had to arrange a bank loan in order to buy it. I hadn't much option, really. The outside inspection routine fizzled out. Ron Cottle, who'd been good as his word and kept me well supplied with commissions, moved on to other things; and I turned down so many jobs in the months I spent looking after Glynis that they finally stopped asking me. 'The chap's simply not reliable.' Fair enough. So I managed to gain employment, off and on, with a local company designing heating and air conditioning systems. They had informal links with an architectural practice, somewhat avant-garde, which meant I was constantly required to work out heat losses for structures fabricated from novel materials whose thermal conductivity was a mystery to all concerned. Even then, I was doing most of the work from home – and there's my old drawing board in the corner to prove it. Eventually I got cheesed off. *Bien fromagé*, as one used to say. Besides, I could see the revolution in working practices that was about to swamp us – everybody could. So I took a crash course in computerised design – I'm not sure who was expected to crash first, the computer or me – and meanwhile ferreted out some of the more interesting contacts from my days in the maritime section. I secured the bank loan on the strength of a letter of intent from Covington Submersibles guaranteeing me work on one of their new craft: routing of pipework for maximum efficiency and optimum use of space. And that's what I'm doing. A pleasant enough bunch of people, who refer to their products, jocularly, among themselves, as U-Boats. Tactless. But they're not to know. All the same, it's a lonely business. The companionship of labour – *though cowards flinch and traitors sneer* – is evidently a thing of the past.

My constant presence here is perhaps becoming something of an irritant to Morwen, who has taken to bringing a boyfriend home. I noticed yesterday that she's fitted a bolt to her door. It's not a big, heavy bolt; which means that she trusts me not to try and break the door down. I appreciate that. The truth of the matter is that she's not far short of the statutory age; and it's been a long time since the flat has heard the sound of joyous bed-springs. Once in a while, of course, I've tried muttering to her about precautionary procedures – hard-hat areas, so to speak – but all I get is, 'Dad – please – I *know*.' It would help, though, if her beaux could be a bit more talkative. I have sometimes wished she'd have an affair with one of her teachers – either sex, it wouldn't bother me, so long as it was someone with whom I could have a decent chin-wag. It might help her exam results, too. After all, if we're into the era of market morality, there's no point in being the last one left with principles. But no, that's too cynical. Glynis wouldn't have accepted that for a moment. As it happens, Morwen comes home alone this evening. She dumps her bag alongside my chair and says:

'You know *Ozymandias*...'

'Met him once or twice. Diamond geezer.'

'No, seriously. You know *Ozymandias*. Well I'm having this mega disagreement with Jacqui. See, I reckon that when it says, "Look on my works, ye mighty, and despair," that means look how everything's broken and destroyed and I used to be so powerful; but Jacqui says no, the words were on it when the statue was first put up, so all it's saying is look, I'm this powerful and I can have the biggest statue in the world. So what do you think? What does it mean?'

'Don't you think it could mean both?'

'T-tt – you're at it again!'

'At what again?'

'Hedging your bets.'

'I'm not bloody hedging my bets. I'm suggesting to you that you can take it both ways. It's legitimate to take it both ways. In fact I'd go so far as to say that that's the whole point of the poem – the irony.'

'What, you mean Shelley may actually have intended...'

'For us to be aware of both meanings? Yes. Why not?'

It's one of those moments. I'm reminded of when she first saw the moon. What's just happened is that Morwen has seen the Red Sea divide, has seen a vista open, not simply upon a particular poem, but onto a whole new way of looking at things: a way that says, 'There may not be a right and a wrong answer to this;' or perhaps that should be, 'The best approach to this may not be by looking for right and wrong answers; and it may be all the more interesting for that.' Why didn't her teachers make this clear to her? Maybe they failed to recognise the barrier she was confronting. Anyhow, this is a moment I shall remember to cherish, because there aren't likely to be many more of them – not, that is, with myself as the agent of enlightenment. And when it comes to parenthood, that's as good as it gets. Come to think of it, was I conscientious in letting my own parents know when I'd benefitted from their wisdom? Of course I wasn't. I was too busy flaunting my intellectual independence.

A manilla envelope with my own handwriting. A crease down the centre where it has been folded to go into another envelope. All submissions must be accompanied by s.a.e. No need to ask: it's another batch of poems returned from one of the literary journals. Back at my desk, postponing the start of my legitimate work, the work I actually get paid for, I cut the thing open. All so professional, a manilla envelope; so sturdy. These are ones I felt good about, felt I stood a chance with. Compulsively – it's something I nearly always do, though I despise myself for it – I reach for a copy of the magazine, the one I chose with such considered regard for the editor's preferences, and look at some of the poems in it. Some come out to meet me; others simply die on the page. What makes the difference? And surely my own, placed aggressively alongside them, measure up in their own way – have at least one or two clearly identifiable points of ignition? Am I wasting my time: all this effort for an average of two poems accepted per year, and not all of those eventually published? When my first collection came out, I thought the door had opened for me. Granted it was a very small publisher. The Steggun Press. That's 'nuggets' backwards; but they had a sten-gun for their logo, no doubt in acknowledgment of the rigour of their typesetting. Anyway, the anarchic aura appealed to me; but they went down the swanee after their fourth publication, mine being their third. I guess I'd simply dropped onto the right desk at the right ascension of the meridian, or whatever it's called. I've been toying with the idea recently of adopting a more classical verse-form. Sonnets, let's say. It would at least take some of the subjectivity out of the process of assessment. I mean, you'd at least be able to claim that they had the right number of lines, the right number of feet, a recognisable rhyme-scheme. Your work would only have to be judged on what was left over after such criteria were satisfied. So it's back to the drawing board? If only!

'Dad, do you have a philosophy of love?'

'A *what*?'

'A philosophy of love.'

'Now why are you asking me that?'

'Never mind why. Do you?'

'God, you really want me to put my head on the chopping block this time, don't you? Look, I can tell you one small thing, that's all. You need to remember that your partner is a real person, a person in her own right – his own right – engaged in a project that even she or he doesn't quite under-stand, bringing his or her meanings into the world, and...'

'And what?'

'I suppose I'm saying that if you try to lay claim to that project, to possess it, even under the guise of understanding, you'll end up destroying the very thing that fired your love in the first place. OK?'

'Hang on, let me get this straight. You're saying people shouldn't try to understand each other? Is that it?'

'Well, we use the word "understand" in different senses, don't we?'

'Aha! Here we go...'

'Shut up. If "understanding" means "sympathy", then that's fine; but if it means knowing exactly how someone else thinks and feels, so that you feel their mind is almost in your pocket, and you can judge their conclusions before they've even reached them, then I suspect that isn't fine. In fact I think it amounts to aggravated trespass.'

Morwen laughs. 'You do realise, don't you, that you're taking up arms against all the advice in all the self-help manuals in all the station book-stalls in Christendom?'

'That's my mission.' It dawns on me that she's grown up.

Jesus, the pain! What time is it? I hurry stiffly to the loo, hardly able to restrain my bladder. I expect a great gush; but nothing. I massage my front. Nothing. Relax. Getting tensed up won't help. A hot drink? It might shift something; but if not, it would just end up filling my bladder more. Lie down for a bit. Give things time. But how can I relax with this? Look, this is actually serious. I've been having a bit of trouble recently; just didn't imagine it had gone this far. But it has. Got to face it – it has. Phone the doctor? You'd only get the answerphone at this time of night. 'Please phone for an appointment.' Phone the hospital? Casualty? I think you're just expected to turn up, preferably bleeding. Jesus, I can't take this! Am I being a wimp? It doesn't matter; the thing is to do something. Desperate for a pee. Fill a hold-all with – what? – towel, change of clothes, dressing gown, soap. Wake Morwen? No need. Tooth brush. Leave her a note: Gone To Hospital; no, that'll put her into a tizz; bin it; Had To Leave At Short Notice? What the hell'll she think that means? Just put: Back Soon! OK? I'll phone her in the morning and explain. Now. Think. Car keys. Driving'll take my mind off the pain. But if the pain gets suddenly worse I may have an accident. No sign of traffic in the street outside. I'll have to phone the local mini-cab firm, then wait in the street so they don't wake Morwen ringing the bell. 'Ten to twelve minutes? Right – I'll be waiting outside.' I've got the panic you get when you know you're about to pee and you're in the middle of the audience at the theatre, or something. Except that in this case the one thing I'm not about to do is pee; but the body's not used to that, doesn't have a built-in adjustment for it. 'I can't pass water.' 'For how long?' 'Well, I'm not sure, I woke up like it,' 'Very well, if you'd like to take a seat over there...' Five minutes. Fifteen minutes. An hour. Writhing, not knowing what to do with myself. I try the loo, but no difference. Most of the people who've come in since I did – bottle and knife wounds from fights outside clubs, a woman hit by a car and brought in on a stretcher – have been taken away for treatment. A change of shift. I go to the counter again. 'Any idea when I can be dealt with?' 'Your problem is...?' 'Retention of urine.' 'Retention? Why didn't you say so?' Five minutes, and I'm on my back in one of those ridiculous hospital gowns that's supposed to tie at the back but doesn't have anything to tie with and somebody's pushing a green plastic bodkin with a blob on the end up my cock with dollops of KY jelly, and it's atrocious and yet at the same time it's not quite pain it's more like... and the blob seems to engage with something inside me like the tumbler of a lock falling into place and suddenly the bliss of feeling my bladder emptying.

Urology and nephrology. That's right – nephrology. There's something indefinably peaceful about this ward in spite of what goes on here. Just the five of us. I've noticed already that there's a set of subtle conventions regarding privacy. Except for the occasional shared joke when something out of the ordinary happens, the rule is to pretend each other isn't there: each on his own liferaft, as it were, occupying his individual space. And this space has tacitly accepted boundaries, which extend roughly a foot – two foot – beyond the edge of the bed, chair and locker. If, while stretching your legs, you feel like chatting to somebody, the procedure is to skirt very close to this boundary and exchange a glance. The other person will then either initiate a conversation or, as if benignly pardoning your infringement, ignore you. My own case, though, is a little special. I happen to occupy a bed next to the window. People naturally like to look out of the window from time to time; and this perforce involves them in violating my sovereignty. We feel close to the sky up here on the eleventh storey. Far below, silent with the double glazing, there is a street corner with a newsagent's and a bank and one or two other shops. Little red single-decker buses take the bend cautiously under the perforated canopy of the plane trees which scatters the sunshine. It is as if we were gods surveying the mortals in the aimless yet strangely endearing scurry of their lives. I'm reminded of those characters you used to be able to buy to populate the platform of a Hornby train set: the guard with his red and his green flags; the porter pushing a trolley piled with luggage; the spruce middle-class family off on their holidays. Did they but know it, the train they awaited would be capable only, after completing its oval or figure-of-eight circuit, of delivering them to the same station from whence they had departed. And what could be more comforting than that? Jack, from Bed 3, has come to stand alongside me:

'Just think, they reckon they can get the whole of the Oxford English Dictionary onto one CD-ROM these days, but you still got to piss the way you always did. Doesn't seem fair, somehow.'

'I know. It's particularly galling for me, this business. I used to be a wizard at mechanics of fluids when I was younger.' We hold our gowns behind us with one hand for modesty, using the other to gesture with, in a curious parody of Roman senators – thus doubtless bestowing on our speech a gravity it has done nothing to earn.

'You an engineer, then?'

'Yes. You?'

'I'm a turner.'

'What – capstan lathe, you mean?'

'That's right. Ever handled one?'

'Yes – but not for my living. So what line are you in – marine, aeronautics..?'

'Nothing so glamourous. I've spent my life with a small company manufacturing fairground equipment – merry-go-rounds, big dippers, water bullets, star trippers – taming technology for the kiddiwinks, and all in a quiet residential street with wonky flagstones where they passed on their way to school, swinging their snazzy plastic satchels and pulling each other's hair and never guessing. But that's all over now. I've joined the immortals.'

'The what?'

'I've been immortalised. That's how they put it. Had all my skills fed into a computer programme. "Every blink, every tremor, the underlying rhythm of your breathing, every microsecond's hesitation, it'll all be there in perpetuity, every time the computer repeats your actions." Of course, it means they don't need me any more. But I'm coming up to retirement anyway, so the firm offered me a deal. Quite generous, actually.' Ephemeral memorial. *My name is Ozymandias...*

They've been doing tests on me all day: rectal examination, blood, urine sample to the lab and so forth. They're taking me down for an ultrasound scan tomorrow, then with luck they'll be able to do the operation the following morning. Micro-surgery – no need to slice me open. I'm glad they've decided to get it over with rather than sending me home with catheter and bag to await a gap in their crowded schedule. Morwen turns up with peaches and sympathy. She brings me a book by William Gibson which she hasn't read but her boyfriend recommended – said it would take my mind off everything, even myself.

I didn't see who turned out the light. It happened, as if by common consent, at about 10.00. This morning the nurses have been busying quietly since 6.30, keen to get everything neat and tidy and all blood pressures recorded in the Book of Eternity before the day shift comes on at 8.30. I settle into this routine as if born to it. White bedlinen. Contentment. Yes, leave me here long enough and I could grow a new personality, put down new roots the way a broken-off geranium stem will if you shove it back into the soil.

'Nice-looking kid, your daughter. Leastways, I'm assuming she's your daughter.'

'Yes.'

'And the wife?'

I shake my head. To be honest, I'd rather get on with the

Gibson book – Morwen's boyfriend was right about it – than get into too intimate a conversation with Jack. But he seems in expansive mood.

'Ah, pity. A girl needs a mother. How long has she been without her?'

'It's been six years now – pushing seven. But even before that, she hadn't seen much of her for a year of two. Glynis was at the Greenham camp.'

'Oh bloody hell. Load of lezzies, if you ask me. Well – sorry – maybe not your missus; but all the same, what other reason could there be? A women-only camp... I mean!'

'Well, aside from anything else, there's the practical consideration. Have a mixed camp, and there'd be bound to be allegations of rape sooner or later; and you've only got to think what the tabloids would do with that. It would have kept them in righteous indignation for months on end.'

'Ought to consider themselves lucky they weren't all raped. Like in Chile. Official secrets. Whisked away and raped with electric batons under the appreciative supervision of the CIA. The Yanks must have been pretty convinced they weren't of any account, didn't represent any threat to their interests.'

'Something to do with the "special relationship", perhaps. Or don't you think there is such a thing?'

'Of course there's such a thing; and I can tell you how it works: our government agrees to do everything America wants us to, and in return we're allowed to keep the external trappings of democracy. Make no mistake, those Yanks know how to deal with dissidents.'

A moment or two of silence, and then I hear myself say: 'I think my wife suffered enough.' I'm shocked at the anger in my voice. I didn't intend or expect it. Neither did Jack, I can see. He mutters an apology and wanders back to his bed. I didn't have the right. He didn't mean to be offensive. He was expressing a popularly touted if pessimistic point of view. I must make some gesture to him tomorrow. Mind you, there was something about his manner. I'm reminded of what I was thinking a while back about there being no companionship of labour nowadays. I used to get so annoyed in the drawing office, the way everything got turned into a joke, the culture of laughing things off, probably for good reason, to avoid serious conflicts developing. Without that culture, people chew on their own fat too long, become obsessive. I'm not sure which is worse. Anyway, it's all clear for tomorrow. Knowing I'll be nil-by-mouth from midnight, the night nurse offers to make me a cup of tea and a couple of slices of toast. Nye Bevan's spirit lives. I accept with gratitude.

It must be the early hours. I've woken up thirsty; but there's no point in asking for a drink. There's a roaring sound in this place at night. It may be there in the daytime too, but I've never noticed it. It's obviously the air conditioning; but it sounds like the engines of an ocean-going liner. Hearing murmurs, I open my eyes to a strange sight. I haven't bothered to close the curtains around my bed, partly because I like to see dawn break and partly because everyone else closes theirs, so I've all the privacy I need. Now, with all but the blue safety lamp extinguished, I see that there is a glow from within the curtains of three of the other beds, accompanied by soft-spoken voices. Maybe some extra tests are being performed; maybe someone has pressed his emergency buzzer; maybe a consultant has just finished an exhausting shift and taken the only opportunity possible to explain to a patient the prognosis for his case. Whatever the explanation, the effect is almost spectral: battle tents on the Mongolian steppe; Henry V conferring with his lieutenants before Agincourt; or the teepees, benders and Getaway tents of Greenham, tiny, but enough for two women or three to gather over cocoa laced with Southern Comfort and discuss tactics for tomorrow's raid.

All clattering and banging as the porters discover there are no side bars on my bed and have to dismantle them from one of the others, then wheeled along corridors where grey forms in dressing gowns flatten themselves against the walls at our passing, then down in a draughty service lift to where the pipes are bigger and the trunking exposed and into a small

184

room where a rubicund mustachioed man is preparing his syringe. He injects me in the back of my hand. I look at the clock, which says 11.30. They're running fifteen minutes late. I look at the clock; but I don't understand it. What's happened? I seem to remember coming down and looking at the clock; but I look at the clock and I can't tell what time it's telling. I'm cold. I'm very cold. A woman's voice; and she's saying, 'He's not saying anything.' And then she says, 'Can you wiggle your toes?' In case she's speaking to me, I wiggle my toes, and she must have been speaking to me, because she says, 'Can you nod your head?' and I nod my head, and she says, 'He's obviously conscious, why isn't he saying anything?' and I want to say something but I'm too cold to get a word out, and she says, 'We'd better turn the heater up, the next one'll be out soon;' and the soles of my feet begin to scorch, but I'm still too cold to speak, and then I manage to say, 'Why am I so cold?' She comes into vision over me, upside-down, a middle-aged nurse with bleached hair, and she says, 'It's because they've been sluicing out your bladder continuously with cold water so they can see what they're doing with the mini-camera. The cold gets to the core of your body. It's like a temporary hypothermia. But you'll be all right.' This must be what it feels like to be dragged to safety after five days and nights in the North Atlantic. And that thought stuns me so that I forget to try looking at the clock again.

Feeling that cold, even without any sense of danger – because it certainly never crossed my mind that I might not survive it – but simply feeling that cold, that cold to the core of your being, is qualitatively different from reading accounts or talking to survivors or watching archival programmes on television. It's important, while I remember. He once said, or Mum said he said, that what surprised him was the way some people let go while he hung on, as if they weren't all that bothered about life. But what if what he really meant was that he was surprised not that they let go but that he didn't; or rather that he, out of all of them, was the one who didn't? In other words, why was he special? Does that feel right? No, not really. There's something else: that George Medal. You weren't given medals just for getting through it. He must have done something actively courageous, saved people's lives, delayed his own escape – delayed it too late – by freeing up the boats or the rafts for others. He never actually told us – *did* he? – that no-one else survived the sinking, only that no-one else, except for one greaser perhaps, survived in the water. Yet even that doesn't seem adequate when I think about the things people did get medals for – things I've read about. There must be a whole other area of experience here that I've never even considered. Of course, for all I know he could have earned his medal for something he did on some previous voyage. But, either way, it wasn't something he wanted to talk about, not even to us. And I don't think that was from modesty. I mean, he could easily have found ways of saying it that didn't sound crassly boastful. Come on. I have to think this through while the ice is still at my own vitals. It could, in theory, have been that he'd done nothing remarkable at all, and felt he'd received the medal under false pretences; but no, I never sensed shame in his behaviour. It must have been – *must* have been – that the medal and all it represented, in a word everything that preceded the sinking, had been rendered in his view redundant, irrelevant. That's it: irrelevant. Irrelevant to what, though? Well, to everything that came after it. A barrier to meaning formed of the cold itself: the absoluteness of the cold severing before from after, action from consequence. After all, he didn't suffer his crisis in the psychic isolation of a hospital, where all your quirks and your responsibilities can be surrendered at Admissions. Dad had them all with him as he struggled not to drown. I remember as a child the tingle behind my nose when I'd shipped a mouthful of bathwater. And here's another thing. A medal, if it implies courage, also implies dangers. He'd seen his mates dying – almost certainly dying horribly, even hideously. All right, the idea of hideous deaths being the price of food was commonplace enough during the war; but that's still a different kettle of fish from experiencing them at first hand. All in black-and-white with sea-sick camera angles and dodgy focus? You can't get away from the conventions, can you. Still, no conventions, no communion. So what about those clippings I found from magazines and papers? Were they no more than flotsam he'd grasped at in a spirit of philosophical extremity: of no great significance in themselves; assuming significance only because they happened to be there where so little else was? This hasn't got me far, really, has it? Only the idea of irrelevance takes us a tentative step closer. But then what's to be expected? I remember the inaccessibility I sensed in Glynis towards the end, when her gaze was unfocused and her hand lay cold in mine. My father's inaccessibility is of a similar scale, if of a different order. What was it I was saying to someone about not needing to understand people? I don't remember what the context was; but maybe it applies here. The question is, presumably, what exactly does one look for in a parent? Is it moral example? Is it a disquisition on the conundrums of the day? Or is it something I haven't yet fathomed: an anatomy of the nature of the conundrum?

I can't make my peace with Jack now. He was discharged while I was in the theatre, and there's someone new in his place. 'Ships that pass in the night,' my mother would have said. So I sit moodily manipulating the translucent tube from my catheter, trying to wash down the fleecy, feathery blood-clots which are blocking the seemingly continuous flow of urine. It occupies my mind. Below, people are alighting from buses and going in and out of the bank and the newsagent's. It's easy, from this elevation and in this antiseptic atmosphere, to see the human enterprise as blips on the screen of international finance. You pass a woman in the street. You find her attractive? Your response has been orchestrated by a billion-dollar pharmaceutical corporation in collusion with a billion-dollar ad agency. Our most intimate and personal feelings: mere epiphenomena of the flow of capital across the world's exchanges.

'This is my Dad. He's uncertain.'

'Uncertain of what?'

'Uncertain of most things, actually.'

Christopher himself looks a trifle uncertain how to take this; but he seems to decide to treat it as an obscure family joke – which I trust, by now, it is – and we shake hands.

'Was it you who recommended the William Gibson book?'

'Yes, it was.'

'Well I'm quite certain I enjoyed that.'

Christopher smiles broadly; and I decide, on the basis of no further evidence, that I like the bloke. Morwen has developed an interest in movies of late; and the other day she popped her head around my door to say, 'We've decided we're going to take you to the NFT for your birthday.'

'We?'

'Me and Christopher. You haven't met him.'

'I know I haven't. You don't bring him here.'

'So this means you will. You don't mind, do you?'

'Do I mind being offered a birthday treat? No, not at all. I'm delighted.'

'I meant Christopher. You don't mind.'

'I can't tell you that till I've met him.'

'Curmudgeon!'

It isn't a full house by any means. The lights go down and a piano begins tinkling. I hadn't noticed there was a piano. It's a Soviet silent film. Called *Earth*. And it opens with a very strange scene where an old man is dying amid a harvest of apples, his family watching him, and he perks up to eat one more apple before falling back dead. In fact it goes on being rather strange. There's something you could call primitive about the style. Yes, there's a little of that fast cutting which people always think of when they hear 'Soviet Silent Cinema', but really not very much of it. To show that a man is waiting a long time, there's a shot of him seated at the table, then a fade out and a fade back in to exactly the same shot, and then the same again. The story is about collectivisation of the land.

The people with the most radiant smiles are the nice ones, and they are the ones in favour of collectivisation. It's as simple as that. Some of the shots are very simple too: just a telegraph wire slanting away to the horizon. Almost every scene consists of an interminable succession of close-ups of faces supposedly carrying the burden of an absolute minimum of dialogue. Am I bored? Are other people bored? I don't truly feel bored; yet I'm puzzled as to why I'm not. After all, this is boring, isn't it? Do I just not want to admit to myself that I'm bored when I'm being treated by my daughter and her boyfriend? Yet the rest of the audience too seem rapt. There's a murky shot – dusk, it would appear – where our Bolshevik hero walks forward along the village path with his eyes closed. At least, I think they are closed. It goes on for minute after minute after minute. He begins to dance, kicking up dust in the moonlight – if it is moonlight. Then someone shoots him. There's something here I'm on the verge of grasping, but I can't quite. When the priest comes to the house of mourning, he's introduced as if he were a burglar or a werewolf trying to break in; and when we do see him, and the young man's father sends him packing in another interminable exchange of mug-shots, the contrast between the father's coarse-grained honesty and the priest's dishevelment is so blatant that I suddenly realise it is not propaganda in the normal sense. What I mean is that a contrast so crude cannot possibly be the message. It is the vehicle for the message. And I realise, by the same token, that I have been misunderstanding the entire film. This film belongs to a period where it was recognised that the material of the narrative comprised a photographic record of faces and locations. I'll put that differently. This film belongs to a period when the photographic nature of its component imagery was regarded as, or rather was taken for granted as being, a crucial component of its meaning. All those slow successions of faces – sad eyes, bristly whiskers, bad teeth – are there not primarily to communicate the sense of the dialogue through the occasional flicker of facial expression; they are there to ground the story in the photographic reproduction of a material world. The faces are not the bearers of the information: they are the information; and the longer they stay on the screen the better. I must remember to thank Morwen for affording me this insight. Because that's what it is. Comrades, I have seen the moon! The film ends with loving close-ups of apples and melons drenched by a shower of rain. The sort of thing you'd find in a commercial? No, the commercial would be far more sprightly and wholesome.

We sit by the river sipping our beers. Seagulls swoop over the drum-shaped buoys, lugged and studded, nubbed and bossed, which look remarkably heavy for buoys now that I think about it and which haven't been re-designed in my life-time. In fact they're probably the same ones as were here when barges had red sails in the sunset. Red ochre sails. Suzette Tarry... ah yes...

'A pity, really, but you have to admit it was a load of old codswallop,' Christopher is saying. 'By all accounts the collec-tivisation of the Soviet Union was little short of genocide.'

'Mmm.' But why can't I accept that it was codswallop? 'I suppose it comes down to whether you think the poetry tran-scends the specifics of the historical situation.'

'You mean whether the poetry transcends the socialism?'

'No. The socialism is factored in to the poetry.'

Christopher glances at Morwen: 'He doesn't seem as uncertain as all that.' And we all laugh – laughing it off.

*Ker-chink, ker-tiddle, ker-chink, ker-tiddle – kak-kak-kak-kak...*
Poor old Anderson shelter's on her last legs, I'm afraid. Every time I take her for an MOT I expect them to tell me she's for the knackers' yard. I've always vaguely hoped she'd see me through to my bus pass. But that's some years away yet. The question is, how long does a year seem to a car? Is it like dogs, seven for every one of ours or somesuch? Never mind, I think I can still rely on her for a spin to the outer suburbs. Leafy suburbs. That's the word they use, isn't it – leafy. As if the leaves were what mattered – and they're only here for half the

year, when all's said and done. It's as if they had something to hide. As if what they had to hide were what mattered. Synecdoche – is that it? 'Leaves' for the things they're concealing. Like fig leaves. No, not quite. Anyhow, the public library is one of those neo-Georgian edifices, its portico finely calculated to make you feel privileged without making you feel over-awed. Inside, oak light-varnished, like the waiting room of a crematorium. The reference section, that's what I need. I've finally tracked it down to here – a copy of Andriessen's *Cyclopaedia of Merchant Shipping*. And there it is on the top shelf, tooled and aloof. I tilt it backwards and take its full weight as it cants into the recoil of my palm; and I carry it with both hands to the reading desk, spreading it like a bible on a lectern. The paper has the smell of a long-empty jar of rosemary, a vitreous memory-trace. In the Contents I find Gartside Wilberforce & Sons, better known as the Green Chevron Line. Turning the pages in unwieldy stacks, I reach the general vicinity: details of the vessels listed chronologically by date of launch: the Wharfedale, the Airedale, the Nidderdale... and I'm there: the SS Calderdale: 1925, Palmers Co. Newcastle; tonnage 7482g, 4503n; engines, single screw turbine double reduction geared; two double-ended boilers, 5050 shp; speed 13 knots; destroyed by enemy action November 1941. That's it: my father's ship. It's a mystery how the human mind works. I already knew that date; yet to see it here, unadorned by sentiment, on these authoritatively stiff pages, is to feel a steely chill the length of my spine: both that it really happened, and at the same time that it has been consigned to this mausoleum of data. There's a photograph too: re-printed from a postcard, to judge from the hand-written white caption: the SS Calderdale docked for provisioning at Port Said. Must have been on the Far Eastern run at that time. It's a smudgy image. There are a few cultivated palm trees. The ship has a wheel-house, a bridge, davits, chevron on the funnel – what you'd expect. On the harbourside there are some blurred shadow shapes, one or another of which may have been my father in his tropical whites glancing back from the slatted shade of a palm at the grass, pea, moss, sage, ivy or apple green of that chevron. There's no knowing. Besides, what difference would it make? Now that I'm confronted with it, I don't know why I went to such trouble to root out this information. To confirm that my father existed for others as well as for us? But that was obvious, wasn't it? I gaze for a moment longer at those smudges one of whom may have been my father; and I'm just about to close the book when the significance of it strikes me: I've never once imagined Dad on his ship, part of a community with a community of purpose. For me, his existence had begun with him in the drink, isolated, clinging to his spar.

On television there is an archival programme, recent history, concerning the collapse of the Soviet Union. Sobchak, now mayor of Leningrad, gives an interview about the blessings of perestroika. He's a man of seeming integrity, who you can believe might be able to stop the rot until you remember that his fellow-citizens have already voted to eradicate the name of the city which, not all that long ago, held out against the Nazis for nearly three years. Behind him, on the wall, is a painting of Lenin; and I find myself giving more attention to this than to Sobchak's analysis of events. The picture is in landscape format, unusually wide. From the left, Lenin, his shoulders hunched, walks diagonally towards us along the bank of a river, or perhaps it is a canal, beyond which lies a desolate and almost featureless landscape, the colours dun and ashen. He seems, though it's difficult to be sure, to be glancing away across the river or canal towards the immensity of Russia which is to be ruled, saved, sovietised. It is one of those moments when you have a fleeting glimpse of an insight too vast to be grasped. It has something to do with the seemingly straightforward human decency of Sobchak; but it has also to do with the complete assurance of the painting even in its portrayal of a moment of loneliness and perhaps doubt; and this against our long-standing assumption that 1917, for better or worse, bespoke the reality of history against which doubts could be represented as already, at least on one level, resolved. The programme has moved on, but I'm no longer taking much notice. What was it? One of those juxtapositions which you feel could generate a whole *roman fleuve* from its fissile potential: a juxtaposition of irreconcilables. Boxes within boxes? A picture within a TV image. Was this the intuition nearly within reach – or at least a part of it? That as we probe ever deeper we encounter different universes? First, let's say, there was the historical Lenin and his tracts and his actions – plus, of course, his recollections of his home and family, of the spectacle of his brother publicly hanged by the Czarist police; then there was the set of strategies and improvisations variously summed up as Leninism, with all the contentious subjectivities attributed to the man – I once saw another television show which interviewed no fewer than three actors who had regularly impersonated him in naff movies where as often as not he was seen accepting avuncular advice from Stalin – and finally we have the new era in which the whole shebang is simply bracketed as 'all that', a statue to be toppled, a city to be disowned. And somewhere on this continuum is a moment, real or imaginary, where a man walked alongside a river or a canal and questioned what was to be done – or possibly what had already been done. It defeats me, this image. Perhaps what it is telling me is that there are moments impermeable to experience: I mean 'impermeable' in the sense that the past cannot get through them to the future: my father bumping and slithering into the sub-zero water; Glynis wincing in pain as I drove her back from Greenham. I'm reminded suddenly of that fellow Clegg – must be a goner himself by now – in the old drawing office, who was like a radio permanently tuned to one station; and that station was the Battle of the Somme. Whenever you switched him on, he was already in full tirade, vehement, vituperative. The anger never wavered and never diminished. And perhaps, after all, he was right.

The days are still sunny, but it's already dark by six o'clock as I arrive back at the flat. The light is on in the kitchen, and there's an agreeable aroma. There is also a manilla envelope propped by the door: four of my most recent poems, at least two of which I'd have thought no editor in their right mind could decline. I take them to my work-room, where Morwen lolls in the leather chair, legs swung over its arm, reading a book.

'Hi, Dad. Glad you've made it back on time. I'm doing a cottage pie for us – should be ready in half an hour or so.'

'Sounds great.'

'I've been reading these poems of yours. I'd forgotten. Some of them are really good, you know.'

'Well, I thought I knew.'

'I like these ones in three parts.'

'I'm glad. No-one else has ever commented on them. It was a bee I had in my bonnet. I thought of them as cyclic poems. The principle was that the first section would describe an incident in plain words, the second would elaborate on the relationship between these words, and the third... to be honest I don't quite remember what the third was supposed to do, but at any rate it was supposed to crank the language up to some higher metaphorical level.'

'I like them, though.' She shuts the book. 'What on earth possessed you to call them "Treacle"?'

'Eh? Well, you did.'

'What d'you mean, I did?'

'You made me promise. Don't you remember?'

'When?'

'You'd have been about seven.'

'Dad, you can't expect me to remember that! You still write poems sometimes, don't you? What are your recent ones like?'

I chuck the manilla envelope into her lap. 'I'll just go and wash the dust of travel off me before we have supper.'

She calls after me: 'I've got us a bottle of plonk as well – celebrate your return home.'

'But I've only been away two days.'

'Not complaining again, are you?'

'No.'

Standing in the shower, a pig being hosed-down in its sty, I start wondering what Morwen will say when she gets to University and her up-market new friends start asking her about her family. 'Well, I've got this dad who's a proper basket case. Writes poetry. Started when he was in his teens, and never grew out of it.' It's worse than catching sight of yourself in a mirror, these sudden apprehensions of how you must seem to other people. Best avoided.

We clink glasses. It seems a long time since we've sat face to face for a meal. 'Hey, this cottage pie is really good. How long have you been keeping these culinary talents to yourself?'

'Oh, I kind of thought it was time I started training myself to be a proper little wifey.'

'Watch it – you'll turn me off my tucker, talking like that. How is Christopher, by the way?'

'Defunct.'

'Ah. Well, I won't inquire. Are you going to tell me what you thought of the new poems?'

'I liked the one about the peasant aunt slicing a big cart-wheel loaf towards her, holding it against her bosom – sounds a bit risky, actually – and all the stuff about relation-ship to the soil, allotments and that – life as a succession of fresh rootings. Yeh. She put me in mind of a photograph – Depression era – dustbowl – this woman stringy as an old runner bean, kids sort of packed around her like fruit in a box – you know the one...' Yes, I do know the one, though I'd never made the connection. 'Come to think of it,' she adds, 'it's them being packed like fruit that's so touching. Was she a real auntie of yours?'

'Well, yes and no.'

Morwen pluffs atomised potato onto the table as she collapses into helpless laughter: 'Dad – you don't change, do you!'

But maybe it's time I did. Things can't go on like this.

Rejection upon rejection. The trouble with poetry is that you're working with the very substance of your consciousness: the words you're made of. I find myself envying artists who manipulate tubes of colour or blocks of stone, and can stand back from what they've done and look at it with other people and say, 'Yes, this works, I'm not so sure that does,' or, 'I think it's quite a good likeness, don't you?' But when all you've got is your synapses, neuro-transmitters and so forth and so fifth, well, what it comes down to is that inadequacy of the product is indistinguishable from inadequacy of the self. You're always trying to exceed yourself, of course: to let the poems strain ahead of you like hounds on the leash. I'm not actually sure Morwen was right about the phantom aunt poem, in fact, though I'm chuffed that she responded to it. But there you go. How can you even think in terms of something 'working'? You can scrutinise your own output until you can't tell any more whether it does or doesn't: analyse it until it falls apart in your hands: falls apart into constituents that simply won't fuse any more as if they were tired of the struggle, felt you'd stopped loving them so why should they make the effort to go on performing for you? *Like a wraith or ghost in the grimy colonnade...*: that's a line from one of my early compositions that still sings to me; but would it sing to anyone else? 'Why "wraith or ghost"? Don't those words mean more or less the same thing?' 'Well, you see, it's about a teenage girl; and I thought "wraith" had an echo of "waif"...' 'Oh dear me, we've got a right one here...' But surely there remains an undercurrent of intuition which tells you when a thing simply feels right? Or is that mere Romantic fancy? I try to be workmanlike. There are poems of mine that have had their punctuation revised three or four times in the space of a year. Sounds ridiculous; but then you wouldn't argue that punctuation made no difference, would you? Even when something does sing to me, I hear the voice of the traitor whispering, 'Can't you see it's bathetic, clichéd, calculated, contrived, self-regarding, over-wrought...' Suppose I were to send a batch of my stuff to some consultant or practitioner, pleading for enlightenment. Would that be likely to help? 'The rhythm here is faintly reminiscent of Eliot; the diction has a flavour of Auden...' Well of course they do. How many possible rhythms are there; how many words to choose from? If the totality doesn't spark off something, then there's no point quibbling about the details. But you're left with the question, 'Why doesn't it?' Doesn't the fault have to lie in the details; or is there something in the totality which is inherently unacceptable? In other words, since, as I've said, my poetry is my consciousness, is there something in who I *am* that is unacceptable? Oh come on now, calm down. It's a bit pointless getting prickly about criticisms I've only imagined. All the same, talking of Eliot, I saw something interesting recently in a Sunday paper: a selection of his early, abandoned poems that someone had brought out into public view. Most of them were pretty awful, and you could see why he'd withdrawn them. But at the same time, some of the awful ones were so close in spirit and style and imagery to the ones we know and admire that you could set them against each other and be at a loss to tell where the difference lay, this difference which nevertheless seemed so absolute and insurmountable; and you were left wondering whether, after all, there was any more to it than the awareness that this one was canonical and that one wasn't. In which case, how was the poet himself to know? As for detail, there are cases where the totality can override it. Arnold, for instance, weakens the word 'roar' in *Dover Beach* by using it twice; yet no-one complains. I remember, in my teens, snipping out from a copy of *Punch* a piece of doggerel which, though I was not in the slightest doubt that it was doggerel, seemed at the same time to encapsulate the unanswerable despair of the human state. And what about all those snatches from the lyrics of popular songs which I used to jot down in my notebooks the way an art student will sketch fragments from a plaster cast of the Winged Victory? *I see the moon, the moon sees me...* Also, as I recall, I made a habit of roping in quotes from catalogues and technical specs –

presumably, among other things, as a strategy for curbing subjectivism. But in the end you're still left with the same dilemma. To stand outside your own work means to stand outside your own being. Of course, you could claim that the attempt to step critically outside your own language was a second degree of the struggle which enabled you to liberate words in the first place. It sounds quite heroic when put that way – except that the question is precisely whether you did liberate words in any useful sense. That's the worst of it. I used to have some theory to the effect that the poetic event, so to say, emerged from a dialectic between the verbal excitement of a moment of perception and the hard, gritty substance of words perceived as extrinsic to the self. Something like that. At any rate, I felt some measure of confidence that I was able to recognise the moment and to grasp it. Now, however, I have the feeling that it has stopped happening to me, that peculiar dialectic between things as words and words as things. Is it one of those knacks that desert us in later life – like no longer being able to hear the piping of bats as they pass, furrily furtive, teasing the edges of the eye? Not that I've lost my pleasure in the visible or auditory world; nevertheless, it could be a question of function decay. It's as if the dough had become stiff under my kneading hands. But no, no, that's nonsense. Many people write poems in old age – good ones, too. Maybe it's that I exhausted all my meanings through my engagement with Glynis, with her politics, earthing all my potential in the attempt to become guarantor for her truth. Look, wait a minute... To be honest, I think I could live with the idea that I'm no good. What gnaws at me is the possibility that this perception may be an imposition of the class enemy. Or don't we believe there is a class enemy any more? Hands up anyone who doesn't believe there's a class enemy; and when I say 'hands up!' I mean surrender. All right, all right. But all the same, there was always a social element to it, wasn't there. But look... And that's where the difference lies between poetry and advertising: because with advertising there really are objective criteria of judgment: you judge a slogan by how many packets of New Formula Crud it's sold. Good. That's progress. It means that poetry's unjudgeability is the very thing which makes it antagonistic to capital: ideas still infused with the savour of Chinese vegetable gravy. But when I... Look, this isn't really the point any longer... Hang on, there's something here I've never thought of before. I've always been sheepishly proud of the fact that I didn't rat out on my milieu. It wasn't that poetry seemed any big, knocked-'em-in-the-Old-Kent-Road deal; it was just what I saw myself as able to do. And I tried. I stayed. I didn't desert my post, scramble to be first on the rescue barges. It's rather that my post has deserted me, that the society of which I felt myself an integral part has shifted, crumbled, the roads re-routed and the names of cities changed. Lili Marlene no longer loiters outside the barrack gate. Even the pre-fabs have vanished, and I never set foot in one – those pre-fabs you used to see as you rattled over the points into Waterloo, which seemed to nestle up against the Houses of Parliament, though of course they couldn't have done because there was the river in between. Seemed vaguely symbolic. But what I'm trying to say is this: if I stayed in my job for the sake of my scribblings, the implication is that without the scribblings I might have chucked the job out of sheer restlessness and tried something else. And what would I be doing today? Quarrying rock, breeding greyhounds? This isn't one of those grand historical imponderables, such as: If Lenin hadn't seen his brother hanged, would that film-maker ever have found himself shooting *Earth*? It's a simple and dismaying fact. Poetry, which I've always treated as something of a sideshow in my life, an optional peripheral, turns out to have been significantly if only negatively responsible for its course. Fine; I'll have the rest of my days to absorb the implications of that; but now: what was it I was trying to think, or nearly thought, a moment or two ago? Something else altogether. Something more primal: to do with a trace, a skid-mark in time. Come to that, what is an appropriately-formed thought? I once saw that asked somewhere, and it nags me still. I remember first hearing my own voice and not recognising myself in it. I only knew it was my voice because it was clearly not that of any other of our little group gathered around the old Grundig with its pale blue perforated padded plastic sides – a group of friends two of whom I find myself no longer able to identify by name or by face, recalling it seems only the conclave atmosphere of the room, a distillate of mauve dust. I'm sure I'd be quite as shocked to hear that recording again now. My accent, like everyone else's, must have changed unnoticed over the years. So what is a poem? A record of the self which holds good only because you don't recognise yourself in it? Consider those images you get on television, video images, a road at night with a succession of cars; and as each one passes out of frame it leaves behind a fading worm of luminescence, the trail of its headlights briefly outlasting its brevity. Is that all it's really about? Grave-goods briefly outlasting those who have loved them? My thought snakes back towards something it cannot reach, cannot descry in the fogs of memory, which was never precise in the first place because still unformed. What else is lurking in this murky dish? I feel I know what things were like; but I don't. I hear echoes without hearing what's echoed. I call to mind the atmosphere of a house or street, but cannot call to mind the house or the street. Somewhere, my sentiments tell me, there is a ribbon of lights that curves its way over a hill, elegant as a theorem, a purple-veiled blueness: and it's assuring me the world can be made a better place if only I can find my way back to that hill. Did such a hill ever objectively exist? Frontier-permeating popular longings encoded in ditties; last husks of feeling? Scattered phrases from my youthful poems seem about to grant access to the past; but the spaces they disclose are empty. Is that all my life has been, then: a succession of empty rooms stuffed with the illusion of furniture, of framed pictures designed for moral uplift, of pot plants refractory though cossetted? Was there nothing there in the first place;

or was it I who was immaterial, the spectre at others' feasts? I see a bus stop, and beside it a street lamp crowned with its self-fashioned helmet of virid leaves snagged with swags of unspooled ferrous oxide audio tape Christmasly twinkling amid a snuffy smell of weed-rot; and I see myself, after a day spent with a gaggle of colleagues discussing trade-offs between bulk and rigidity or between temperature and pressure, standing under that light, looking at the crescent moon and thinking – what would I be thinking? – that it's actually on the wane, so you can hardly call it a crescent, it must be a diminuescent; and I gather my courage and stride up to myself and say, 'I need your help. What would you do if you were me?' And I reply, 'But I am you. And you can see what I'm doing. I'm waiting for this frigging bus.' Right. Now what about the poetry? I don't mean the principle of the thing, which I've just discovered has been the hidden determinant of my life; I mean the actually-existing poetry, the stuff I've actually hammered or sweated out. Well, either it was never much good at all, or it was good but unpublishable in an élitist culture, or it was good as an élitist game but would never have made contact with the people for whom it was ultimately meant, or... I'm sure there are countless other ways of looking defeat in the face. And what could look more defeated than those collections you find in the farthest recesses of provincial bookshops: stapled wads of paper hand-made from a kit with text in lino-cut; flaking leaflets laboriously made up with a John Bull rubber stamp; and as for sonnets, where was it I saw that posthumous volume – Kingston-on-bloody-Hull, wasn't it? – graveyard slabs of verse metrically impeccable printed locally in the typeface used for obits in the parish mag. Why does anyone bother? I've been trying in the last year or two to get a bit of social consciousness into my stuff; but I wonder whether that isn't something better done in fiction than in poetry. So maybe it's back to those stories I used to mess about with. Either way, though, what matters is to reach behind the formulae, behind the desiccated formulations however compelling: to recover

The ledgers bore the name Reucastle & Sons, and spanned the period 1887 to 1939. At this point it was not noticed that one of the ledgers bore no date.

Inquiries at the City Hall revealed that Reucastle & Sons had been a small firm of brassfounders and finishers taken over in 1939 by their larger neighbour, the shipbuilders Ogram & Lazenby (known by a quirk of local usage as O&G). By 1946 Ogram & Lazenby had absorbed all the little ancillary companies which had once clustered about them, and their works stretched the entire length of Poseidon St; but in 1953, having over-extended themselves in expectation of post-war prosperity, they prudently withdrew to more modest quarters near Beverley; and it was at this time that Witteringham's Biscuits acquired the site. Back in 1941, however, the buildings housing the brassfoundry had been destroyed by a high-explosive bomb. In the urgency of wartime the cellar areas had been cleared of rubble and the walls asphalted to serve as a static water tank for firefighting purposes. In the process the old records store of Reucastle & Sons was isolated from the remainder of the factory and, since the information it contained was never required, forgotten. Having been re-discovered, their provenance established, and the navvies having spent their tea break marvelling at the Lilliputian prices quoted for labour and materials in the earlier volumes, the ledgers were loaded onto a truck for transportation to Beverley, where they were again consigned to storage. Ogram & Lazenby survived, through a series of judicious retrenchments, until the early 1980s. When they were finally forced into liquidation, their old paperwork was bought for a song by the local Historical Society and transferred to the vaults of the Archive of Municipal Records. Here they gathered fresh dust until a student, preparing a thesis on the City's shipbuilding heritage, was given permission to consult them. It was he who, his eye falling upon the un-dated volume, opened it to discover that it was filled not with accounts but with sonnets. He drew these to the attention of Mr Myton, a schoolteacher who had for some time been engaged upon a search for some undiscovered local talent with whom to launch a long-gestated publishing venture. Thus Melchior Wright's efforts, resurrected as it were from their third crypt, appear at last before the public in a slim and limited edition.

> Kingston upon Hull, where even the wrinkles of the elderly poor seem scoured to antiseptic whiteness by the saline estuary breezes, city of the gilt equestrian statue of William III who, as every child is told, dismounts his horse on hearing the Holy Trinity clock strike midnight and circumambulates the plinth before resuming his accustomed and immobile posture. Like all children for whom the penny has yet to drop, little Melchior must have made elaborate plans for nocturnal escape in order to witness this unlikely phenomenon; but the plans were never realised. If you don't call the bluff, you won't see the deception. This, perhaps, was a lesson in politics.

Perhaps. The simple facts are as follows. Melchior Wright was born in 1893 on the fringes of the old City, an area of drysalters, ships' chandlers and merchants of fent and dross. Leaving school at the age of fourteen, he took a job as office dogsbody with Reucastle & Sons. He escaped service in the Great War as a result of lameness – either a congenital club foot or some deformity due to a childhood bout of rickets – and, except for being laid off for some months in the early '30s when the company were obliged by the slump to operate on a skeleton staff, remained with Reucastle until their absorption into Ogram & Lazenby, by which time he held the position of Chief Clerk in the forwarding department. He was kept on by O&G, though with lowlier status and at a reduced wage, until his death in an air raid in 1941. His wife, whom he had married in 1925, had died in 1937; and they left no children.

By upbringing, Wright was a Primitive Methodist; and the earliest of the poems, which may be dated on internal evidence to the later years of the Great War, seem designed to promote the nonconformist values of temperance and industry:

> The tang-a-rang man ties his halting mare
> To toss a yellowed nosebag's wage, while he
> Plays Chopin on the upright, out of key,
> Breathing exhaled and alcoholic air
> Where curses linger in the smoke-fouled light
> And dreams take flight in shapes he cannot see.

Mr Myton devotes considerable speculation to the source of Wright's poetic impulse: to

> how we may explain the emergence of this embryo talent in the ambience of heat and din attendant upon the manufacture of elbow joints, instrument housings, valve casings, ornamental toasting forks and propellers for lesser craft; an environment of bills of lading, of requisitions hastily impaled on spikes, of day-books whose pages, edged with rainbow ripple, are ceaselessly flicked with a sucked and grimy thumb

and he suggests that the daily sight of the statue of Andrew Marvell, which in those days occupied the junction of Bond St and Smeaton St, may have encouraged him, as a boy, to pay attention to his English lessons. Certainly there can be few cities in England where a poet, MP or no, is honoured by a monument so placed as to impede the flow of traffic; but while Wright may display some of Marvell's terseness of argument, the caustic playfulness seems alien to his temperament. As for the poetry he encountered at school, it is improbable that this extended far beyond such faithfuls as 'The Burial of Sir John Moore at Corunna'.

It would, however, be a mistake to overemphasise the element of the naif – of the Sunday poet – in Melchior Wright, for he was far from insensitive to the multiplex values of words. We may note, for example, the play upon 'halting' in the first line of the above quotation. More significantly, we may ask exactly what is to be understood in the sixth line: are the dreams 'taking flight' in the sense of 'making their escape', and can the tang-a-rang man not perceive their shapes because he is too befuddled by alcohol; or are the dreams rather 'taking wing' in shapes which he cannot see because they are the 'shapes' of music? And, having asked this question, we are almost bound to ask ourselves whether the man is playing Chopin 'out of key' because he is a poor pianist or because the instrument on which he is obliged to perform has been pounded to destruction. Here we have an ambiguity which Wright's more bigoted brethren might justly have regarded as an evasion. At all events, the balance of his poems soon shifts noticeably, and there is an increasing concern with the individuality of the subject at the expense of moral pre-judgments, as in the sonnet 'To a Trawlerman':

> ... whose wealth, from catch to catch,
> Sustains a meagre purchase on the land
> To harbour his misgivings, where the stones
> Unfathomably mock his hopes – to snatch
> Brief chills of solitude from watch to watch
> And, if the swell be cheated of his bones,
> Brass screws to close his casket in the end.

With the exception of one or two very early and very late works, the sonnets adhere strictly to a complex, interlocking rhyme-scheme: abba bccb acbbca. This has affinities with the Petrarchian model, but differs from it significantly in that the sestet introduces no endings not previously used in the octave. For Mr Myton, in one of his rare attempts at disinterested criticism, Wright is here seeking to compensate for his amateurism with an excessive, hence equally amateur, display of purely technical accomplishment. But this seems a needlessly ungenerous way of putting it. Aside from two poems printed in his Chapel newsletter during the early '20s, there is no record of the publication of any of Wright's work during his lifetime. On the basis of conversations with people who remember Wright (though their recollections, when not unaccountably hazy, are suspiciously sharp) Mr Myton is satisfied that he made considerable efforts, at an early stage, to reach a wider public. It therefore seems reasonable to assume that his adoption of this difficult pattern – demanding four to six rhymes, or at least assonances, for each ending – was an attempt to reassure himself, despite the evidence of countless rejection slips to the contrary, that what he was writing was really and truly poetry.

It is hard to pinpoint the moment at which political awareness makes itself felt. The development is continuous, Once the ethical puritanism has been left behind, concern with individuals seems to lead naturally into concern with their situation and hence, inevitably, with those social co-ordinates which define and limit their possibilities. Then, gradually, the place left vacant by the moral exhortation – delivered, in the first poems, in a straight Shakespearean couplet – is reoccupied by a meditation, emerging subtly out of the octave into the sestet, in which the individual subject yields an image for the wider social reality. It is impossible to doubt that Wright's complicated rhyme-scheme, perhaps the fruit of idle invention, played its own part in this growing integration between the universe of observation and the universe of moral choice: indeed, it may be no overstatement to say that his literary career is the history of his attempt, not merely to integrate these two elements in poetry, but, through his poetry, to explore ways in which they might be reconciled in life. At this point it is worth looking at a full example of Wright's mature style. 'A Woman Convicted of Burglary' is characteristic:

Perhaps she preferred her nightmares to her dreams
In some misguided residue of hope
To give her bitterness sufficient rope
To hang itself. Without success, it seems,
She sought in her petty larcenies the scope,
Grudged by her lowly circumstance, to prove

Not, as the doctors guess, her claim to love,
But rather her capacity to cope
Without it. We, conniving at her schemes
For dignity by theft, might not approve
Yet could not quite condemn her – we who broke
Faith with our daily futures as we woke
To doubts which pawned our longings: where the dove
Hangs crucified, and naught but cash redeems.

It was in 1931, perhaps towards the end of his period on the dole, that a small but critical influence came to bear upon the worker-poet: and on this, for once, Mr Myton's researches seem to have turned up concrete results. The only extraneous document to survive, slipped between the leaves of the ledger where Melchior Wright assiduously copied out his sonnets in that flawless copper-plate of which his generation were the last exponents, was a cutting from The War-Cry in which an ex-convict, who had incurred a stretch of penal servitude by visiting GBH upon his nine-year-old daughter while under the influence of the demon drink, testified to his conversion. The final paragraphs describe his experiences in solitary confinement, on a bread-and-water diet, for some unspecified infringement of prison discipline:

> ... and the water came – they gave it you in the same can you used for p***ing in – and the bread, just a hunk, stale on the outside so's you could have sandpapered wood with it, and there was these grey hairs on it, and I couldn't see any tooth-marks, but I thought it's rats, I can smell 'em – you know the smell of rats anywhere – and the hatch clanged shut.
>  And gradually, what with nothing else to do, I started trying different things with it – chomping the bread hard with my front teeth like a rat, or dipping it into the water and pressing it on the roof of my mouth with the back of my tongue, or screwing it into a hard ball in my fist then sucking it like a gobstopper. And the water too, things like sucking it up into a fine spray into my throat. And

suddenly I realised I'd never known before just how many tastes you could get out of just bread and water, like being a nipper all over again and the world's new and you'll try anything, and I saw in my mind that picture of Jesus we'd had in the classroom at school, and I suddenly realised, This Is It! With so much good in the world I could do anything, give up the drink, anything. All God's gifts had been there all the time – everywhere, if you see what I mean. This is it – the Kingdom of God on Earth.

It is clear that the phrase 'This is it,' untarnished by the associations of its later vulgar currency, held a unique power for Wright; and Mr Myton offers relatively plentiful evidence for his belief that the words were scratched into the leading edge of his desk at the factory.

Just as Pascal sewed into his shirt-lining the very date and hour of his salvation, so did Melchior Wright carve into the woodwork of his cubby-hole, among all the holiday postcards from colleagues in Brid or Filey, in that parallel-line script peculiar to the use of a broken pen-nib as an engraving tool, the slogan of his new enlightenment.

But for Wright this slogan bore little promise of the Kingdom of God. He seems to have understood it rather to mean that progress can begin only from where one happens to be situated, and that moral absolutes are of little practical help. He tried to express this idea directly in the poem which begins,

So this is it, here where the 'prentice stands
Fettling the casting, blistered by the brush...

and proceeds to the suggestion that, whilst every moment must be considered unique and precious, there should nonetheless be more to life than a variety of ways of savouring bread and water. Just as his 'temperance' poems had seemed to portray drink less as an affront to God's passion for sobriety than as a dulling of men's minds to life's better possibilities, so he chose now to affirm that, whilst 'this' might be it, 'it' must surely have more to offer than this. Yet it is a strange paradox that, although the attitudes represented by this talismanic phrase had long been foreshadowed in his poetry, his conscious espousal of them led his poems slowly into decline.

Throughout the 'pink' decade, Wright engaged himself, within the limits of his capabilities, in political activity: working in his ward, pasting up posters and addressing election literature at trestle tables in draughty halls. For him, as for so many indispensable voluntary helpers, the taste of socialism must have been the gum on countless envelopes. More and more he tried to use his poetry for explicit analysis, as if to have it provoke, rather than merely reflect, his evolving awareness. He appears to have attempted to raise money for the Spanish Republicans; but, as Mr Myton has it, 'legends of the impecunious wives of the unemployed casting their wedding rings into the collection boxes were not to be re-enacted under his aegis.' The obligatory poem 'To Spain' shows his work at its most didactic, manufactured and ill-at-ease, beginning,

The blood that clots the sand in deadly sport
Now soaks in earnest through the soil of Spain
Barren and ochre...

and progressing into an amalgam of homily and second-hand local colour. Only at the end, after the dispersal of an Arms for Madrid rally, does the authentic Wright tone reassert itself:

Here, through the gentler rain,
Uninjured save in conscience, we re-tread
Our lonely path unbettered save in thought.

To commit his poetry to political purposes when he had long since accepted its prospects for publication as negligible must have involved Wright in an increasing sense of dislocation. As the '30s drew to a close, an unmistakable air of disillusion – perhaps with politics, but more probably with the sonnets themselves – begins to pervade the work. The complex pattern is no longer rigidly followed, and assonance is more frequently substituted for rhyme. There is a concomitant loss of logical cohesion in the thought. It is as if Wright had no longer cared to maintain, even to himself, the illusion of professionalism. Yet with this abdication of high purpose, technical and social, there emerges in some of the late poems a lightness of touch amounting almost to a dour vivacity:

> A coddled child, I scarcely ever swam
> In mucky water. Now at last I'm free
> To go at will – no-one to mourn for me
> If I am trundled over by a tram.
> Simply in sum of years I've paid my fee...

With the onset of World War II, Ogram & Lazenby began to re-tool – at first almost absent-mindedly, but later, after Dunkirk, with grim rapidity – for war production. When the Hull blitz began, early in 1941, Melchior Wright took his place on the works roster for fire-watching on the clock tower over the factory gate.

> Every few days he would set off in the morning with his heavy-duty marine binoculars, his gas mask in a rexine-covered box and the khaki canvas satchel containing his thermos flask and his fishpaste or dried egg omelette sandwiches in an Oxo tin. He knew that, barring disasters, he would sleep again only in thirty-six hours' time.

It was during these hours of vigil that the sensory impact of the air-raids, the maritime environment and the traditions of a city which still congratulates itself corporately upon the abolition of the slave trade fused in Wright's mind to spark off his final poem:

The city yaws and pitches in the blast;
Tall buildings ride the billows of the smoke
Towards the fiery centre of the night
As if bewitched, bearing their sordid freight
Of souls calloused by hardship. From the holds,
Unmanacled, they swarm to douse the masts,
To prime the pumps, to scale the teetering height
Of shrouds and smouldering ratlines, swing the boats
And man the wheelhouse where the steersman chokes.
Well may the masters of this flame-wracked fleet,
Crewed by its human cargo, muse aghast
Upon the powers, devotion, skill and might
Which, exercised within a happier state,
Had brought the whip upon their meekened backs.

That this sonnet would have initiated a new period in
Wright's work is sufficiently attested by his total reversal of
the rhyme-scheme: the sestet now precedes the octave to
create an impression, not of the broadening of the field of
vision, but of the sharpening of its focus. The intuitive
handling of ambiguity is once again manifested, this time in
the last few lines. Our historically-conditioned reading,
which the grammatical construction permits, is that the
whip would have fallen on the backs of the workers/slaves;
but the grammar strongly favours the interpretation that it
might instead have fallen upon the masters: and the word
'masters', though here meaning primarily the skippers of
ships, has the meaning of 'slave-owners' scarcely concealed
under its surface. The tone of weariness, almost of resignation, never entirely absent from Wright's previous poems, is
missing. It is as if, having throughout his life sought to
balance possibility against actuality, he had, in his last few
weeks, discovered that the possibilities had always been
greater than he had supposed.

Mr Myton makes great play with the mystery of how,
after the fatal air-raid, Wright's manuscript could have found
its way into a storage vault blocked by collapsed masonry. He

then produces the solution with a flourish. According to information readily available from the registrar's office. Wright died not in the raid which crippled the factory but, while on fire-watching duty, in an earlier one. A large splinter of shrapnel penetrated his tin hat, splaying it inside his skull like a rivet. It may be assumed that, after his death, someone removed his tome to the cellar without bothering to look inside it.

That, in a sense, is the end of the matter. But certain misgivings clamour to be voiced.

To begin with, what value must we truly accord to the work of Melchior Wright? Not merely did his poems remain unpublished in his lifetime, but it seems reasonable to doubt whether they could ever have been published until such time as their intrinsic virtues had become patinated with the adventitious charm of the literary oddity. Mr Myton states it thus:

> In the '20s they would have seemed insufficiently "poetic" to those nurtured upon Tennyson, whilst the denizens of *The Waste Land* would have found them regressive. Despite their social content, they would have compared poorly in technique with the virtuosities of MacNeice and Auden, whilst their modesty, with its hint of utility carpentry, would not have commended itself to those who trumpeted the New Apocalypse from the bastions of a beleaguered isle. Their unflinching humanity would have seemed ill-bred to those post-war poets who strove to eliminate from their *terza-rima* all propositions neither purely demonstrative nor capable of verification, whilst devotees of folk art would have frowned upon their lack of anonymity.

Our natural response may be that this does not affect the status of Wright's products as works of art, to be judged upon their merits: but if a work is unpublishable, it is incapable of communication; and if it is incapable of communication, what merit can it claim?

A further misgiving centres upon Mr Myton's introduction. Despite his jaunty air of well-researched assurance, his narrative is supported by altogether too many constructions of the form, 'There can be little doubt...' or, 'It is well-nigh certain that...' or, 'It is not unreasonable to suppose...' For example, the clause, 'We may imagine him, club-footed astride his Hercules bicycle...' is surely too good to be true. Is Mr Myton really sure that Wright's bicycle was a Hercules? Admittedly Myton himself queries the veracity of some of his information; but this may be merely a tactic to pre-empt scrutiny of a catalogue of 'facts' to many of which he can hardly have had access. As for 'dried egg omelette sandwiches,' powdered egg was not introduced until June 1942.

There, then, they rest on the pages of his great volume, uniform slabs of slate-grey indelible pencil trimmed with the emphasis of the occasional purple lick.

Is this, we are constrained to ask, the effervescence of abundant scholarship, or is it a smoke screen calculated to conceal an underlying ignorance? If it is the latter, we may well begin to ask how much Mr Myton has really found out about his subject; and, if it is as little as we may begin to suspect, we may further ask how much there ever was to find.

At this point the question becomes somewhat delicate. But it is worth reminding oneself that there is, in the centre of Hull, a thoroughfare called Myton Gate, which once gave egress from its fortifications. Is the name G. Myton therefore to be construed as a pseudonym? And, if so, is it just possibly a pseudonym for some person unknown who may also have adopted the pseudonym Melchior Wright?

Without wishing to stray into the realms of libel, one may perhaps be permitted to observe that *if* there were any truth in this hypothesis it would cast a strange light upon the whole enterprise: for Mr Myton's introduction, which seems an attempt to invest with the savour of lived experience a life which, for all we may finally know of it, remains mute as an epitaph, must then constitute a meditation upon himself and a withdrawal of his own utterances, the poems, behind that threshold of incommunicability upon which he is at pains to insist. What motive might one advance for this strange introversion? Is it a mere exercise in low camp? A plagiarist's attempt to hoodwink experts? Or, assuming the purpose to be serious: were the poems written to lend subjective substance to an otherwise skeletal biography deemed significant as fiction, or was the biography erected to supply a key to poems which, once written, their inept author recognised as being couched in a style rendered opaque by the vicissitudes of fashion: i.e. to provide a framework which, though not rendering the poems emotionally and culturally accessible, might at least posit them as *having once been so*; or, to be more precise, as having once held the potential for so becoming, if only in a better world?

# SIX

The sea trials of the Elpenor have been a complete success; and there's a good deal of restrained back-slapping as we stand clustered on the gently dipping deck of the research vessel and watch her being winched up, breaking surface accompanied by a couple of guys with aqualungs who've been monitoring some of her manoeuvres at the upper levels, water sluicing from her in that natural way, as if she were some large marine mammal, that gives you instant confidence in the rightness of the design. Briefly I see once more the wire-frame model revolving in the virtual aquarium of my computer. The scoop, the camera extension, the sampling nozzles: everything retracts to present an almost smooth, sculptural curvature; and much of this was my doing. Covingtons have always been relaxed about embracing people's contributions, even those of freelancers; and I've always had the tact not to try and exploit this as a means of enhancing my remuneration. I'm particularly pleased with the distinctive way the robot arm arches back over the body of the craft when at rest. I suggested, on the strength of this, that we ought to name her 'The Scorpion'; but it was decided that this would be inauspicious, being the name of an American nuclear powered and nuclear armed submarine that had sunk itself with one of its own torpedoes somewhere off the Azores in the late '60s and was still, so far as anyone knew, sitting on the seabed waiting to launch its arsenal as soon as seawater seeped through to the electrics – assuming, that was, that there remained an active source of current, and so on and so forth – anyway, it wasn't a good idea, and the name 'Elpenor' was chosen because he was someone who had gone down to the underworld and come to report back. Yes, I remembered the line from the *Odyssey*: 'But first Elpenor came...' Someone pops the first bottle; and foam bursts up and slides clingingly down. To be honest, I'm always a bit uncomfortable with champagne in the context of submarine technology. You'd think the idea of gas bubbles forming with the release of pressure would have painful connotations for divers. But no-one seems to be bothered by this; we just drink the stuff. And only now am I made fully aware – though I must say I had my suspicions – that this is not simply a celebration for the successful completion of the Elpenor's tests; it is also – hence my invitation to attend – to a lesser extent a farewell party for me:

'You'll have noticed, I'm sure, how the work's been thinning out of late. The bald truth is that we've no further orders on the books once the Elpenor's delivered. One or two whispers, of course; but in the nature of things, even at the most optimistic estimate, it'd be years rather than months before we'd be likely to have enough work to contract any out.'

'That's right. Even our permanent staff – well, we're going to have to hold a meeting to discuss prospects...'

'Mm. What Keith's hinting at – and this is just between ourselves and the little fishes, OK? – is that there's a company in the States that wants to buy us out. But even that wouldn't necessarily guarantee continued employment for us. There's good reason to suppose their only interest is in eliminating a competitor.'

'It's called the free market,' Harry laughs, rolling down his wetsuit to expose the flattened black rug of his chest. 'It wouldn't be economic for the Yanks to produce anything of this quality, so their only option is to scuttle us.'

The conversation turns to the shoddiness of American technology:

'Remember that Mars probe not so long ago? Billions spent on it, right, and it didn't work. And why didn't it work? 'Cos they'd mixed up their imperial and metric units. For God's sake! You went to college, didn't you? What was the first thing they taught you?'

'Always keep your conversion factors at the ready,' I say.

'Exactly; and I bet you still know them, too.'

'But you know what the Yanks say: "Only a fool manufactures things".'

'Yes. That's because material objects impede the process, the process of the generation of wealth. It works best in the vacuum of pure ideation. Money accumulates fastest on paper.'

'Paper? What's that?'

We all laugh. The air out here is so pure you want to inhale it by the cubic metre.

Alighting at Euston, I decide to cut through Bloomsbury to Oxford St. Somewhere here I once came upon an incongruous little second-hand bookshop. I've developed this infantile but harmless habit: whenever I see a second-hand bookshop, I pop in to see if they have a copy of *Treacle*. So far, I've never found one. I've been wondering recently, having had no success with my stories, whether I might not be able to repeat the trick of gathering a few poems written during a former phase – in this case before my ill-fated deviation into prose – and trying to get someone interested in a booklet. I could call it *Growing Things*. Or even *Scorpion*. Or maybe Morwen could come up with an idea. There it is: in an otherwise normal city street, this low building almost smothered in wisteria as if it were on the fringes of a market town, where things are getting a bit decrepit, no longer part of the tourist itinerary yet not quite in the country either. The window is dusty. Visible in the gloom are a copy of Auden's early poems – probably a first edition – and a bumper boys' annual showing a lad in white flannels and fluted shin-pads hitting sixes. Also something about the theatre. Despite a notice saying it is open every weekday from 10.00am to 5.30pm, the shop is closed. If I were young now, I sometimes ask myself, what would I think? From what would I take my bearings in this present society in order to still to be, in some sense, the me I know and am? Damned silly question! I pass a Woolf Mews and, shortly afterwards, a Virginia Court. Of course: they were called the Bloomsbury set, weren't they. When I first went out to work I started reading *The Years* – I think it was *The Years* – in my lunch breaks. I'm not even sure if I ever finished it. I dare say it's on Glynis's shelves some-where. I'll look when I get home. As if with conscious intention, my steps have guided me to the street where – just across the road there – is the building at the top of which I embarked on my career in that drawing office the shape of a Roman galley. Gazing up at the row of dormers, I half expect to see my adolescent face staring back at me, eager and imperious and scared. Virginia Woolf, even then, was a dead classic author being re-issued for a new generation of readers. Yet only the other day I saw in someone's newspaper an interview with Frances Partridge, who knew Woolf personally and is evidently still with us: the whole trudge of my life encompassed in a backward glance over her shoulder. Our white coats had buttons, which we removed when they were collected for laundering, held in place by a sliding brass clip: buttons of ersatz bone; or perhaps it was real bone filched from some hapless animal. What was the name of that bloke, the first one to get the elbow? Bob Bobson. That's right, Bob Bobson. Oh well, if I had to lose my last foothold in the world of gainful employment, now is as good a time as any. Only a couple of months, and I'll be able to start drawing my pension. Travel pass. Black-and-white television if I can find one in a car boot sale. Concessionary rates at one thing and another. I reckon I'll be able to survive. I've started doing calculations on scraps of paper – proper sheets of paper would make it too serious. For example, if I settle for being a touch less scrupulous about my bodily odours, I can skip every other week at the launderette and save £3 a go for the occasional luxury – bottle of wine once a fortnight, cheap paperback once a month – that sort of thing. Of course, the rational plan would be to sell the flat, which is on the large side for one person, and buy a property in a depressed area. Salford, perhaps. Or Hull. Hull: I remember going there on site visits when the Humber bridge was being built, just the catenary spanning the two towers, an inverse hyperbolic cosine curve limned in pencil on the fog, an arc of passage so pure that the bird of poetry had vanished and only its flight remained: the more beautiful, somehow, because one knew the formula for it: because it had a sweetness, the simplicity of the line matching the simplicity of the algebraic expression. Mathematics: the triumph of Analogical Reason. Not that I'm sure to this day what a formula is: the ultimate shrinkage of description; the attempt, always failed, to extirpate subjectivity? In any case, you can't wish for life always to be like that. Already I'd arrived too late for the heroic days when trawlers were launched sideways into the river at Beverley – because if you'd launched them the normal way they'd have run aground on the opposite bank – then towed by muscular little tugs towards the oil-dark sea for final fitting in Prince's dock. Still, that's no reason for going to live somewhere. It would mean missing out on museums and exhibitions and what-have-you, and on – oh, I don't know – just familiarity, streets with memories, balconies blessed by a frail sun. Besides, how often would I see Morwen, let alone anyone else I know? Yes, I'm sure she'd make the effort to come up and visit me; but it would be an effort. Human relations only really work when they're casual. Or is that a primitive, knuckle-scraping, pre-postmodern, superstitious, tactile-materialist, rurally-idiotic way of looking at things?

I've found *The Years*. Standing on a high stool, I'd withdrawn it from the squeeze of its companions and had already blown the dust off it before it struck me that this was dust that had begun to settle as soon as Glynis last replaced the book on its shelf. These things get through to you sometimes, usually when you least expect them. As I glance around the flat, its familiarity drains away. That tiny framed reproduction of a blue period Picasso, two gaunt people drinking absinthe: I remember seeing it beside the kitchen door the first time I came to visit Glynis here; and there it is still, grease-spotted and wrinkled. I'll never know now who gave it to her – if anyone did. Everything is here, but without its pre-given reason to be here, and therefore burdened with the task of constituting that reason from its own resources. Yet here I find myself. Did anything in my schooldays prefigure it? Was my fate sealed when I first donned my draughtsman's white coat whose cuffs already bore those successively bleached pen-strokes speaking of my predecessors, of histories trodden in strange sands? All the complex motivations of our early lives: they flare up, fade, die or are re-structured, and they leave us with the consequences of our choices, the residue, the arbitrary reality of residence or of relationships: all the passions, for example, not to mention flukes of fortune, many of them forgotten, which ended up with me beached here in this flat I never chose but love. Possibly people who 'take command' of their lives – as if they were armoured divisions – never experience this. You might even say that my not knowing the provenance of that Picasso makes it the more eloquent: eloquent of the absoluteness of Glynis's existence as indeed of her absence, bulwark against her dismantlement, against the shrivelling of her memory. And what of this room, which began to be designated 'my' room even before Glynis departed for Greenham: what is on the walls? What would an inventory tell us? Pride of place, if only in the sense of its being hung over the long-blocked-off hearth, properly framed with black wood and wide margins, is my prized graduation drawing, the exploded isometric of a non-return valve. *Answer me, O Lord above...* The lines of the dye-line print are faded to pale chestnut, almost indiscernible in places. *Say what sin have I been guilty of...* Would it, if I were to remove its frame, still give off a faint odour of ammonia like an old man's bedlinen? Framed in ornate and tarnished silver is my parents' wedding photo: a purely iconic presence, since it is far too formal to remind me of them in any true sense. Then there is a pre-war studio portrait of my mother, businesslike hair-do already in evidence, which does seem to capture, if this is not too weighty an interpretation, something of that political stance which almost defined her even as a mother: a belief in the efficacy of small-scale effort; a conviction that the system can be reformed from the inside by people simply refusing to collude in its values. There is no other photograph of my dad; but blu-tacked to the door is a photocopy of a reproduction of a postcard of the SS Calderdale berthed at Port Said. One or two colour snaps of Glynis and Morwen are wedged into the edge of the mirror; but most precious, and pinned above my computer, is the only one I possess of Glynis and myself together, taken by I've-forgotten-whom in a pub in our early days. Lastly, three things occupy clip-frames. One is a poster of a Braque still life which I bought years ago simply because I liked it – because Braque seems to me to reclaim the physical world for our non-Euclidean century as surely as did Chardin for the Enlightenment. This, you might I suppose want to say, is the image which reflects my taste with least intervention from circumstance. Second is the last birthday card Glynis sent me. It is big as birthday cards go, is hand-made, and consists of pressed leaves and flowers from the vicinity of her dwelling laminated onto a mount; but, with a mordant humour typical of Glynis, the vegetation consists of buttercup, deadnettle, clover, convolvulus – all weeds. Third is a silver print I bought quite recently through the internet: Raissa Page's famous photograph of a ring of women dancing on top of the Greenham missile silos. Somehow it sums the whole thing up for me. Odd, though. After all, I wasn't there. Even Glynis wasn't there – she'd come home after taking part in the embracing of the base and didn't go back until the following spring. Yet there it is. You don't notice at first, but the picture is composed in an unusual way, in almost self-contained horizontal bands. At the top there is the fairy circle of women, holding hands, semi-silhouetted against what appears to be the dawn glow of the New Year's sky beyond, though much of the illumination seems confusingly to come from two disembodied searchlights to the far left. The second band comprises the top of the silo itself, presumably concrete but looking more like a natural, stratified geological formation erupting from a dark and undifferentiated mountain mass. Next comes a narrow strip composed simply of an elongated coil of barbed wire. This crosses the picture so crisply, and is so delicately lit, as to have the appearance of a purely graphic convention. Finally, at the bottom, are two police cars, angled to echo the concrete above and seemingly flattened by the perspective. It's the barbed wire that does it, that reminds me of something. Paul Klee. A tiny drawing called *Gartenbau*, likewise assembled from horizontal elements each of which is identified by stylised and repetitive signs for vegetation: like a quilt; like an allotment. Oh. I'd forgotten. There is one other visual image in this room: pasted long ago on the side of my desk where it is seldom now seen, tobacco-brown and fragile: an illustration from a newspaper of Picasso's drawing of Stalin. I wonder if I haven't happened upon the answer – an answer – to a question which even now exercises me at the edge of sleep: What would I, had it been asked of me, have chosen to peg to the fence of a nuclear weapons facility whether as affirmation or as repudiation or – a term embracing both of those concepts – as sacrifice, a calling to witness of the future dead? Well, since I didn't know of the ship in those days, and the portrait of Stalin might have lent itself to misunderstanding, only the non-return valve would have been truly appropriate.

It's a long walk from the bus stop. Hard to believe, but I've almost forgotten this district. Things aren't quite where I thought they were. But this, surely, must be the right street. Yes – there it is: camouflaged by the regularity of the terraced housing until you get quite close, this gap between buildings which begins as an alley but quickly degenerates into a lane and then a bumpy path and here, between iron gateposts which never to my recollection supported a gate, is the entrance to the allotments. Affixed to one gatepost is one of those Official notices where you've no choice but to read the small print because it's all in small print: due to diminishing demand for plots and bearing in mind the provision of new and better-appointed Leisure Gardens in another part of the borough and the re-sale value of the land this-that-and-the-other ordinance notwithstanding the Council has taken the decision to reclaim this area available for development in the wider interest and; it's to be shut down as from September, that's what they're saying. I've only just come in time. The sky is like an old blanket. A straggle of trees struggles for precedence. Everything is so life-choked that it's difficult to tell where one person's plot ends and another's begins. Dad's shed I just about recognise, though it has been extensively patched with sheets of linoleum and is well-nigh suffocating in old man's beard. Black-eyed, tip-tailed, a wren peeps out and flits back. A farthing's-worth, no less. There's no longer a greasy area where he used to lean against the door jamb; but by pushing aside with my foot a clump of toadflax I expose the herringbone layout of bricks, now porous and black with the excreta of micro-organisms, which I remember he once told me had all been salvaged from the rubble of bombed houses. I doubt whether even the ghosts still walk here as I used to imagine them when I was a child, shadowy, searching vacantly for their demolished dwellings. There is a pane of begrimed glass, perhaps a remnant of a cloche which once nurtured those pale, foetal cucumbers. But there's scarcely a trace of Dad's quasi-Rosicrucian neatness – visible manifestation of an inner state, no doubt – his elegant exactitudes hewn out of rugged matter: as if of an order where concepts come first and the world of phenomena follows because it must. A mode of knowing no longer current. Domain of youth – or of youth frozen? Or simply of memories. Is that it? From somewhere not far off comes the shrill discord of an infants' school playground. That's something I don't remember. But of course I only came here at weekends or in the evenings. Dad would have heard it, though, generations ago, sounding no different, fresh as a shower of rain. I hear the scrape of a spade. There, thirty-odd yards away, a man is still defiantly working his land. How typical of allotment folk! Does he think there is still the chance of a reprieve; or doesn't he care? I'm reminded of those women at the camp who planted rows of parsnip and turnip, knowing perfectly well that the authorities would almost certainly spot them and would churn up the soil with their off-road vehicles to destroy such potential for nutriment. It was Page's photograph that brought me back here. The link with Klee. The patchwork. The more I think about the way we represent things, and the pleasure or enlightenment this seems to bestow, the less I feel I understand it. It's one of the most profound pleasures in life; but at the same time it poses a challenge we feel has to be met. So what does this patchwork most closely resemble: the convoy of ships; battle tents on a plain; a network of Party cells or Union branches; the desks of a classroom encoding the individuality of ambition and consequently of subjection; the isolation of survivors bobbing in the swell? Or is the whole point of it the fact that it's another pattern altogether? And then Dad: what did he find here, having, I suspect, passed through that point of emptiness where all doubts cease, or at least cease to interest us? Was this place, for him, a term in some system of oppositions I haven't yet thought of: rectilinearity versus randomness, friable earth versus evasive water, sterility versus growth? I somehow prefer those to the idea that he was taking a stand for isolation in preference to community, the sea in preference to the ship. I've never truly believed that, though in some ways it's the easiest thing to believe. Perhaps, in the end, his experience had simply convinced him of the importance of a nation's being self-sufficient in food. And who could quarrel with that? I consider strolling over to chat with the man still labouring in the distance. But he hasn't once glanced up to see who has intruded. I'll leave him, this solitary Adam, delving and levelling at his leisure.

Community. The concept of community. I wonder what it actually says now. My obsolete screen stares back at me emptily. Absurd to think of all this computational power devoted to the odd letter to the Benefits Office or to tinkering with the odd lame poem; but its re-sale value is nil. Caught in stasis, the women execute their roundelay upon the lid of terror. Yes, Greenham was a community without a doubt; but it was a community defined essentially by what it opposed. Meanwhile, the representatives of one of the last true work communities, the colliers, were being frog-marched through glass doors and beaten silly by guest constabulary in every tin-pot cop-shop throughout the carboniferous world. Ironically, it may be that the only solid, old-fashioned work-based communities left to us are the police and the army. Fancifully I take solace in the corre-spondence from the Benefits people: single-spaced typewriter script on wartime-quality paper; no poncey duotone letterhead; untouched by the world of bright brochures, of smiles and lies. It's as if the years had been scraped away to reveal the original machinery of the Beveridge Plan still miraculously functioning: an office with wooden filing cabinets and In, Out and Pending trays and rubber stamps and weighty breath-dulled black telephones with chrome dials and flex sheathed in a frayed brown fabric; and people are working out my entitlements by hand and getting them right because they were taught at school to get things right. How many such fancies would it take to regen-erate the past in all its prolixity – the eyelids flickering, the corpse beginning to stir? For that matter, how much did it take when it was alive in the first place?

Keys jingle outside. It must be Morwen – though she's uncharacteristically fumbly about getting in. As I rise to go to the door, it opens. The weight of her rucksack is on her right shoulder; and her left arm is in a sling, in fact it's in a heavy plaster cast: plaster half way up the upper arm.

'What the hell's happened to you?'

'Genoa. That's what's happened to me – Genoa.' She drops the rucksack by the kitchen door and flops down at the table. Her face looks pale as the plaster.

'Coffee?' She nods. 'You mean you were at the G8 summit?' Another nod. 'And Roderick – was he with you?'

'No.' A short, mirthless laugh. 'He's at a conference in Oslo.'

I make coffees for us both, and sit down facing her. 'So – do you want to tell me about it?'

'I've never seen so many people.'

'At a demo?'

'Anywhere, I don't think. Maybe.'

I sip my coffee, trying not to stare at her – as if she were some freakish person opposite me on a train. And I'm her father. 'All they showed on TV were burning cars and a few smashed windows and a lot of people running about.'

'Of course.'

'Yes.'

She rallies a little. Lack of sleep, I suppose. It occurs to me that she may be on pain-killers. 'So odd, right from the start. I mean, there was a group in white overalls, Italian organisation, committed to non-violence, but they were all padded up... There was the usual carnival stuff as well as the Trade Union banners, slogans, but, well, there were these guys on stilts, jugglers, but they were wearing gas masks. And it wasn't a surrealist jape. The gas, the gas, everywhere – I've still got it clinging to my clothes, in the back of my mouth... The whole scene was a mix-up of a political march, a circus and the '14-'18 war. Not much live ammo, I'll admit – though one guy did get shot; but get hit by one of those gas canisters and you'd know it. They'd got fins – could have cut your face open...'

'And the Men in Black – how about them?'

'It wasn't a fucking joke, Dad!'

'I wasn't trying to suggest it was.'

She says nothing. I try to lighten the mood by asking if she'd like me to autograph her plaster; but she doesn't consider that worthy of anything more than a shrug. When did it start, this contemptuous – or perhaps not contemptuous, quite, but dismissive – this dismissive attitude towards me? I've tried to pin-point it, but I can't. Was it just that terrible moment in every child's life when you realise all of a sudden that your parents are simply two people, like any other two people? Or did I once say something, unwittingly, that revealed some quality in me she saw for the first time and despised? I'm not up to much, I know that: compared to Glynis, for example; or even to someone like Andrea, who's given her life to administering – indeed administrating – the relief of pain. But how far can you take such comparisons? Even the Elpenor could be used, at a pinch, for attaching limpet mines to ships' hulls; but I don't feel bound to assume guilt on that account. Anyway, I'll not be asking Morwen why. Once something's framed in words, it becomes irreversible, and then...

'Sorry – you were asking about the Black Bloc. Well, what was odd was that the police, carabinieri, whatever, seemed to take no action against them. Everyone said.'

'You think they were provocateurs – or some of them, at least?'

'Possibly. That was one theory, and I guess it would be amazing if some of them weren't. Another theory is that the police were too nervous to take on anyone who looked as if they might be prepared to return violence with violence.'

'Oh dear, the battle-shy Italian soldier! It's unbelievable how long these stereotypes can last.'

'I know. The other theory – and it's the one I'd subscribe to – is that they'd received instructions not to move against anyone who was attacking property, because those were the images they wanted to be available to the media. That way, it would make no difference whether the Blacks were provocateurs or not; and the police could turn their attention to the peaceful demonstrators, because the media wouldn't be bothering with them. And they did. A huge crowd of pacifists, women and children among them, and they'd painted the palms of their hands white as a symbol of non-violence: they were just sitting quietly, and the cops weighed in at them...'

'And is that when you...' I nod towards her arm.

'Oh no. Oh no. That was when it was all over – at least, we thought it was. Late evening. A bunch of us were kipping down in this school, made available by the Genoa City Council, I believe – they still have left-wing local councils over there. We were all asleep in our bags. Or at any rate I was asleep, probably everyone was. And I was woken up by a trampling of boots and there was this carabiniere – riot shield, respirator, the lot – towering above me with his baton raised, and he crashed it down on my arm; and I heard it break – actually heard the crack as my bone broke; and I sort of assumed he'd stop then, but he didn't, he went on doing it, over and over again; and there were shrieks all around me, and these dull thumps, and these great big figures thrashing at people...' She rummages one-handedly in her rucksack. 'I've got the X-ray here. They gave it to me.' The X-ray is rolled up, but has been pressed flat by being packed, and is difficult to flatten against the window, against the light. It's funny how bones show up white on X-rays. Nothing to do with the fact that bones are white, of course; but we tend to read it that way. I don't immediately recognise what I'm looking at; then I see the point of fracture: the fragmentation; the pointy shards disconnected. It's as if someone had embedded the several blades of a Swiss army knife in her muscle. 'The Italian doctor said he'd done the best he could, but the damage was so extensive that I might have to have it broken again and re-set once this had healed.' I've sometimes, at morbid moments, wondered what it must be like for a parent to have a child abducted and tortured by a pervert. Well now I know.

'You must be all in. Finish your coffee; I'll make up a bed for you in a minute.'

'It's all right. I can manage.'

'Morwen, for Christ's sake! I'll make up a bed for you. OK?'

Eventually she says, 'There's something I can't get out of my mind. We were sitting near the barrier of the Red Zone, and this line of paramilitaries were facing us with their gear and their clutter and their uniforms with fluted pads on the shins and hips; and there was this one, quite close to me, gripping his baton in both hands the way they do, and he was gazing down with a preoccupied expression, and I suddenly thought, "He's got a kiddie who's ill with chicken-pox, or something, and he's worrying about her, whether she's going to be all right, hoping it won't leave her face scarred." I can still see him now.'

'You're saying there's a glimmer of hope – professional thugs can show a touch of humanity?'

'I'm afraid I'm coming at it the other way round. It doesn't make a scrap of difference how much humanity anyone has – you, me, the government, the police. The system's got its own logic.'

'And that logic will override any individual?'

'It'll override *all* individuals. Always.'

I don't think I've seen Morwen cry since she was about three; but there are tears streaming down her cheeks now. I move to the other side of the table and put my arm around her, and she lets her head rest on my shoulder. I offer no words of comfort. You can comfort someone for private grief. But this is not private grief.

I was just about to bin the Sunday paper when I spotted it: at the Serpentine Gallery: 'The Big Tune' – video installation and ancillary works by Alice Cave. Kensington Gardens has always been a trifle frowsty: all these paths laid out according to an aesthetic, a geometry, now lost to us. Even the autumn leaves fall primly, as if schooled in decorum. I like it like this. I like to think there may still be grey-uniformed governesses pushing high perambulators on the broad-walk, little boys in sailor suits with hoops and sticks. All before my time, of course; but when you've become part of the past, who cares which part you choose to appropriate? Actually, dress codes aside, I dare say the place hasn't changed so very much. There are still people plentifully dotted around enjoying the Indian summer. In fact it's a place where, without speaking to a soul, you can experience a sense of community – the community of the lassitudinous. Most of these individuals, or twos, or threes, seem to be students poring over their set books – their whole lives ahead of them, poor sods. Now what the hell made me say that? Is it what I really think – or am I becoming a grumpy old man? And am I talking aloud to myself? Not that it matters nowadays, as people will think you have a mobile phone of exceedingly discreet design. And that really is the first sign of madness. But all the same, all these students. I know what it is. The other week, when I went to that experimental theatre production, I became acutely aware that nearly all of the audience were drama students – and the few who weren't seemed to be relatives of the performers. And I'm willing to bet most of the visitors at the Serpentine will be art students or lecturers or critics. Something wrong is happening. I remember once reading that in Holland during the war, when it was an offence carrying the death penalty to publish anything in English, a press brought out a clandestine edition of Gray's Elegy. Imagine that – risking your neck for Gray's Elegy! Yet most of these kids probably haven't even read it. Oh come on – that's not fair. Well, I know it isn't; but for all that, there's still something wrong. When the arts were sneered at, you knew where you stood. And now? The time's not far off when it'll be illegal to write poems or stories if you haven't got an NVQ in Creative Writing.

The first gallery contains only one exhibit: on a table, protected under glass, lies a drawing on good old-fashioned cartridge paper labelled 'The Serpentine Gallery – Plan'. It has all the usual boxes for company name, client's name, drawing number and so forth. But the drawing itself consists of nothing but a compass indicating North. The table is not placed square to the sides of the room; and there seems every reason to suppose that the North arrow has been correctly aligned. Yet surely there are still too many variables here. An architect's drawing is normally aligned either with the axis of the building represented or with the points of the compass. In this case it must seemingly align with neither: which is logically possible, but quite inexplicable since the drawing contains no information. So why does the drawing contain no information? I'm baffled by this until my eye is caught by the

legend: 'Scale: 3 feet to one inch.' What is schematically represented here is less than one square inch of floor area. In the
next room is a glass case labelled 'Studies for The Big Tune',
and it contains four stands. Of the inner two stands, one is
labelled 'One' and holds a tattered copy of Giuseppe di
Lampedusa's *Il Gattopardo*, a book which I remember
enjoyed a certain popularity in the 1960s; the other is labelled
'Zero' and holds – appropriately enough – nothing. The two
outer stands are labelled 'Infinity, Left' and 'Infinity, Right'.
Each is made of a continuous brass ribbon and has the look
of an infinity symbol – the toppled 8; but closer inspection
reveals that they are both Mobius strips on which are etched
a continuous succession of arrows. Not only that, but the two
strips seem to follow a different configuration. It is madden-
ingly difficult, since they are spaced at opposite ends of the
case, to judge whether they really do differ – a left-hand twist
as against a right-hand twist – or whether simply turning
them around, or upside down, would reveal them as identical.
And then there are the arrows: would it be essentially different if they were pointing the other way? In other words, we
are left agonising over whether there is only one pattern here
after all, or two – or even the implication of four. Now, on the
walls, we come to some framed works in crayon consisting
mainly of dots and blotches with the occasional wavy line
visible at the outermost margins; and these are described as
'The Big Tune – Sketches'. Then there is a light-trap through
which we enter a cubical space, each wall almost completely
filled by a video projection; and immediately it becomes
apparent that what we have just seen can hardly have been
sketches *for* this installation but must rather have been
sketches *from* it. A leopard is prowling around us: circuitously,
hungrily, relentlessly; pad soft, breath tongue-rasped, spots
stroboscopic; tail giving the occasional flick, head thrust low,
skin rippling hypnotically over bunched muscles as it passes
sometimes almost brushing the camera, sometimes seen at
full stretch, sometimes reversing direction with every appearance of lethal impatience. What's this got to do with a tune?

One's first reaction is fear – a naked, unabashed, animal fear. Then fascination. Only after a while do we – or I, at any rate – begin to wonder how these images have been obtained. It seems unlikely that the leopard was pacing in a tight circle around an array of only four cameras. Animals pace to and fro, don't they? The cameras must have been placed in a row, probably looking in through the rails of the compound. But if that were the case, the leopard would always turn round at the same point, wouldn't it? And it doesn't. Sometimes it continues in the same direction for quite a long time. It may be that the continuity between the images is an illusion, and there were many more than four cameras. The surroundings are not specific enough to give many clues. And maybe those moments where the leopard fills the frame are the points where a little cheating has taken place. But however I look at it it doesn't quite make sense; and it occurs to me that this is a feature of all Alice's work: that it appears perfectly simple until you start to think about it, from which point it gets progressively more puzzling, pulling the rug from under your phrasing of the world, sense being exposed as the flip side of nonsense – and none the more worthy of trust. Was that true of Alice herself – when we were young, I mean? Was I simply too crass to notice the light-trap where the contradictions began, the entry to her other world? As I turn towards the exit, Alice walks past me. I half expect her to notice me, to say something to me; but of course she is entering a dark area from a lighter one; and she might well not have remembered me in any case. She is one of those women – not so rare, as it happens – who become more attractive rather than less as they grow older. Her calves and arms are like rope; her iron-grey hair is bound casually; her stride is feline and predatory, so that you half expect her to give voice to a growl like the ignition of a blow-torch. Leaving, I notice that the full title of the work is, 'The Big Tune Will Come Back One Day' – and then, in smaller lettering, 'But Probably Not In Our Lifetime'. That's a great help.

Ought I to have made myself known to her? From the

bench where I've sat down for a breather before toddling on home, through the thinning trees, I can see the buff and red curvature of the Albert Hall. I've only been in there once, and that was when Alice took me to a concert in those long lost days beyond recall. But that's hardly sufficient ground for a re-acquaintance. In any case, I don't think I treated her all that well. And now, besides, she's a public figure: not that her name is always in the papers; but I assume you have to be pretty well thought-of to get a show at the Serpentine. There's something I'm missing, though: some link I'm groping for. Was it to do with an hour-glass: a winged hour-glass? The Albert Hall, the queue. Something Alice said? A lissom young woman jogs past me on her white techno-soles and gives me a nice smile. Ten years ago, that wouldn't have happened. A young woman can smile at me now, not because she finds me an appealing proposition, but because she sees me as past it, out of the running, no threat. And I've got it. The Great Eastern. Alice said she'd always been been inspired by one of Brunel's drawings of the Great Eastern, which she'd seen in the Science Museum. For all I know, it may still be there.

It's tucked away in the corner of the entrance-and-exit hall of South Kensington station: brown, furtive, dingy, as if there were something shameful about it: the gateway to a cata-comb frequented only by persons mired in pagan depravities, or more likely the access route for electrical and mechanical and hydraulical services. But it is the public tunnel to the Natural History and Science Museums: a short cut under the busy traffic. The walls and the ceiling are surfaced with white tiles, brick-sized, which obviously date from when it was built. But there is something sordid about them, as if, over the decades, dirty dishwater had managed to seep between the slip and the glaze. A certain distance along, there is a slight bend beyond which is revealed a longer vista; and, beyond this, another bend which reveals a longer vista still. I have a faint recollection – or I think I do – of having been wheeled along here in my push-chair as an infant. What

I am sure of is that, for several years during my childhood, I believed I had dreamed it, and was startled eventually to discover there really was such a place. Of course, I'd almost certainly dreamed it as well; so it is only a matter of which came first. Why am I walking with such determination? Am I afraid I might give up from limpness of spirit before reaching the end? No, it is merely that there is no choice but for everyone, before and behind me, to maintain the same pace. People maintain too, I notice, a near-superstitious silence. It is not exactly creepy, but it is sepulchral, calling to mind not so much the dead as those who serve the needs of the dead. For moments at a stretch I am confused as to whether I'm passing through the real tunnel or the dreamed one. The faces of those approaching from the opposite direction are pallid in this light; and when a family passes me wearing plastic skeleton masks I do not register it as anything particularly unexpected. To the right, breaking the monotony only for it to reaffirm itself with redoubled insistence, is a locked, painted, dirty iron door framed by ornate but rusty iron columns: forbidden passageway to the queen's mortuary chamber with its long, small, direct channel for beaming her up to Betelgeuse – cutting-edge Old Kingdom science, no less? *Such ghosts as haunt the ghost of thought/ Hanging in drainpipe corners/ No longer countenanced/ Or sought* – that's from one that didn't even make it into *Treacle*. But whose were those ghosts I always envisaged awaiting me in hushed places or ready to materialise on a deserted station platform where the blue clock of my youth was already clicking away the seconds? Can't say I've ever found out. They never came, that's why; or if they did, I failed to recognise them. Tender, destitute, unbearably wise; but only one more strand – in an argument, in life's tapestry, in a clew of twine – that didn't lead anywhere. The floor, though much patched and bodged, seems to retain a good deal of its original surface: an elephant grey composition in which, at intervals, is sunk brass lettering reading sometimes, 'Wilkes & Co. Devonshire Sq. E.C.' and sometimes, less frequently, 'Wilke's Metallic

Flooring Co. Ld.' So what are we to believe about that rogue apostrophe? Was the man called Wilke or was he called Wilkes? There's not much else to think about in a corridor a third of a mile long. I tell myself it is just a perfectly ordinary underground conduit for tourists, even if the light is a little dismal and the acoustic a little wobbly. But the dream tunnel is a different question altogether. And it's definitely here too. *Then first Elpenor came, saying, 'Leave me not unburied in a strange land...'* And from the strait and sunken portal of an Anderson shelter, easily mistakable for a wisteria-choked bookshop and flanked by statues of hieratic storks, the shades clamber after many a night of unsettled sleep craving refreshment, craving recognition, demanding restitution of their jobs and, while we're about it, the reinstatement of the machinery for free collective bargaining.

I navigate the museum with somnambulistic confidence: past the Newcomen engine in whose deep pit, under whose Doomsday beam, a waxwork stoker fuels the simulated blaze. Will the imaginary fire melt the imaginary man? It is entirely a matter of whose fantasy is the stronger. I pass Matthew Murray's self-contained condensing beam engine and Sir Marc Brunel's diagonal oscillating engine of 1822. I pass the pump labelled Old Bess with its sooty photograph of bewhiskered attendants with clay pipes and broad vowels, the very people who really would have called her Old Bess... And there it is, framed: the lithograph of a drawing of the Great Eastern, a longitudinal section, one eighth of an inch to the foot: not by Brunel himself but by his partner in the enterprise, J.Scott Russell Esq. The thing is a good six feet in length. The paper is biscuit coloured; but perhaps that is age. The galleries echo with the voices of unseen children as long-forgotten movements ghost themselves onto my hands: reaching for the stock of the T-square to make sure it is snug against the runner; testing the flow of the ink against my sleeve; sliding my father's yellowed celluloid set-square into place, securing it with the tips of my fingers while I angle the pen to avoid ink seeping under: the briskness, the delicate firmness of successive motions each the embodiment of a quantum of choice: as if the precision of the engineering, with even the tolerances and margins of error meticulously prescribed, indeed the touch of the hands on the wheels and the levers which would control this gargantuan tonnage of iron once built, could – should – be foreshadowed in the skill of hand and eye of the draughtsman. I'd forgotten the Great Eastern had an axial propeller as well as its paddles and, just to be on the safe side, sails. Wasn't it this ship of which it was said that, when she was finally broken up, the skeletons of two rivetters were found between the inner and outer hulls – though I've heard that story told, with a kind of corporate pride bordering on relish, in almost every shipyard I've ever visited. The way the light falls in this drawing is startling when you notice it: not from local lamps or apertures, but as if the vessel had been physically sliced down its length to expose its interior, the source of illumination being notionally at about 45 degrees both to the vertical and to the picture plane. It's a light the real ship would never see. Tremor of muted familiarity. Hence the shape of the shadow has been calculated for both the upper-sides and under-sides of staircases, and a scimitar of graduated darkening describes the inner curvature of the bows. Yet despite this recourse to naturalism, the walls of coal in the hoppers – coal from Barnsley, or from Ebbw Vale, which clearly occupied a huge proportion of below-decks volume – remain undisturbed, vertical, a cliff-face. Not only that, but the bronze alloy collars of the shafts are rendered in yellow against the grey of cast iron, as if in conformity with a colour coding still familiar today and self-assured as empires jostling on an old map. In short, the contradictions here are worthy of one of Alice Cave's exhibition pieces. If the light is natural, why doesn't the coal spill out? If the colours are conventional, then the dark blue buttoned leather upholstery of the banquettes – similar to those found in repro at the Pope Joan when I first met Glynis, and doubtless packed with horsehair

– must represent wrought iron, mustn't it, and the curtains copper. The most astonishing thing, though, is the detail. Not only is every lump of coal highlighted; the visible facets of the tiniest steel nut – in reality some three inches across – are individually shaded; and some of the lines are so fine that you'd hardly believe ink could escape from such a narrow setting. The instinctive assumption which I realise I've been making is that this is a reduction print of some sort from a larger original. But there were no such things in the mid-nineteenth century. I feel a sense of helplessness in the face of this piece of work, as if my 2H pencil, craftily sharpened to a chisel point, had fallen from my numbed grasp. My handskills desert me because our culture denies the hand and the gift of the hand. This drawing represents everything I once valued; yet in the end it defeats my empathy. Its presence here, in a public space, is profoundly subversive. It escapes censure and censorship solely through its venerability, the dust of years making it politically invisible. Perhaps that is why Alice's art leaves such a bitter aftertaste. It enacts the demise of our physical imagination. 'You know, don't you, that forty percent of merchant ships were still coal-fired at the start of the Second World War?' A scruffy old man is standing beside me. 'The U-Boats loved 'em – could see the smoke from miles off.' I glance into his Arctic eyes, give a short affirmative grunt and turn away towards the café area.

The café area, demarcated by a barrier of punched aluminium sections, has a utilitarian feel, a bit like a factory canteen occupying a space that was not really meant for it. The chairs are of punched aluminium too, and squeak against the floor. There aren't many people at this time of day. I join a small queue, and withdraw with a coffee and muffin to the periphery. A couple of tables away, a bald and portly man casts me a grin: 'Takes you back, eh?' I nod and smile briefly; and the man rises and lumbers over towards me with his sandwich and drink: 'Remember me, don't you?'

Not a glimmer. 'Sorry.'

'I'm Frank. Face from the past, eh?' Bloody hell – Frank

Rillington. He of the Tottenham flick, no less. 'OK if I join you?'

'Of course. Sorry I didn't...'

'Not surprised. The old barnet's not what it used to be, and that's just for starters.'

'True enough. So what have you been up to since we last met?'

'I stuck around in the business – engineering. Went aeronautical, though. I decided that's where the future was – and it turned out I was right, more or less. You hear that – "Where the future *was*." Says it all, dunnit?' He laughs.

'You still working, then? A bit younger than me, weren't you?'

'Yeh, due for my pension next year; but I took early retirement. Or was I pushed? Never mind, it was quite a good settlement. I'd made it to Project Manager by the time they caught up with me – would you believe? – yeh, Project Manager. But the pressure was on, I could tell – management all getting the jitters – so I sort of saw it coming. Not that I minded that much. The kids were off my hands by then, and I'd lost the missus a couple of years previous. So there you go. C'est la-bloody-vie! How about you?'

'Similar story. Wife passed on; daughter in her twenties. I managed to keep earning pretty well up to my retirement, but a lot of the time it was touch and go.'

'What we ought to have been was designers. That's where the dosh is now – and the kudos. But they didn't have designers in them days, did they?'

'Interesting thought. Someone must have been doing it, doing the stuff that's now called designing – must have been – but we didn't have the word, and so you couldn't aspire to it. In our day you were either a commercial artist or you were an inventor.'

'And an inventor was someone with hair like a chimney-sweep's brush who made explosions in the attic.'

'That's right.'

We both sip our drinks, suddenly uncomfortable at the

thought that maybe fifty-odd years have not supplied us with enough fresh experiences to sustain a conversation. Then Frank chuckles: 'What I mainly remember about you is the poetry.'

'I didn't even know you knew.'

'Oh yes. I remember being very impressed with a poem of yours about Gina Lollobrigida.'

'Gina Lollobrigida?'

'You know – Italian film star.'

I remember the film star all right; but I find it hard to believe I ever wrote a poem about her. A cat with green eyes and its paws in a flowerbed was more up my street. All the same, I'm flattered. 'I'll tell you what it was,' I say. 'To be honest, I don't think I've ever told anyone this before; but you were sort of on the spot, so... What happened was that one day I was having trouble with my slide-rule – remember slide rules?'

'Blimey, slide-rules! My dad – he was an engineer too – he used to have a joke that went: What is an engineer? An engineer is someone who multiplies two by two on a slide-rule, gets an answer of three-point-nine-nine and says, Call it four for all practical purposes.'

I laugh: 'You're not going to believe this, but my dad once told me that joke too.'

'And now people are saying with all this 3D software you don't even need maths to be an engineer. Still – sorry – you were starting to tell me something about the poetry.'

'Ah, yes, well, there was this occasion when I was having trouble with my slide rule, it kept jamming, wouldn't run smoothly; and one of the blokes said, "Here, give it to me," and he took it and ran a lead pencil along the groove and he said, "There you are"; and I tried it and it was fine. So I said, "What made you think of lead pencil?" and he said, "Well, graphite's a lubricant, isn't it." And that... well, it's difficult to explain what I saw in that, but it was to do with the way he'd taken two things, a stiff slide-rule and a lead pencil, and from those two things he'd as it were *generated* the concept "lubricant". I mean, it's not as if he'd always looked at a pencil as a lubricant only waiting to be used on a slide-rule. And that's exactly the way poetry works – two dissociated words generating a fresh insight. That was the moment, the real core moment, when I decided there couldn't possibly be a contradiction between poetry and engineering. Words make things – like the word "designer" we were talking about. There had to be a way of making it work. The rest was just a question of method. Unfortunately, it's a question I never managed to resolve.'

'Hmm. I have to admit I've always had my doubts.'

'About what – poetry?'

'Well, not as such; but it's always seemed to me that you can't write about working class life – leastways, nobody does seem to – without first turning it into something, namely literature, which it isn't and which excludes it by definition.'

'By definition? We could argue about that until the cows come home.'

'And they never do.'

'Right. Talking of the arts, though, do you remember Alice Cave?' He looks blank. 'Alice Cave: used to be a tracer; I was a bit sweet on her for a while...'

'Doesn't ring any bells. Why?'

'Oh, she's turned into an artist, that's all – got an exhibition on at the moment.'

'Ah. You go to exhibitions much, then?'

'Quite a bit. Fills in the time. How about you – I mean, filling in your time. Any special interests I couldn't begin to guess at?'

'Haydn.'

'Haydn? The composer? Didn't know you were into music.'

'I never was, until quite recently. Just came home one evening, crashed down with a beer, switched on the radio; and you know how it is sometimes, when you switch on just as something's about to start, and there's this silence which gives you a sort of tingle – well, it was like that, and I was suddenly alert, like a cat, waiting for what was going to happen; and what happened was this piano, and there was something about the precise nature of the sound, the room it was recorded in, maybe just the level I'd got my radio, but at any rate I couldn't stop listening as these strands of music started exploring that space. The pianist had his back to me, I was sure of that, and he was playing one of those square pianos they had in the old days – you see them in the V&A. Like I say, the room was empty, and every note was precious; and the way the music explored the notes, it was like you see a kiddie with a tangram puzzle or a cat's cradle, totally absorbed, seeing what shapes he can make... So when it was over they announced such-and-such – I don't even remember which one it was – such-and-such a sonata by Joseph Haydn, and I said to myself, "Frank, me old fruit, this is it." Next day it was down the HMV shop, and I lashed out one-hundred-and-nine smackers on the complete Haydn sonatas. The lot. And you know what, I never get tired of them – never. Exploration of what's possible, that's what it's about: tracing little mazes among the keys... I've had a go with other stuff, but it doesn't do it for me: always seems to be trying to say something. These Haydn sonatas aren't trying to say anything. All they're doing is trying to find all the things you can do, all the paths you can weave; and I reckon that's worthy of a lifetime – his or mine.'

'And what about other music by Haydn? He must have written other things besides piano sonatas.'

'Yes, he did. But I'm not bothered. After all, there's masses of music in the world; and you can't listen to it all – you'd drown, wouldn't you. Besides, I've never been one to make life more difficult than I can help. There's a whole world in those sonatas. It'll do me...'

It'll do me. What was that – 'It'll do me? It'll...' That's it: it's what Dad said to me once about his allotment: in some sense, for better or for worse, accepting that circumscribed world as sufficient in its self-containment to represent the totality of what might be. Frank is still talking; but I no longer listen. There's something I want to know. I want to know precisely, to five significant figures: what is the relationship between Frank's man with his back to us, playing the piano in an empty room, and all those police with their clubs and their visors and their handcuffs and their perspex shields and their children with chicken-pox and their tear gas? Yes, it's a ludicrous question; but that's how the human mind works, and I want to know.

'I gave you an image.' Astonished, I see my father seated beside me. 'What more could you ask of your old man?' His dressing gown is wet and dripping onto the floor. 'What you make of it is up to you.' His pyjamas – burgundy with pale blue stripes – are torn open, his flesh white and corrugated as the underside of some unappetising sea creature. 'It all happened in the bath. Haven't you ever fallen asleep in the bath and woken to find the water perishing cold? They had to prise my fingers away...' How many memories make a truth? An old blue plastic Grundig, perforated, in a room full of twilight?

I feel a hand on my shoulder, and the Old Man – the old Old Man, that is – is saying, 'I always knew you'd do well for yourself, son.'

'Actually, sir, I'm unemployed...'

'Yes – always knew you'd be a credit to me.'

A tape spool with my old voice on it. Somewhere. Perhaps here, in one of these cabinets. Blodwen, supping her cawl, glances up: 'Can't even trust our grandmothers to suck eggs any more. That's what I say.'

Small working models of overwhelming engines; fugitive light oils; a clatter of bones on a tin plate: Alice is tackling a pile of spare ribs. Meanwhile Cassandra, slicing a solitary onion on a wooden platter, says, 'Since Beeching abolished our branch line, the village has been cut off. Only the most intrepid have plucked up courage to leave, and fewer returned. Food has become limited to what we can scavenge. Congenital deformities have begun to multiply. Idiocy is rife.'

'And Iwan?' I ask, turning to Blodwen.

'Poor soul,' she murmurs, dipping her eyes in remembrance as a bone yields loudly to Alice's molars. 'All those funerary pyres – all that meat-smoke...'

Cassandra's husband's ghost strolls through in uniform, taking pinches of grated carrot – government truth fodder – from a cocktail dish. No-one else seems to see him; but I imagine that is because they're too intent on their own mastications.

The Old Man leans forward to retrieve some crumbs from my muffin and to mumble into my ear: 'You know why you're here, don't you? The museum has acquired the Elpenor for its permanent collection. A bronze plaque will mention you by name. Thus your future is guaranteed secure.'

'But she's only been in service for a year or so,' I say. 'You must be telling me the future is obsolete.'

'Unless the yes-men and the car-noddies get here first.' Stallworthy is eating meat and two veg from a thick plate, courtesy of a British Restaurant circa 1944. 'Even Marx saw no future in the lumpenproletariat. And we're all lumpen-proles now. You, me, the youngster shooting up in a squat and the twelve-year-old hawking herself around King's Cross to support his habit – we're all as one in our uselessness to the Revolution.'

Jill, selecting delicacies from a bowl of forest roots and berries, nods in agreement: 'During one of the evictions, one of my friends – Glynis, her name was – had all her letters, diaries, even her notebooks, taken by the bailiffs and thrown into the muncher. She said to me, "I no longer know who I am. I am a tabula rasa, a blank charge-sheet."'

Somewhere a long way off I think I hear commands being barked.

Blodwen shakes her head: 'It's the oil in their wool that makes them burn so fierce.'

'So what would you have done,' I ask Stallworthy testily, 'if you'd received the command to continue the advance eastwards?'

'I'd have obeyed orders, same as we all do.'

'And leave me to sort out the collateral,' Andrea pipes up, tucking in to her tagliatelle. Alice's jaws crack another bone. The German Shepherd, sprawled in anticipation of scraps, favours me with a complicitous wink. Jack is stalking round the backs of the chairs, noshing a Mars bar, swinging a length of rubber piping, flashing a hairy bum where his gown has fallen open and chanting, 'Get them in the kidneys, that's the style.... Nobody'll know... Bugger their waterworks...' Frank follows behind as if dancing the conga and trying to revive the Tottenham flick for today's fashion-hungry youth.

I seem to hear the stomp of marching feet; in fact I seem to have been aware of them for some time. Dad is gnawing at a mackerel he has grabbed, more I'd imagine for its content of fresh water than for the nutrition of its flesh. The drips from his clothing have formed a small rivulet and are trickling towards an electric socket. And now, terrible, Cassie demands:

'Why did you leave me?'

Alice's voice is the draw of air up a crusty flue, her eyes embers locked in amber, as she spits, 'He left me as well.'

'He does it to everyone,' Andrea sneers with a soupçon of self-righteousness.

The tread of the marchers sounds ever nearer, ever louder, and the suspicion grows upon me that they are the legions of those I have never met. But no – they are The Enemy Within: the enemy within us each and all:

Sodom and Gomorrah

Say, 'Call again tomorrah'...

'I'll tell you the story, and allow you all to judge' Cassandra resumes. 'When our village began to starve, I said to my nephew, "We are reduced to eating the seed-corn. There will be nothing to sow for next year's crop." He said to me, "I am a man now. I will leave the village and return with corn." And sure enough, after three months' absence, he returned with a bulging sack of corn over his shoulder. I did not ask how he had come by it.' The vanguard are now thronging the staircases. We can hear the clip of bayonets being fixed – a clip without a clop. We've always known they would come one day, but have behaved as if we didn't. What could we have done? 'Then one day I said to my nephew, "The piano has fallen prey to woodworm. The keys crumble under my fingers and the floor is adrift with dunes of sawdust." And he said, "Wait for me. Do not despair. I may be away longer this time, but I shall return."' Cassandra has now to raise her voice above the pandemonium as booted feet approach along the galleries from every stairhead, from every direction: 'And again he spoke the truth. He was away for a year, and I was beginning to think he had gone for good when I saw him one morning in the dawn light approaching across the furrowed fields, his back bent under the weight of a new piano.' I think I detect the distinctive fishy smell of faulty electrics, ozone from sparks arcing; but maybe it is only Dad's breath. 'Finally the time came when I said to my nephew, "Everything is collapsing around us. The well is choked with dead kittens and my jam kettle is rusted through. Only one thing could solve all our problems, and that is money." And my nephew said, "I shall go and..."' There is a blinding blue flash and the lights all go out and the marching feet halt in mid-tramp and the ambient sound of machinery one had not even been aware of hearing plummets through the bass frequencies into silence; and in the silence, already, the screams of disoriented children can be heard. The German Shepherd twists and hefts himself upright. Cassie grabs my hand. 'Come on,' she says. 'Let's get out of here.'

*When fear cometh as desolation and their destruction cometh as the whirlwind, when despair cometh upon them...*

The field rises to a ridge that seems to come no closer. To the west, clouds bank up like termite towers. The light over the crops is already crepuscular, though there's no tolling knell; but far above, a long, blood-soaked feather deepens perceptibly from scarlet to crimson: a disintegrated vapour trail. The wind is getting up. Each of us carries a switch with which to swipe the heads off thistles. 'It's better than just letting them spread,' you say; but there are an awful lot of thistles.

I say, 'You didn't finish your story.'

You say, 'All stories have the same end; and it's not what you'd want to hear.'

I say, 'Morwen's gone with Roderick to America. He's a bio-chemist, and he's got a job there. For all my lackadaisical approach to politics, I think I'd have thought twice about that.'

You say, 'So there's only the two of us now.'

I say, 'Yes. Only the two of us.'

After a pause, you say, 'Why did you leave me? You haven't been near me for years.'

I say, 'I was jealous of your husband.'

You say, 'With eleven free games, you'd no call to be jealous.'

So I say, 'I think I felt I had to face up to the fact that you were a false memory.'

You say, 'What does that matter? It's the false memories that are the good ones, the creative ones. True memories leave us no farther forward than we were already.'

I feel ashamed. You cast aside the switch and take my hand with surprising gentleness, your fingers nestling in my palm. Not knowing what to say, I ask, 'It's barley in this field, isn't it?'

You say, 'It looks like barley; but for all I know it may have had coelacanth genes spliced into it. You can't tell what anything is by looking at it any more.'

I say, 'Yet hasn't that always been so? Isn't it only in childhood that we take things for what they are? In fact isn't that almost a definition of childhood? It occurred to me quite recently: I doubt whether I've ever seen a dog in my life that didn't owe its shape – even its temperament – to generations of human intervention.' The German Shepherd glances up at me, seeking comfort.

You say, 'True; but the dog, even if you rear it as an

investment, still commands a margin of choice. The modernistic buildings of the 1930s still had wooden surfaces that could be dented and scored, glazed stoneware sinks that could be chipped. Now they have materials that can replicate on command the hard lines of the architect's drawing. There are no more givens. I remember you once saying the reason computers were so ugly was to persuade us to disregard the tangible world, the world of things. And that's true enough. But it only serves to conceal the fact that the world of things is being re-made by the computers. And you can't blame it all on the binary principle. Your argument that poetry has its origins in the concrete – graphite on the slide-rule – is true enough too, but it ignores the fact that the poetry of tech- nology, distilled to those terse mathematical phrases you've always admired – ultra-violet to poetry's infra-red – has finally dissolved real things: dissolved them into a miasma of malign wish where all that's left in the world is what we imagine and put there to fulfil our imaginings: nothing but emanations of our own consciousness peering back at us. Yes, matter has reappeared, but in spectral form: the return of the repressed. Physical objects, whether flocks of sheep or fields of rye or skyscrapers, have become little more than prosthesis, the last word in Hollywood hokum, a mere exten- sion of the insides of our minds – or rather, of the corporate mind of the system. Soon you'll be able to generate a phantom aunt in the flesh if you're affluent enough. And then what will fantasy be worth – or memory? Those stories of yours: I know you like to think of them as post-Stalinist fiction; but in fact they're nothing but nostalgia. It's far too late to be putting in a good word for the inhabitants of the Cities of the Plain. The human project is bankrupt.'

'So socialism never stood a chance?'

'Once, possibly; but now – well, you might care to try again after the next ice age. And I don't mean that figura- tively; I mean it literally.'

You put down the candle on the chest of drawers as the wind thumps and punches at the walls of the cottage. 'Come into bed with me,' I say; and, as you slide down at my side, I put my arm around you so that your rough linen night-dress rides up over your hips and I feel your pubis brush like static against my thigh. 'So what's going to happen?'

'Are you asking me in my capacity as a seer?'

'Yes.'

'The truth is, I don't know.'

'I don't believe you.'

'I knew you wouldn't. All right, I'll give you two scenarios, and you can choose between them. First: capitalism collapses, not from its internal contradictions but from the fact that it has made itself redundant. With nano-robots that can put together anything, animate or inanimate, from elementary particles – and there's no shortage of particles in the universe – human beings cease to be required on either side of the economic equation, either as producers or as consumers.'

'So it's still a bosses' world, even at the sub-atomic level...'

'Exactly. The ruling class can have anything they want. Of course a sort of vestigial, low-performing capitalism will persist among the remainder of the population; but this will compare with the capitalism we know today as a slime mould to a rain forest.'

'I don't buy that one. I reckon capitalism is robust enough to survive even if no-one at all benefits from it. Few enough do now.'

'All right. The second scenario is that the weather wins. Climate change is so radical and so sudden that all human cultures as we know them are wiped out. Only the rich and ruthless will survive – along, of course, with the rats and the cockroaches – and it won't be enough to be rich or to be ruthless: you'll have to be both. And God knows what they'll have mutated into by the time things have settled down again.'

'How will it start?'

'It's started already. Can't you hear the wind? For a while, everyone'll plod on as if it were nothing more than an inconvenience; but the day will come when so many homes are flooded, so many roofs blown away, that the damage can't be mended before the next big storm, and it'll dawn on people that things are going to go on being damaged faster than they can be mended, and that from now on it'll be normal to live like tramps in homes which are fast becoming ruins, water-proof sleeping bags in our own beds, the banks are not opening their doors and allotments are guarded with fists and knives and lap-dogs roam the streets in packs and the postal services can't get through and all the pages on the web are dead sites because literacy is a thing of the past...'

'Can't say I like that one much either. Do I have to choose?'

*Answer me...* No answer was the stern reply... *then they shall call upon God, but he will not answer.* I stretch my arm out; there's no-one there. Well of course there isn't. I'm alone in this bed as I have always been. No cat is going to burst through the clouds for my redemption. *O leave me not unmourned and unburied as thou settest forth...* I was attentive to my lessons. I worked for my living with diligence, as good people are meant to do. The only duty still required of me is to die. Still, there's no hurry. Perhaps I'll investigate those Haydn sonatas, learn new ways of putting thoughts together. You could extrapolate a political programme from that. Perhaps even now I can be of assistance. I've just noticed something rather odd, though: however far back I look into my childhood, even to when I was scarcely two foot tall and a bee hummed past my ear and I smelled the smell of warm asphalt, I find myself already there; and that cannot quite be true, can it? Perhaps we have to return to first principles. A gorge where a rivulet races pell-mell down the slippery rocks; a zero or infinity traintrack: but that too was an uncon-scionably long time ago. A roof tile slips and slides. There is the creak of strained timber... *as thou settest keel to the unbid-den waters...* Question: What lies on the bed of the sea and quivers? Answer: A nervous wreck. I came across that in a comic when I was very, very young. Likewise many wise predictions, for example: 'Cheap television-in-colour sets will be available after the war.' Water under the bridge, old son. Paul Terhune featured in 'Was it the Gorilla?' As for 'The Truth About Wilson', it was as follows: William Wilson, who invaded the stadium in the 1936 Olympics – wide strides in a hirsute tracksuit – to overtake the legitimate contestants and run a four-minute mile before vanishing into the crowd, had already lived well over a hundred years by dint of slowing down his heartbeat; but I was never able to master the trick. In any case I must be wrong, since they'd not be likely to have had an imperial mile in the Berlin Olympics. 'Gusty Gale Gets Cracking.' From an enormous roll held in a loop of string I am issued a small, puce ticket with the number 22 printed on it, which means that I am twenty-second in line for something or other. Don't ask! Come to think of it, nobody asks my questions any more. The window frames are rattling madly, it's as dark with my eyes open as it is with them closed; my bedside lamp – it used to be Glynis's – declines to function. All fluff and feathers, even my dreams. Never mind: so long as there are two things remaining to engender a third. What was it Graham used to call that? A hurricane blowing with the howl of a bomb falling which never makes impact. NOBODY EVEN ASKS MY QUESTIONS ANY MORE. Yet still the ghost of my voice is somewhere – my old voice, that is, which was my young voice once – formatted in rust and glimmering amid the leaf-gloss. For all it's worth. Trying to signal something. Not too far away I hear what sounds like the splintering of branches and a tinkle of glass; and the German Shepherd grumbles in his sleep. I shall have to buy some putty in the morning.

# THE AUTHOR

Poet, novelist and critic, Dai Vaughan was, for more than thirty-five years, one of the foremost documentary film editors in Britain, author of the seminal *For Documentary*. His previous novels include *Moritur*, *Germs*, *The Cloud Chamber* and *Totes Meer*. *The Review of Contemporary Fiction* describe him as "one of the most skilful writers of our age." He lives in London.